A SUDDEN VACANCY

"How was she killed?" I asked, hoping the question sounded more professional than I felt.

"Stabbed," NYPD Detective Button replied. "Stabbed repeatedly about the face and body with a butcher knife." His slight smile told me he knew very well he was speaking in cop-witness jargon. "Knife's still up there," he went on. "Have to get the scene-of-the-crime boys on it when they get here. Fingerprints, photos, blood samples—you know." I nodded; my work as a criminal lawyer had made me familiar with police procedure.

"How many times..." I began, then faltered, not sure I really wanted to know.

"Let's put it this way, Counselor," Button answered, his voice suddenly grim, "You're going to have to put six coats of paint on the walls before you rent the apartment."

Bantam Books offers the finest in classic and modern American murder mysteries.
Ask your bookseller for the books you have missed.

Stuart Palmer
Murder on the Blackboard

Craig Rice
The Lucky Stiff

Rex Stout
Broken Vase
Death of a Dude
Death Times Three
Fer-de-Lance
The Final Deduction
Gambit
The Rubber Band

Max Allan Collins
The Dark City

William Kienzle
The Rosary Murders

Joseph Louis
Madelaine
The Trouble with Stephanie

M. J. Adamson
Not till a Hot February
A February Face
Remember March

Conrad Haynes
Bishop's Gambit, Declined
Perpetual Check

Barbara Paul
First Gravedigger
But He Was Already Dead When I
    Got There

P.M. Carlson
Murder Unrenovated
Rehearsal for Murder

Ross Macdonald
The Goodbye Look
Sleeping Beauty
The Name Is Archer
The Drowning Pool
The Underground Man

Margaret Maron
The Right Jack
Baby Doll Games

William Murray
When the Fat Man Sings

Robert Goldsborough
Murder in E Minor
Death on Deadline

Sue Grafton
"A" Is for Alibi
"B" Is for Burglar
"C" Is for Corpse

R. D. Brown
Hazzard
Villa Head

A. E. Maxwell
Just Another Day in Paradise
The Frog and the Scorpion

Rob Kantner
Back-Door Man
The Harder They Hit

Joseph Telushkin
The Unorthodox Murder of Rabbi Wahl

Richard Hilary
Snake in the Grasses
Pieces of Cream
Pillow of the Community

Carolyn G. Hart
Design for Murder
Death on Demand

Lia Matera
Where Lawyers Fear to Tread
A Radical Departure

Robert Crais
The Monkey's Raincoat

Keith Peterson
The Trapdoor

Jim Stinson
Double Exposure

Carolyn Wheat
Where Nobody Dies

WHERE NOBODY DIES

Carolyn Wheat

BANTAM BOOKS
TORONTO · NEW YORK · LONDON · SYDNEY · AUCKLAND

WHERE NOBODY DIES
*A Bantam Book / published by arrangement with
St. Martin's Press*

PRINTING HISTORY
*St. Martin's Press edition published July 1986
Bantam edition / June 1988*

*Grateful acknowledgment is made to The Clancy Brothers and
Tommy Makem for permission to reprint lines from "Isn't It
Grand Boys?" arranged by Pat Clancy, Tom Clancy, Liam
Clancy, and T. Markem.
Copyright © 1966, 1969 by Tiparm Music Publishers, Inc.
International Copyright Secured. All Rights Reserved.*

*Edna St. Vincent Millay excerpts appearing throughout from
Collected Poems, Harper & Row. Copyright © 1921, 1934, 1948,
1962 by Edna St. Vincent Millay and Norma Millay Ellis.*

for Harriet:
precious friend, you will be there

"Childhood is the kingdom where nobody dies."
—EDNA ST. VINCENT MILLAY

1

The morning sun poured through the window like a blessing, suffusing everything it touched with a golden glow. It reminded me of Sunday services when I was a kid, except that this halo was produced not by Presbyterian stained glass, but by a thick coating of filth. One of the many differences, I reflected, between church and Family Court.

I glanced at my client. She sat primly in her chair, her tiny feet barely touching the floor, her hands folded in her lap, gazing at the judge with the rapt expression of a kid with a crush on the teacher. She was the picture of a child whose parents were fighting for her custody. On closer inspection, the truth emerged. It was the kindly golden sun that softened her hard edges; the deliberate schoolgirl pose masked a profound sexual awareness. Linda Ritchie was the mother.

I didn't like Linda. She was the kind of woman who came alive only around men, who boasted that she had no women friends. Yet I had to respect her. She'd gone from high-school dropout–battered wife to congressman's secretary with no help from anyone, least of all her ex-husband. Now Congressman Lucenti wanted her on his Washington staff, and Brad Ritchie was doing everything possible to stand in her way.

I looked at Brad, sprawled in his chair, his football player's legs wide apart. Strands of dishwater blond hair fell across his forehead. His face was set in its habitual pout. From star high-school athlete, Brad had gone on to screw up his college hopes. He dropped out to marry a pregnant Linda, and the cycle of lost jobs and wife-beating began. If Linda was playing teacher's pet for the judge, then Brad had never outgrown his role of class bad boy, always on the edge of expulsion.

Judge Bettinger interrupted my reveries. "Miss Jameson," he said, "I believe you said earlier that your client is willing to make certain concessions with regard to visitation?"

"Yes, Your Honor," I answered, quickly summoning up my notes. I was bleary-eyed and my reflexes were slow—a side effect of having my client living upstairs from me. I'd been up half the night trying to persuade Linda not to be a ballbuster or she'd risk having to choose between her new job and her daughter. Even now, she was only half convinced.

"My client agrees to visitation one weekend a month," I began, hoping Linda wouldn't say anything to undercut me.

"Big deal," sneered Brad. "Sure, give me one weekend a month when you know I'm out of work. How's Dawnie going to get here from Washington, huh? Answer me that!"

I did. "Mrs. Ritchie," I addressed the judge, "has agreed to pay for Dawn's fare to and from Brooklyn," I said calmly, keeping my eyes fixed on his face and away from Linda. I didn't want to call attention to the glare she was probably giving me; that particular concession had come only after serious arm-twisting at one A.M.

"Mrs. Ritchie also agrees to send Dawn to Brooklyn every other Christmas, Easter, and Thanksgiving," I went on. "Plus she will let Dawn spend every summer with her father...."

"Sounds very fair to me," the judge murmured.

I suppressed a victory smile. That was precisely the judicial state of mind I'd hoped to engender. Now came the hard part. The one A.M. argument over the plane fare for Dawn's visits had been a piece of cake compared to this one. In all honesty, I'd had to admit to Linda that it was going to be tough to sell the judge on it. Once she'd heard that, she was all for dropping it. Which wouldn't have been bad strategy, except that what we were talking about was the most important thing in her daughter's life.

I took a deep breath, aware of my own tension, heightened by the anxiety I felt radiating from Dawn. "Judge," I began, "the only exception to the summer visitation will be the three weeks Dawn spends at tennis camp. Mr. Ritchie will also be responsible for seeing to it that Dawn gets to all her summer matches."

"*Tennis* camp?" Judge Bettinger's voice boomed. "Do you seriously mean to tell me, Counselor, that this child is going to some fancy-shmancy tennis camp instead of spending time with her own father?" He snorted his indignation.

I wasn't surprised; everyone in Brooklyn Family Court knew Bettinger for a divorced father who lived for his kids' visits. It wasn't easy representing the mother in his courtroom.

The tension level in the courtroom jumped about ten degrees. I could sense Linda's I-told-you-so; I could feel Dawn's near-panic; I could even sympathize with Brad's ambivalence. He was proud of his daughter's accomplishments, yet at the same time he had to resent the fact that her tennis time would come out of his visitation.

I put on my mental blinders. I couldn't let myself be distracted by anyone else's needs. My whole attention had to be concentrated on the judge, on making him see what I knew—that tennis was Dawn's one talent, the thing that set her apart from other unhappy divorce kids. I found myself wishing I could show him a videotape of Dawn on the court. I'd gone to one of her matches with Linda's sister Marcy, and what I'd seen had taken my breath away. The slight heaviness, the twelve-year-old gawkiness of Dawn's body had disappeared. The Dawn I knew had been transformed into a white-clad sprite, who danced around the net, her racket flashing, her face knotted with concentration yet radiant with joy. It had been thrilling; if Judge Bettinger had seen it, Dawn could have lived at the tennis camp. Instead, my words had to do the job. For a moment, I wondered if they would be enough.

I'd done my homework. I'd dug beneath the surface of the Bettinger everyone knew, and discovered that he'd gone through college on a track scholarship. I played my trump card.

"Judge," I began earnestly, "Dawn has a very special relationship with her father." I tried not to think how Linda was reacting; I hoped at least that she wouldn't make her contempt obvious. "She loves her father very much and has no desire to cheat him out of visitation time." Bettinger nodded his approval. I smiled. We were getting somewhere.

"But," I went on, "Dawn Ritchie is a nationally ranked tennis champion. Her coach thinks she's Wimbledon material. There's a good chance she could win a college scholarship.

Her father is the last person in the world who would want to stand in her way. Why not ask him what he thinks?"

It was as big a gamble as I'd ever taken in a courtroom. I had no idea what Brad would say. His obsessive hostility toward his ex-wife definitely carried over to me as her lawyer; he'd made that clear every time I'd seen him. Yet he'd come alive on the football field the way Dawn did on the tennis court. Despite all that had come later, I hoped for Dawn's sake he could remember that feeling.

We were all the way off the Richter scale for tension. Judge Bettinger looked expectantly at Brad. Linda looked smug, waiting for the disaster she'd predicted the night before. Dawn seemed ready to faint; her face was white and she bit her lips convulsively.

Brad shot me a furious glance that gave me a momentary pang of guilt. What I was doing to him was, I knew, unconscionable. It was also necessary for Dawn's happiness, but I didn't expect him to recognize that in this decade. The irony was that he included Linda in his rage, little realizing that she'd fought tooth and nail against Dawn's tennis as a priority. Then Brad looked at Dawn. The anger in his face died, replaced by a tender sadness. As Dawn's tight face relaxed from within, my breath came out in a long sigh of relief.

Brad turned to the judge and nodded. "Okay," he said in a thick voice that sounded as though it was coming through a lump in his throat.

"One more thing," Judge Bettinger said. "I must be certain that this arrangement is in the best interests of the child." He intoned the stock phrase as though he'd invented it on the spot. He turned to Dawn. My eyes followed to where she sat in a posture of unnatural stillness. It was easy to see Brad in her—the height, the broad shoulders, the gold in her light-brown hair, the full lips and slightly heavy legs. Her mother's contribution was more subtle—honey-colored skin, liquid brown eyes, and a way of holding herself. Dawn copied Linda's schoolgirl pose, hands folded, eyes straight ahead. But her hands showed quick-bitten nails, and she chewed her lips until small spots of blood began to appear. Dawn was not the teacher's pet but the shy child in the back of the room who wets her pants because she's afraid to ask permission to leave the room.

She was always like this on court days. Other times, she

was just your basic twelve-year-old. Everything in Dawn's world was either "neat" or "yucky." So far, although she never said so, I was afraid the move to Washington fell into the latter category. I was hoping she wouldn't choose this opportunity to express her feelings.

"So," the judge began in a hearty-uncle voice, "you want to be another Billie Jean King?" I winced; even I, tennis ignoramus that I was, knew that younger heroines had supplanted the great pioneer. But Dawn, head down and face beet-red, mumbled, "I'll never be *that* good."

"But you like the game?" the judge pressed her. "You're not just in it to please Mommy and Daddy?"

Dawn looked up with incredulous eyes. She had fought her mother over her tennis for as long as she could remember; Linda thought it was stupid to spend so much time on a pastime not geared to meeting boys. Brad, the failed athlete, supported his daughter, but from a distance created by circumstances. It was Marcy, Linda's unmarried sister, who paid for the coaching and the camp and saw to it that Dawn got to her matches. Dawn looked up, solemnly assuring the judge that she was not in tennis because of pushing parents.

Judge Bettinger relaxed, gave Dawn what passed with him for a fatherly smile, and said, "Submit order." We had won.

Linda rewarded the judge with a dazzling smile, her tiny even teeth white in her dark face. The sound of chairs slamming behind me was Brad's only response. I thanked the judge and promised to get the order in as soon as possible. Now that the case was over, the adrenaline that had kept me going on four hours' sleep abruptly dissipated. I was bone-tired. I picked up my down coat and my leather briefcase, eager to exchange the dingy, overheated courtroom for the crisp January air.

Linda grabbed her fur jacket and purse, then stood tapping her foot as Dawn struggled with the zipper of the pink ski jacket. Dawn glanced at her mother in mute apology, but her shaking hands refused to grip the zipper and she continued to fumble, making little noises of frustration. Finally, she got it zipped and stood expectantly, like a dog waiting to be walked.

Looking at them together, I was struck forcibly by the contrast. Linda, tiny and trim, dressed meticulously, wearing clothes that fitted perfectly and choosing colors that flattered

her dark beauty. Yet the pink of Dawn's ski jacket was all
wrong for her honey skin, and she had grown so much in the
last year that an inch of wrist showed white against the frayed
cuff. I shrugged; it was none of my business, but I found
myself hoping that, once in Washington, Linda would give
Dawn's wardrobe even a quarter of the attention she lavished
on her own.

It must have been my tiredness that put me off guard.
I'd actually expected to be able to leave the courthouse and
get some lunch without interruption. I should have known
Brad wasn't finished.

He walked up to Linda, towering over her. She stood
unmoving, looking up at him with a challenge in her eyes,
daring him to start something. "Okay, Linda," he said quietly
enough, but with an air of menace. "That was round one. You
won it on a technicality." He glared at me, then turned his
attention back to his ex-wife. "But round two"—he stabbed
the air with a thick finger—"that one's gonna be mine. Just
wait and see."

"What's that supposed to mean?" Linda's voice managed
a weary indifference, but her eyes narrowed with suspicion.

"You gave me no choice in there." He pointed at the
closed courtroom. "You put me on the spot. I couldn't say no
to Dawnie." His face clouded. "It was a dirty trick," he
added, like a kid who'd been cheated at marbles.

I was inclined to agree with him and opened my mouth
to say so, when Linda cut in, her voice artificially sweet. "All's
fair in love and war, Brad," she said. Brad's hands clenched
into fists, and he moved one step closer to his tiny antagonist.
I stepped back instinctively, but Linda never moved an inch.
"Besides," she added with a toss of her head, "it was for
Dawn."

"Don't give me that!" Brad exploded. "You don't care
about her. You never did. You only wanted her in the first
place because you knew how much it would hurt me. And
now"—his voice cracked—"you're taking her away." He turned
his head sharply but not before I saw his eyes fill.

I turned toward Dawn. She was as rigid as her mother,
but her fingers, still shaking, played uncontrollably with the
zipper of her jacket. She was biting her lips, her teeth
making little bloody indentations. Linda waited coolly for
Brad to compose himself, then said softly, "You'd better get

used to it. Dawn's coming to Washington and that's that. There's nothing you can do about it."

"Oh, yeah?" Brad was in control again, his grief transmuted into belligerence. "I can come back into this court tomorrow if I want to and get another judge to modify the order."

I wasn't surprised at Brad's mastery of the jargon. He and Linda had been coming to Family Court regularly since their divorce, each trying to one-up the other on matters of custody, support, and visitation. "You might have to make a lot of trips in from Washington to come to court," Brad taunted. "How will your new boss like that?"

Linda laughed. It was a silver laugh that held no humor. "Is that all you can find to threaten me with?" she asked. "If you think Art's going to fire me—"

"Art?" The name came out like a slap. I'd grown so used to Linda referring to her boss by his first name that I no longer noticed it, but to Brad it had only one meaning. "You're having an affair with him." His face was a mixture of shock and deliberate blankness. I knew him well enough by now to know he was masking a deep hurt.

"Jealous, Brad?" Linda's silver laugh sounded a little tarnished the second time around. Her smile was the same one she used when someone complimented her on a new outfit.

"You think I care who you—" Brad's rough voice stopped just short of the word, after a hasty glance at his daughter. "Just be careful in front of Dawn," he warned, his fist slamming into his open palm. "I don't want her exposed to your filth, Linda. Understand?" The sound reverberated through the hallway. It was, I knew, simply Brad's equivalent to Dawn's playing with her zipper.

Unfortunately, the court officer who'd been watching this exchange didn't see it that way. Stepping quickly between Linda and Brad, he laid a hand on Brad's clenched arm and said, "Calm down, buddy. I don't want no trouble."

It was the worst thing that could have happened. Brad, whose rage had been checked by Dawn's presence, turned on the officer, eyes blazing. "Get your fucking hand off me," he snarled, twisting out of the officer's grip. It may not have been meant as an aggressive move, but Brad had a good eight inches on the court officer, who fell back against a wall. He shouted for help, ripped his handcuffs off his belt, and lunged at Brad.

Brad set his feet apart and spread out his arms, ready for a wrestling match. His breath was coming fast, and he seemed almost glad that things had moved to a physical level. He dared the officer to come at him. I looked around; six officers were about to weigh in on the side of law and order. "Listen, Brad," I began, hoping to avert disaster. But Linda had other ideas. Turning to one of the officers, she murmured, "Just don't let him hit me. He's always trying to hit me."

"Don't worry, lady," the officer answered grimly. "We know how to take care of guys like him. Tough guys who like beating up on women." He jumped into the fray, whirled Brad around, and before he knew what had hit him, Brad was standing in the center of a circle of blue, chained like a baited bear.

"What the fuck—" Brad cried, as puzzled as he was hurt.

"Shut your foul mouth," the officer who had cuffed him yelled, punching him on the arm for good measure.

"Not till I finish talking to my wife," Brad shouted, his face bright red.

"She don't want to talk to you," the officer replied, prodding Brad in the ribs.

Brad pulled away and faced Linda, his breath coming in little gasps. "Your fault," he panted. "You bitch! You'll be sorry for this, Linda. I swear you will." One of the officers told him to shut up, jerking him along like a puppet on a string. As they led him away, he shouted, "I'll kill you for this, Linda." Double doors banged, and the phalanx of officers led Brad, still shouting, behind them.

Linda watched, calm as a summer breeze, her dark eyes unblinking. Then she turned to her daughter. "Come on, Dawn," she said briskly. "Show's over."

Dawn, whose eyes had been fixed with mute sympathy on her father, put her trembling hand to her bleeding mouth and did what her Aunt Marcy had told me she did before every one of her tennis matches. She threw up. Personally, I thought the kid had a point.

2

Thank you, God, I prayed silently, forgetting for the moment that I'd become an atheist at twenty. Relief flooded through me; sweat poured in rivulets inside my down coat. My breath still came in icy gasps that stabbed my lungs, and my legs were rubber. But it was all right. My house was safe. It wasn't a fire.

Then the medics brought the body out. I must have gasped audibly. Someone in the crowd said, "It was that woman who lived on the top floor. The one with the daughter."

Linda! My head reeled as I tried to assimilate the news. It had been a week since our victory in Family Court. A week full of cases and clients and a thousand other things that had almost driven the memory of Linda's triumphant smirk and Brad's hate-twisted face out of my mind. Almost—but not quite.

"My God," I breathed. I stood a moment, trying to readjust my mind from relief to shock to sorrow. Then I trudged slowly up the steps, stopped at the top by a uniformed cop.

"Look, lady," the cop said wearily. "You can't go in there."

"I live here," I said, pointing to my name in gold on the parlor floor window. CASSANDRA JAMESON, COUNSELOR-AT-LAW. It winked at me through the strobelike flashes of the police lights. I didn't wait to be asked for ID, just turned the key in the lock and went into my office.

I headed straight to the filing cabinet, opened the drawer marked CONFIDENTIAL, and took out the bottle of expensive Scotch Matt Riordan had given me when I opened my own office after leaving Legal Aid. I poured a little into my coffee mug and drank it neat. Its warmth felt good, but it didn't stop the shaking. I sat down hard and took another sip. I was still shaking, but now there was an overlay of giddiness. Not a good state in which to talk to cops.

A voice came out of the silence. A voice I recognized from the past, from another murder, another body. It felt like the instant replay of a nightmare. I jumped, spilling whiskey on the desk.

When I looked up, I sighed with relief. It wasn't a nightmare after all. The man in the doorway really was Detective Button, the cop who'd shown up when I'd discovered my dead lover's body nearly a year ago.

"Christ, Button," I said with feeling. "You scared the hell out of me. What are you, the only detective in Brooklyn?"

"Seems like it sometimes," he agreed. "'Course, this is different," he went on, moving toward one of the clients' chairs. "You didn't actually find this one, did you, Counselor?"

"No, thank God," I replied, taking another drink. If we were going to talk about Nathan's death, I was going to need one.

Between the shock and the booze, I was feeling reckless. Gesturing toward the bottle, I offered Button a drink, fully expecting him to decline. He didn't. He poured a generous amount into the coffee mug I kept for clients, took a sip, and said, "You private lawyers sure can afford good booze."

"It was a gift," I answered glumly, watching my office-warming present on its way to warming Button's insides.

"Nice office, too," he commented, looking around appreciatively. "I like the pictures." Button's gaze rested approvingly on my Depression-era photographs of farm families.

"Must cost quite a bit, a place like this," he went on.

"I owe the world," I answered lightly. If Button really wanted a report on my financial situation, he could get it in ten minutes. "The bank, my parents, my brother Ron."

"Must be nice to have rich relatives."

I thought of Ron, who for years had lived in the VA hospital in Brecksville, Ohio, near our hometown. Out of boredom, he'd started investing his spare cash in the stock market, until he'd amassed a tidy sum. Now that he had discovered personal computers and ham radios, he had his own expenses, but he'd been more than generous about sharing his money with me.

"Yeah," I replied. "Silver spoons and all that." I looked at the detective across an expanse of oak desk, feeling a little like Nero Wolfe. Button had changed not a hair since I'd seen him last. His close-cropped Afro had exactly the same amount of gray, his cheeks were still chipmunk-round, and he still looked like the first black loan officer hired by a midtown bank.

"How was she killed?" I asked, hoping the question sounded more professional than I felt.

"Stabbed," he replied. "Stabbed repeatedly about the face and body with a butcher knife." His slight smile told me he knew very well he was speaking in cop-witness jargon. "Knife's still up there," he went on. "Have to get the scene-of-the-crime boys on it when they get here. Fingerprints, photos, blood samples—you know." I nodded; my work as a criminal lawyer had made me familiar with police procedure.

"How many times . . ." I began, then faltered, not sure I really wanted to know.

"Let's put it this way, Counselor," Button answered, his voice suddenly grim. "You're going to have to put six coats of paint on the walls before you can rent the apartment."

"I wish you hadn't said that," I murmured, picturing the upstairs apartment spattered with Linda's blood. Somehow I'd conjured up a vision of a peaceful, Sleeping Beauty kind of death. My mind flashed back to Family Court, to Brad, handcuffed and shouting threats. "You'll be sorry," he'd told Linda. I recalled his pained cry: "I'll kill you for this." Had it been the bluster of a man driven beyond endurance, or had it been a promise?

I'm a born defense lawyer. It's a reflex, not a choice. Start bad-mouthing Attila the Hun, and I'll probably come up with a defense. So if Detective Button had been trying to sell me Brad Ritchie as the killer, I'd have bent all my energies on thinking of reasons why he hadn't done it. But Button said nothing of the kind. Suspicion of Brad came from somewhere deep inside, unhampered by my habitual defense orientation.

I told Button everything. How Linda had overcome her usual prejudice against women and hired me after her first lawyer had retired. How I'd gone to court at least eleven times in three months to fight the petty motions brought by Brad and his succession of lawyers. How Brad had reacted when Linda boasted of her affair with Art Lucenti. How Linda had gotten Brad arrested and how he'd threatened her. How Dawn had stood, shaken and sick, in the aftermath of her parents' hatred.

Thinking of Dawn undid me. My recitation stopped as I choked back a sob. Linda's death I could handle; Dawn motherless I couldn't. I pulled three Kleenexes out of the box on my desk and buried my face in them.

Button waited. He was good at that. I threw the wet Kleenexes away, noting dispassionately that most of my make-up had gone with them. Then I took another drink; this time I felt it.

"Where is the daughter?" Button asked.

"Marcy's, I suppose," I replied. I was feeling exhausted from shock and emotion. "Linda's sister. She lives in Manhattan," I explained. "She always takes Dawn when Linda has a date."

"Oh, why was that?" Button asked, all innocence.

"Because of Brad," I answered with weary patience. "Linda had to be careful about the men in her life. If Brad ever caught her—" I broke off at the sight of Button's smug smile.

"I didn't say he'd kill her," I retorted. My defender's instinct was returning. "But he'd have used anything to get custody of Dawn away from Linda."

"How would he know?" Button asked.

"The man's a fanatic," I had to admit. "She told me once how he followed her, tapped her phone, went through her garbage. Believe me," I told Button, "he'd know in a minute if she ever did anything he could use in court. He's a professional ex-husband." I kept on talking, too engrossed to notice the way Button took it all in, feeding me straight lines, until I'd said more than I intended to. With all my years in the system, I couldn't figure out that I was rapidly becoming the prosecution's star witness.

"Of course," I went on, "he's not even supposed to know where she lives. If he has to talk to her, he calls Marcy and she calls Linda. Then Linda gets back to him. Visits are the same way. Linda takes Dawn to Marcy's, then leaves. An hour later, Brad comes, takes Dawn, brings her back, and Linda picks her up an hour after that. It's a total pain, Linda says, but it's the only way to avoid contact with Brad." I was not only unconscious that I was making a formal statement, I was oblivious to the fact that I was still using the present tense.

"I'd say a little contact took place tonight," Button said grimly. "Before I talked to you, I'd have said she walked in on a burglar, but this fits better. Nothing was taken, even though there's a lot of disarray." He shook his head. "Besides, that number of stab wounds—hell, no ordinary burglar would do that unless he was on angel dust. But an ex-husband, especially one with a history of wife-beating, he's capable of anything." I looked at Button curiously. The slightly bitter edge to his tone gave me the feeling he was speaking from experience. But I knew better than to ask.

Button picked up my phone. Automatically, I nodded the permission he hadn't bothered to request. "Where does the sister live?" he asked. "I'll have to get a policewoman to stay with the kid while she identifies the body."

"You don't need a policewoman," I said hurriedly. "I'll go with you."

"Well," Button looked at me, calculation in his eyes. "You *are* a lawyer, and a friend of the family." He put down the phone.

If I'd been operating on all eight cylinders, I'd have realized then instead of later that I'd been set up.

I watched Button's face as he rang the doorbell of Marcy Sheldon's East Side apartment. Impassive, schooled, with an underlying tautness that spoke the anxiety his features refused to reveal. How many times, I wondered, had this man stood in a doorway, waiting to bring death inside?

Marcy opened the door and let us in without a word. A tiny woman like her sister, she was different from Linda in every way that mattered. Where Linda had played up her little-girl look, Marcy was strictly dress-for-success. Where Linda had been a self-described man's woman, Marcy ran her own public-relations business and was independent to the point of fanaticism. She was about ten years older than Linda and held herself with the assurance of a much taller woman.

As Marcy motioned us inside, I looked around for Dawn. I didn't see her. What I saw was a standard-issue single professional woman's apartment. Stark white walls, chrome-and-glass tables, track lighting, wall units with smoked glass doors. A blue and green Rya rug. Framed posters of modern art shows from the Whitney and the Guggenheim. The living room struck me as looking about as personal as a corporate conference room.

The funny thing was that Marcy's office was the exact opposite. There she'd gone in for sumptuous upholstery in shades of mauve, black and silver lamps, wonderful Art Deco antiques and highly polished redwood. Vases of peacock feathers and framed 1920s *Vogue* covers had completed the look. It was stunning—and sensuous enough for a boudoir.

Marcy motioned me to the couch. I sat gingerly, not wanting to make myself too much at ease, as though death required some sort of discomfort. I decided Marcy must have furnished her apartment fifteen years earlier and hadn't given the place a second thought since.

She handed me coffee in a thick Danish mug edged with heavy blue stripes. I sipped it gratefully, needing it after the Scotch I'd put away. Marcy drank hers slowly and watched Button with expectant eyes. She'd been told on the phone that Linda was dead, but I didn't know how many details she'd been given.

I wondered how Button would play it. He could be sympathetic or brutal, and his choice would have nothing whatever to do with Marcy Sheldon's needs. Button would say whatever it took to open her up.

He chose the crisply impersonal yet regretful tone of a newscaster describing a four-car collision on the Major Deegan. It wasn't the way I'd have spoken to a woman whose only sister had been stabbed to death in her own apartment, but Marcy visibly relaxed and answered in kind.

Even when they got to the hard stuff, both Button and Marcy never wavered from the six o'clock news version.

"Did your sister have many men friends?" Button inquired, his face the same bland mask he'd worn since entering the apartment.

"I knew she was dating," Marcy replied, "but I didn't know the details. She was very taken up with her new job, of course," she added, then shook her head regretfully. "Such a good opportunity," she commented, as though Linda's murder had been an unfortunate career setback.

"What was her relationship with Congressman Lucenti?"

Marcy flashed me a glance from under mascaraed eyelashes and hesitated only a fraction of a second before replying smoothly, "He was her boss, Detective, nothing more."

I got the unspoken message. It was time for me to see Dawn. "In the bedroom," Marcy murmured, pointing to a door. I wondered what she would tell Button once she had me out of the way.

I walked toward the bedroom, my heart pounding. I cracked open the door, suddenly wishing to God I'd kept my stupid mouth shut and stayed in Brooklyn where I belonged. What right had I, I accused myself, to come blundering into this child's grief?

Then I caught hold of myself. I hadn't come as a sightseer; if I weren't here, some faceless lady cop would be pushing open this door. Dawn might as well be harassed by someone she already knew.

I opened the door and stepped into the room. Dawn sat on her bed still as a statue. A trance of grief, I told myself—until I saw the earphones. I tapped lightly on her shoulder, and she turned off the tape-player.

"Do you like the Police?" she asked.

"Well," I began, startled by the question. "Detective Button's okay."

"No," she giggled, her laughter slightly edged with hysteria. "not the police. The Po*lice*." She pointed to a cassette.

"Oh, the group," I said lamely as Dawn continued to stifle nervous laughter. I felt about a hundred and three, remembering my attempt to explain the Rolling Stones to my Grandma Winchell.

"I came to stay with you while your Aunt Marcy..." I broke off, not knowing how to finish. Or maybe the word *morgue* stuck in my throat.

Dawn nodded. While she didn't replace the earphones, she didn't talk either. We sat in silence for a moment, me perched awkwardly on the edge of the bed, my eyes darting around the room in search of something to talk about. A Culture Club poster, two Michael Jacksons, a teddy bear holding a miniature tennis racket, three tennis trophies—Marcy's guest room had been decorated with one guest in mind. A white bedroom suite, with green and yellow accents to match the patchwork comforter on the bed. Remembering the jumble of secondhand furniture in Dawn's own bedroom, I found myself warming to Marcy. She may act like a cold fish, I told myself, but if material things can show love, then she loves her niece. It was the one good thought I'd had since Linda's death. It comforted me as I watched Dawn look longingly at her earphones.

The silence was becoming oppressive. I wanted to say

something, but I knew instinctively that what I said had to be exactly right or I'd lose Dawn forever. Twelve is like that.

I relaxed slightly as I recognized the feeling. It was the same one I'd had when I'd started at Legal Aid, sitting in dark pens with accused criminals. For the first time in my comfortable, middle-class life I'd had to communicate with people so different from me as to seem wholly alien. Hell, I snorted silently to myself, I hadn't even known their *names*. Oh, sure, I knew to call them Julio or Anthony, Mr. Ramirez or Ms. Jackson, but those were the names they gave the Man. On the street they were Chico or Freeze or Mr. Cool. Once I'd learned that, I'd begun to loosen up with my clients, to learn their language.

I looked at Dawn. What secret name did she go by? What was the key to her private language? I tried to reach back in time to my own twelve-year-old self. Then I factored in Nathan. Less than a year earlier, I'd had to come to terms with the murder of my lover. What I'd needed as much as—more than—sympathy, had been truth, solid, rock-bottom truth—no lies, no sugar coating. My momentary question about Dawn's ability to handle truth evaporated when I recalled how many harsh realities she'd already faced in her life.

Suddenly I knew what to say. The words that had carried me through ten years at Legal Aid. The words that had started as an office joke, then became a catch phrase, and finally a summing up of the whole criminal-law experience. "It's a tough business," I said, keeping my voice as neutral as possible. The words themselves would mean nothing, but I hoped the tone would be more welcome than the phony sympathy she was probably expecting.

Dawn stopped biting her lips. Her tortured mouth relaxed into a brief smile of relief. She picked up a phosphorescent-yellow tennis ball and began squeezing it with her right hand. It was a strengthening exercise, but she used it the way her father had used his fist-slapping movement—to relieve the tension. It seemed a step forward.

"Did you find the body?" Dawn asked.

I cleared my throat. This honesty stuff was going to be harder than I thought. "No," I answered. "I came home just as the medics were taking her out."

"Who called the cops?" Her muscles knotted and relaxed, knotted and relaxed as her strong hand squeezed the ball.

"I don't know. Nobody does. Detective Button told me there was a 911 call, 'Burglary in progress.' Whoever called didn't leave a name."

Dawn's face relaxed from within. It was the same look she'd given her father in Family Court, when he'd finally agreed to the tennis camp.

"Burglary," she said. It sounded like a sigh. "Just some crummy stupid junkie who killed my mother for the TV."

She'd obviously seen a lot of six o'clock news programs, I thought. I would have given a lot to be able to leave it there, to agree with her that it had been a crummy burglar and the world was pretty crummy too, if such things could happen over a color TV. But I'd already agreed to a different proposition altogether. No lies.

"It could have been a burglary," I said carefully. "The police are checking on that too. But," I added, "they'd like to talk to your father."

"No!" Her voice was a moan, but the very depth of its protest told me the thought was not a new one. She had been hiding in her bed from the ugly possibility, drowning her fear in her music. For a moment, I wanted to lie—or at least give her back her earphones—but I knew the reality would have to be faced sometime. Brad was a prime suspect, possibly a guilty one. She might have a lot more harsh reality to face in the near future.

"There *is* a case against him," I pointed out in a deliberately professional tone, as though this were a billable hour. "He said some wild things that day in court." I looked into Dawn's solemn face and put the case for the prosecution as baldly as I could. "Let's face it," I began. "He didn't like your mother's relationship with Congressman Lucenti. He hated your mother taking you to Washington. Those are pretty good motives." Not to mention Brad's history of violence toward his wife. I was sure Dawn, who'd been eight when Linda had sought sanctuary at the Safe Haven shelter, hadn't forgotten.

Dawn gave the tennis ball a final death-dealing squeeze and flung it with all her might. "I hate Congressman Lucenti!" she cried passionately. "It's all his fault!"

There was a tinkling crash as the tennis ball hit the mirror above the white-painted dresser, sharding it into a million glittering, sharp-edged pieces. On top of the dresser, a yellow china dog sat, decapitated by the falling glass.

"Oh, God, I'm sorry, I'm sorry," Dawn moaned, jumping out of bed.

"Get back in bed!" My voice was sharpened by shock. "Your bare feet!"

"I'll get a broom and clean it up," Dawn promised, her voice tight. Her lips were working again; the look she gave me was the same mute apology she'd given her mother when she'd had trouble with her zipper in court.

"Get back in that bed," I ordered. Dawn did, but her eyes still darted as though she expected an angry Linda to come through the door and scold her. "I'm sorry," she said again.

"It's okay," I told her, trying to smile. My stomach was knotted in a sympathetic response it took me a moment to recognize. When I did, I had Dawn's secret. The deepest fear a child can know: It's all my fault.

"Oh, God," I said, my eyes welling with tears. Of course—Dawn blamed herself for her parents' divorce, and the permanent custody battle had only reinforced the feeling of guilt. Now it seemed that her mother was dead and her father a suspect because of her.

I forced a laugh. "No harm done," I said lightly. "What's seven years' bad luck?" Dawn gave me a wan smile for my effort, but then we sat in silence, trying not to think about it. Finally, Dawn broke the stillness.

"He wouldn't," Dawn insisted. "He said crummy things sometimes, but he didn't mean them. He was just acting out," she explained, her voice a parody of her Aunt Marcy's professional tone. My throat tightened as I listened.

"He didn't mean it," Dawn repeated. "I know he didn't." She pleaded for my agreement.

"Detective Button's a good cop," I said seriously. "He'll check out all the angles. He's not looking to pin it on anyone. If your father's not guilty, he'll find out who is." I hoped to God I was right. The problem was I could be right and so could Button. Brad Ritchie could be guilty.

Then Dawn's agitated movement stopped and she fixed me with a calm, clear gaze. "He was going to take me away," she announced. "That's what he meant when he told Mom she'd be sorry," she confided. "He was going to pick me up on Sunday for my visit with Granny, only instead of going to Bensonhurst we were going to drive all the way to Florida."

Dawn's voice was confident, but her eyes were still pleading. "He said I wouldn't need my clothes and stuff; he'd buy me everything new in Miami." She looked at me expectantly, waiting for a ruling. I knew the signs. The kid was a born defender, and her lifelong client was Brad Ritchie.

Judge Jameson signed and gave counsel for the defense what she wanted. "I'll tell Detective Button," I promised. "It might make a difference if he knows your father was planning to kidnap you." I hadn't meant to use the word; my anger flared as I thought about the reality that lay behind Brad's grandiose talk. A sorry trailer park. Dawn left alone while Brad, chronically unemployed, looked for work. Dawn trudging to school in Salvation Army castoffs. No more matches. No more coaching. No more camp. No more tennis.

"It wasn't *kid*napping," Dawn corrected sharply. "The man *is* my father."

"No." I agreed. "Just custodial interference. A mere misdemeanor." The last part I said under my breath.

"Would you really have gone?" I asked aloud.

Dawn gave it serious thought. "I didn't want to move to crummy old Washington," she said finally. I nodded; this was not news. The nod seemed to reassure her and she went on. "And Daddy needed me more than Mom did. Sometimes he'd get so sad when I had to go home on Sunday nights that he'd hold me and cry. Mom never cried."

Epitaph for Linda Ritchie. Mom never cried. Would she, I wondered, have cried if Brad had taken her daughter away from her? Or would she have found solace in the embrace of Congressman Lucenti?

That thought led quickly to another one. Had Brad's obvious jealousy of Lucenti been the final straw, the motive for Linda's murder?

Dawn was still arguing her case. "But if Daddy meant to take me to Florida," she said earnestly, "then he had no reason to kill Mom."

I remembered my promise to tell Dawn nothing but the truth. I looked her straight in the eyes and gave my answer. "No," I lied, my voice steady. "He had no reason."

3

If I'd had a boss, I'd have called in sick. Since I *was* the boss, I told myself not to be a damned fool. Then I hauled myself out of my loft bed, hit the shower, and took my hangover down to the Morning Glory.

I hadn't made my own breakfast since my old friend Dorinda had opened the place six months earlier. She'd been talking about running her own restaurant for three years or so, but only after I bought the brownstone did the idea really seem feasible. She'd rented my ground floor and had been doing a steady business ever since. Any day now, *New York* magazine was going to write her up and I wouldn't be able to get a stool to myself.

Dorinda herself stood behind the counter, her thick, wheat-colored hair braided into a single pigtail. She wore a hand-appliquéd apron; her Lassie's-mother look. She handed me a steaming mug of coffee without a word, knowing better than to expect conversation from me in the morning.

I drank the coffee quickly, letting it warm me from the inside out, waiting for that caffeine rush I'm convinced starts my blood moving every day. As I handed it back to Dorinda for a refill, I pointed to the hand-lettered sign over the counter: *Warm your cockles*, it read, *with a cheese-and-hot-pepper omelet*. "With rye toast," I added, as Dorinda walked over to the stove and started breaking eggs.

The hot peppers burned away some of the fog, and by the time the breakfast crowd had thinned, I was capable of speech. Dorinda took away my plate, then came back, poured more coffee, and murmured, "I heard about Linda."

"Yeah," I replied. "Tough business." I kept my voice low, murder not being very good breakfast conversation.

"I heard they arrested Brad," she went on.

"What!" My voice rose and I attracted curious stares. Dropping my voice again, I asked, "Where the hell did you get that, and me with the cops all night?"

"Ezra told me," she replied. Ezra Varshak was the reason she could afford the Morning Glory. After a lifetime of relationships with exciting losers, Dorinda had finally latched onto a winner. A man with money, eager to invest it in a vegetarian luncheonette in Cobble Hill. Since the place both fed me and helped pay my mortgage, I thoroughly approved. "He heard it on the all-news radio," she explained.

"Poor Dawn," I whispered. "I wonder if she knows yet. I was with her last night," I explained, looking into Dorinda's concerned eyes.

"How did she take it?"

"Linda's death? Not too badly, considering. What really bothered her was thinking about Brad's arrest."

"I can relate to that," Dorinda replied. The bitterness in her voice made me raise my eyebrows in a question I didn't have to put into words.

"Okay, so I didn't like her," Dorinda went on crossly. "I didn't like her attitude and I didn't like the way she treated Dawn." She turned toward her front window, where the sun filtered through the potted herbs that hung there, fragrant substitutes for the boring spider plants that decorated more conventional restaurants.

"I'm five-feet-ten," Dorinda said finally. "I was five-feet-ten by the age of fourteen. The tallest girl Traverse City ever saw. They used to call me the Jolly Green Giant. I felt like a giraffe. Like my feet were these enormous things I couldn't stand to look at." She laughed suddenly and came back to me. "It's okay now," she explained. "I don't mind Ezra's being shorter than I am. But then . . ." She shook her head. "I used to wish I could eat a piece of mushroom like Alice and get back to being a regular-sized person again. So one day Linda and Dawn stop in here after shopping. They had these A&S shoe bags and all Linda did the whole time they were here was make these cute little jokes about how big Dawn's feet were getting. Dawn tried to laugh, but I could see her slipping down into her chair, as though she was trying to shrink herself down to her mother's size. It was all I could do to keep from telling Linda off. If you ask me, Dawn's better off without her."

"She was a difficult woman," I agreed, remembering her demanding attitude as a client.

"She was a bitch," Dorinda pronounced.

We meditated on that thought while I downed my coffee and accepted another refill. This was a three-cup day if I'd ever seen one.

"She made a will," I said at last. "Marcy hired me as her lawyer for the probate proceedings." I almost smiled as I recalled my open-mouthed shock of the night before. Not only had Marcy been incredibly businesslike for someone who'd just seen her sister on a slab, but she'd handed me five crisp hundreds as a retainer. I'd tried to look as though clients willingly paid me cash in advance every day of the week.

"That doesn't sound like Linda," Dorinda remarked. "Making a will and all."

"No," I agreed. "She never struck me as a woman who accepted the inevitability of death." I shrugged. "Maybe she got a package deal with the divorce."

"I suppose Marcy will keep Dawn with her now," Dorinda said, but there was a note of doubt in her voice.

"I wish I knew," I sighed. "I tried to bring it up last night, but all she said was she'd think it over and let me know."

"What about Linda's mother? Or Brad's?" Dorinda asked.

I shook my head. "Linda's mother's out. She had major surgery a couple of months ago. She needs help to care for herself, let alone a twelve-year-old. As for Brad's mother—" I broke off, thinking of the last time I'd seen Ma Ritchie in Family Court. She'd worked herself into hysterics, causing a twenty-minute recess. But that wasn't the worst thing about Viola Ritchie.

"She's a dangerous woman," I said, knowing it sounded dramatic. "She's . . ." I broke off, unable to put words around my profound mistrust of Brad's sweet-faced, gray-haired mother. "She's Willy Loman," I concluded lamely.

Dorinda, mistress of the non sequitur, nodded knowingly, as though what I'd said had made sense to her.

"She pumped poor Brad up with hot air and grandiose ambitions, so that the jobs he could get seemed like a giant comedown. Then, when he lost even those menial jobs, she helped him blame everyone but himself. I can see her doing the same thing to Dawn," I went on, warming to the theme, "convincing her that she's such a great tennis player that she doesn't need to bother with silly things like practicing every day."

"You really care about Dawn, don't you?" Dorinda's steady gray eyes regarded me seriously.

"I just want Marcy to make up her mind, that's all," I replied crossly, ignoring Dorinda's knowing, sympathetic smile.

All night I'd pictured Dawn, alone in her green-and-white room, with her tapes and her trophies for company. What I couldn't see was Marcy holding Dawn, soothing her, letting Dawn sleep in her bed.

If I wasn't sure Marcy Sheldon really wanted custody, I was even less sure whether she wanted Dawn.

If cops fall in love with the street, then criminal lawyers fall in love with the system. It's a mainline shot of primo adrenaline, a daily fix of pure, uncut life. So I strapped up my arm and prepared to stick the needle in. I walked to court.

Mr. Green was on my mind. He was my new boss, and a damned sight more demanding one than Milt Jacobs at Legal Aid had ever thought about being. Mr. Green is the fee, the bucks, the money. Get it up front, that's the first rule of criminal law. On the theory that it's hard getting money from a guy newly employed in the license-plate industry. And if you get your client off, collecting the fee still isn't easy—the sucker will convince himself he was innocent all along and ought to be suing for false arrest instead of paying his lawyer.

It's a great philosophy, get the money up front, and one I was getting used to living by. The mortgage payments, the fuel bill, the office expenses, all helped remove the diffidence I had started with when it came to asking for money. But then there was Hattie Hopkins, who worked two cleaning jobs in spite of her arthritic fingers and rheumy cataract eyes. Who put on her best flowered hat every Sunday and rode three buses to the Foursquare Gospel Church. Who would have given any amount of money to see her grandson Terrell go free. Only one hitch: Terrell was guilty as hell.

"I ain't takin' no flea bargain," Terrell said truculently.

I faced him across an iron table. All around us were the iron sounds of the ninth-floor pens, the clanking of cell doors, the rasp of the huge keys turning in their locks, the raucous shouts of prisoners and corrections officers. The long tables ran the length of the interview room, lawyers sitting on one side, defendants on the other, all having essentially the same conversation.

"Not a bad deal..."

"But I ain't *did* nothin'..."

"You're a persistent felon. It's ten-to-life minimum if you blow trial."

"My woman, she'll come to court..."

I sighed. I'd both heard and said all the above, and now I was about to say it again to Terrell. My life was being measured out in guilty pleas.

I held up the police report and read it to my client. I knew there was no point in letting him read it for himself. He couldn't. "This kid Duane Rogers," I began, "says you showed him a gun in your waistband and said, 'Yo, run the coat.'" No response; I might as well have been reading him the Dow Jones.

"So Duane gave you the sheepskin," I went on, "and then he went home and told his mother, who called the cops. Now here comes the hard part." I looked up from the report and fixed Terrell with a long slow stare. "Duane Rogers not only described you to the cops, Terrell, he gave them your name and told them where you lived. He *knew* you, Terrell."

"He ain't know me," Terrell responded with scorn. He was still slumped in his chair in an attitude of total indifference, but the slight frown creasing his forehead was a good sign. I felt I was getting through in the all-but-hopeless task of convincing Terrell that the case against him was airtight. "He just think he know me, but he ain't *really* know me."

"He knew you well enough to get the cops to your house," I countered, "where, as you know, they found Duane's coat and your gun."

"I told you," Terrell's voice was high with anger and denial, "I ain't *takin'* no flea bargain. What you think my grandmother payin' you for? Huh?" He snorted his contempt, rising from his chair with a gesture of finality. "What kind of lawyer you be, makin' me plead guilty for somethin' I ain't did?" He slammed his way back to the iron door, banged on it, and shouted to be let back in. "I'm *fin*ished with this here lawyer," he announced in ringing tones.

I gathered up my things and followed him. As I walked the length of the room, I met amused or commiserating glances from all the lawyers who'd been in my shoes and contemptuous stares from the other defendants, convinced I was trying to sell Terrell out. That guantlet was a minor one compared to the one I passed after I got into the pen area. I had to avert my eyes in case someone was taking a leak, and I had to ignore the obscene shouts and whistles that followed me down the corridor. I breathed a sigh of relief as I got to the other side of the clanging doors, and wondered how the corrections officers stood it. For eight hours a day, they were as much prisoners as the men they guarded.

Terrell's grandmother waited patiently in the hall, holding the brown paper bag full of clothes she knew full well she wouldn't be permitted to give him. She brought it every time, a symbol of her caring.

"How is he, Miz Jameson?" she asked. "How they treatin' my boy back there?"

"He seems fine, Ms. Hopkins," I answered. I wanted to tell her the truth, that the best thing she could do for Terrell was to lessen her fierce belief in him, to allow him to face the reality of his guilt and cut the best deal he could get. But I had the uneasy feeling that her faith in him was the only thing Terrell had, the only rock in a stormy sea, and that he couldn't bear to let it go even if it meant seven extra years in prison.

I looked into Ms. Hopkins's eyes, their hopeful luster dimmed not a bit by the cloudy cataracts through which she saw the world. No, I decided, let Terrell tell her the truth himself. If he could. As to the fee, I decided it could wait.

I went from Terrell Hopkins to Tito Fernandez. Where Terrell had only one person who cared for him, Tito had a whole corridor full of supporters, slapping his back, poking him, laughing with him. They all wore their colors, against my legal advice. I really think a gang member would rather go naked in January than appear without the jacket that proclaims his affiliation.

They called themselves the Unknown Homicides. Like other gangs, they stuck together out of a need for community and protection in a harsh urban world. They needed both more than most kids do. They were deaf.

I walked up and greeted him with a smile and the one sign I knew—the two-finger salute that meant "Hi." The official sign-language interpreter wasn't there yet, but Frankie, who was only partially deaf, offered to translate for me.

"How's it going, Tito?" I addressed my client, a kid of eighteen whose Colombian parents had had enough trouble learning English, let alone taking on Ameslan. They could communicate with their son only in the most rudimentary fashion. As soon as he met the Homicides, Tito had left his family and moved into the semi-abandoned building they called home.

Unfortunately, sombody'd lit a fire in the tumbledown building, starting with Tito's mattress, and the cops had arrested him on the complaint of the super, a hostile type who objected to the "dummies" taking over his building and who claimed Tito and another gang member had threatened to burn down the building earlier in the week.

I'd talked to the guys many times about the day of the fire, but I'd always had the feeling, born of ten years in the system, that they were holding something back. I knew I'd better find out what it was before the trial.

I turned to Frankie. "Tito says he was with three other guys in Julio's room, right?" Frankie signed and Tito nodded; his hands started rapid movement, his mouth miming words. Frankie turned back to me and said in the dull monotone of the deaf, "Tito says he was with Julio, Marco, and Randy." Here he pointed to a tall black kid with cornrows. Unlike most gangs, the Homicides were integrated. Deafness was the only entrance requirement.

"What were they doing there?" I faced Tito as I spoke, even though I knew his lip-reading ability to be nil. "And I don't want any bullshit!" I said, pointing and scowling as I spoke. "I want the truth!" I punctuated my words with a forceful gesture, then turned to Frankie and repeated it. Whenever I talked to Tito, I found myself using exaggerated gestures and facial expressions to make up for the lack of words. I felt like a silent-movie actress.

Tito and Frankie signed back and forth and finally both turned to Ray, the leader. Ray stared at me with the impassivity I had come to expect from him. He was in his mid-twenties and had an acne-scarred face. He made a living selling cards printed in the sign-language alphabet on the subway. I asked Frankie to explain that if I was going to help Tito out of this jam, I was going to need the truth. While I spoke to Frankie, I deliberately locked eyes with Ray. He stared back coolly. He was a born leader, Ray, and I couldn't help but wonder what he could have been had he been born rich or hearing, or both.

After Frankie finished relaying my message, he looked at me with a steady, appraising glance. I willed myself not to blink. Finally he nodded, a single nod that sent all the fingers in the group flying as the Unknown Homicides proceeded to breach the wall of silence and tell me what had really happened.

"We was in Julio's room," Frankie translated. "We was gettin' high."

I nodded. I had expected something like this. "Tito was helpin' Marco find a vein," Frankie went on, pointing to a skinny, curly-haired kid of about fifteen. "He got skinny arms, and we was pokin' him to get the vein to pop." Frankie illustrated as he spoke, pointing to his own arm, pulling the tourniquet, searching for the vein. "Then Randy smell smoke." Frankie lifted his head and made a sniffing motion. It was such perfect mime, I could almost smell smoke in the courthouse corridor. "We didn't think nothin'," Frankie went on, making a brush-off motion, "but then it got stronger and we all run out." Tito was acting it out now, using his whole body to show how he ran downstairs, opened his apartment door and then recoiled from the flames.

"Stop!" I held up a hand. "Ask him why he went to his room. Why not straight outside?"

Signs flew. "He wanted to get his stuff out," Frankie explained. "But there was too much fire." His hands encompassed a conflagration.

The rest I knew. The super, perpetually angry at the Homicides' invasion, had told the police the boys had lit matches in front of his face. In his view, this had been their way of announcing their plans for the building. This the gang emphatically denied.

"So if you guys didn't do it, who did?" I asked, although I already knew the answer. Their answer. According to them, any rival gang, any Hearing gang, could and would have done it. "They always down on us for bein' deaf," Frankie said in his eerie voice, pointing to his ears. "We always gettin' crap from Hearing," added a plump black kid, whose huge earphones almost but not quite put him in the Hearing world.

Some wonderful defense, I thought as I signed the case in on the clerk's sheet and walked toward the front row of the courtroom. Gang vengeance by an unknown gang for an unknown reason. And my kids no angels in spite of their handicaps. The Homicides might not have lived up to their name, but there were burglars, shoplifters, and drug addicts among them, just as there were among the Hearing.

I needed a postponement. This case just wasn't ready for a jury, not if I wanted to win. I found myself wishing Linda's help had paid off. When I'd first picked up the case, I'd asked her how to go about locating the building's owner to see whether the fire might not have made him a profit. She'd given me advice from her days in a real-estate office, and I'd done my share of sending letters and subpoenas. None of it had borne fruit; the fire had been minor and no big insurance payoff had been made. It was just one more fire in a neighborhood gradually being destroyed by arson.

Still, I felt as though there were things I should know and didn't. Plus I had to see the building, something I'd been unable to arrange due to a heavy trial schedule. When I asked for the adjournment, Judge Kaplan gave me her Dragon Lady smile and asked, "What's the matter, Counselor, afraid to take this case to a jury?"

"Of course," I answered. "Any lawyer who's not afraid to hold a kid's life in her hands is someone I don't even want to know. Especially," I added with a smile, "when the case isn't ready. I'm owed a few things by the DA's office and there are subpoenaed items that haven't come in yet."

Over the prosecution's strenuous objection, I got my adjournment, as well as the fire marshal's report I'd been waiting for. One week in which to work a miracle.

The only person less thrilled by the delay than ADA Bergen was Tito Fernandez. Angrily gesturing, the Homicides demanded to know why they couldn't have the trial today and "get it over with." I tried to explain that "getting it over with" was not the first objective of a good defense lawyer, but they walked away disgusted. There are few things in life less rewarding than addressing the retreating back of a deaf person, but I did it anyway. "For the guys who don't trust Hearing," I muttered, "you're pretty anxious to put Tito's fate in the hands of a Hearing jury."

As the gang passed through the metal detectors, I saw Tito turn toward me. The one-finger sign he flashed me needed no translation.

4

As I surveyed the rack of brightly colored size-four dresses that hung in Linda Ritchie's closet, I recalled some lines of Edna St. Vincent Millay:

> Give away her gowns
> Give away her shoes
> She has no more use
> For her fragrant gowns.

I couldn't remember the middle, so I jumped straight to the end: "'Sweep her narrow shoes/from the closet floor,'" I recited to myself.

It seemed too soon. Linda wasn't even in the ground yet. But I had to admit Marcy was right. Dawn needed her school clothes and tennis things, and there was no reason some charity shouldn't put Linda's wardrobe to good use. And of course there was the fact that I needed the rental income from the top-floor apartment. I would have had to find a new tenant anyway, I reflected, once Linda had made her move to Washington. With that, plus the extra office I'd been trying to sublet, I was beginning to feel like a real landlord.

I looked around, trying to decide where to start. The cops had left things pretty much as they were, which meant a mess. The blood had been cleaned up as well as possible, and there was a film of dusting powder on tables and windowsills. The place had definitely been tossed. Brad looking for proof of an affair, the police had thought. Whoever had done it hadn't found what he came for. I didn't know at first where that certainty came from, only that the impression was strong and instinctive. Then I remembered the "safe." Linda and I had joked about it when she'd first moved in. Brownstone houses with working fireplaces cost more than I could afford; the fireplaces in my building had elaborate mantels under which were ornate gratings, meant to look like real hearths. Behind the grating on each floor was an empty hole just large enough to use as a hiding place. Whatever Linda had hidden— if anything at all—would be there.

I went to the fireplace, pulled back the grating, and found a manila envelope crammed with papers. I took it out, walked over to the window seat and sat looking at it. It was an ethical dilemma.

I finally decided that the contents of the envelope were part of Linda's estate and that I should, as Marcy's lawyer, open it. And besides, I was curious as hell.

I hadn't like Linda Ritchie. After reading the contents of the envelope, I knew why. She'd been moonlighting as a blackmailer.

The papers were well-organized, held together with giant paper clips. One clip per blackmail victim, plus a bankbook with regular entries—all deposits.

First victim: Ira Bellfield. It was no longer a secret how Linda had gotten the job in his real-estate office. Right on top was a Xerox copy of Norma Bellfield's file card showing that she'd been treated at the Safe Haven, the same battered women's shelter Linda had sought refuge in. Ira Bellfield was a wife-beater.

Linda hadn't wasted time once she started work. She'd learned everything she could about Ira's business, and what she'd learned hadn't been too savory. I began to see why Jack Newfield had named Bellfield as one of his Ten Worst Landlords. Linda had lists of his buildings showing apartments to be burglarized, fires to be set—all to encourage recalcitrant tenants to leave so the building could be flipped to a new owner at a profit. There were tapes wrapped in yellow legal paper and bound with a rubber band. I left Linda's apartment, went downstairs to my office, and put one of Linda's tapes in my cassette player. Then I pushed the button for "play."

"This fuckin' coffee's gonna kill me," a voice on the tape said.

"You think you got troubles," a higher-pitched voice

answered. "I gotta eat dinner again when I get home or my wife's gonna think I been out screwin' some broad."

The conversation wasn't moving; I pressed "fast forward."

"I want that guy whacked," the high-pitched voice ordered. "He's been giving me nothing but trouble, him and that fucking tenants' association."

"You want a fire or what?" The tone was bored, as though the men were discussing plumbing supplies. "I mean," he went on, "we done a lot of fires over there, Ira. We maybe oughta try a new tack."

"You let me worry about that," came the answer. The high-pitched voice carried more authority than I would have thought possible. "We got coverage on the fires—and I'm not talking Mutual of Omaha." He laughed, a snigger that went with the voice. "But what the hell, maybe you're right. Maybe we could just hurt the guy. Not even kill, give him a break. Hurt him for life." His voice grew intrigued with the possibilities. "A fuckin' vegetable," he concluded.

"Hey, Ira," the other guy protested. "I'm good, but, like, I'm no fuckin' *surg*eon, you know?"

It was something out of a Donald Westlake novel, or Jimmy Breslin's *The Gang That Couldn't Shoot Straight*. But something told me these guys *could* shoot straight and that the man they were talking about was by this time at least a "fuckin' vegetable."

I fast-forwarded again. "All right," Ira was giving orders. "We got Frankie in as super over there. He's been in a week and he's already busted the boiler and rented 6B, 2D, and 3E to junkies. Now we gotta start the break-ins. Let's do 5G for starters—I hate that big-mouth broad. She's been a pain in my ass ever since I bought the building. Clean her out—TV, stereo, cameras—I don't want her to own a fucking toothpick when we're done. Got me?"

I shut the machine off and took out the tape. Someday I promised myself to listen to all of them straight through, but for today I'd heard enough.

I looked around my office. The oak desk I'd earned as a fee from the owners of the Oaken Bucket on Atlantic Avenue, whose leases I'd negotiated; the brass-trimmed legal-size filing cabinets I'd bought with the proceeds of the Harmon divorce; the green-shaded desk lamp my brother Ron had given me for Christmas—it all looked suddenly very dear, and very vulnerable. The thought of arson hung oppressively in the air, like a heavy perfume.

I shook the morbid thoughts out of my head and went on to the second clipped bundle. Now I knew what Bellfield meant when he said he was covered for arson. Duncan Pitt, senior fire marshal for the New York Fire Department, had investigated fires in some fourteen Bellfield buildings. Even the ones he'd labeled "suspicious" he'd attributed to junkies or winos. No mention of the pattern of Bellfield ownership, no hint of arson-for-profit, came through his carefully worded reports. He was on the payroll.

One address caught my eye. I walked over to my brief-case, took out the report ADA Bergen had given me in court, and compared it to the one in Linda's packet. I'd been right. The Unknown Homicides lived in an Ira Bellfield building. It was the break I'd been waiting for. And Linda had known it. Instead of giving it to me, she'd used it for blackmail.

I traded in my Sam Spade fedora for Antony Maitland's barrister's wig and went back to being a defense lawyer. Would any of this, I wondered, be admissible in evidence at Tito Fernandez's trial? Could I show that Bellfield routinely used arson as a means to empty his buildings, and that he was, therefore, at least as good a suspect as Tito Fernandez and the Unknown Homicides?

The truth: probably not. The rules of evidence were strict; the relevance of other Bellfield fires would be hard to establish. Unless—my mind took a different turn. What if Duncan Pitt, the bribed fire marshall, were being investigat-ed? Surely that fact would be relevant to Tito's jury. The question was how would I get this information to the right people without tipping off Pitt and triggering a cover-up?

Matt Riordan. The high-powered, edge-of-ethical crimi-nal lawyer I'd met after Nathan's murder. If anybody would know how to stir up a hornet's nest without getting stung, he would. I decided to schedule a consultation, then smiled as I recalled that most of our recent conferences had ended in bed.

I went on to the third victim. Todd Lessek, called by local newspapers "the Donald Trump of Brooklyn." A super-developer whose touch was golden, he was a one-man gentrification movement, turning slums into luxury co-ops. If Ira Bellfield's name was synonymous with "slumlord," then the name Lessek meant money and plenty of it. It was hard to believe he'd leave any room for a small-time blackmailer like Linda. Still less likely that he'd actually paid her off.

But Linda's records spoke for themselves. It seemed that a high proportion of Lessek's buildings had once belonged to Ira Bellfield, and that he'd renovated them with considerable help from the City of New York in the form of tax credits and low-interest loans. Could it be a coincidence that the next blackmailee was a city employee named Elliott Pilcher, and that Elliott was listed as a limited partner in Lessek's most grandoise scheme to date?

The waterfront development plan was the biggest thing to hit Brooklyn since the bridge. When it was finished—if the city approved it—it would consist of luxury housing with splendid views of Manhattan, South Street Seaport–style shopping malls and restaurants, and a sports complex. Nobody was saying much about the fact that the plan would dispossess a number of small manufacturing businesses and the artists who had first staked out the area for living space. I knew about the artists firsthand. Some of them were my clients, introduced to me by Dorinda, who lived in a waterfront building and was wholeheartedly on the side of the community and against Lessek.

The most carefully guarded secret in the whole plan was the names of Lessek's limited partners, the people who were to share in the huge profits while keeping their identities hidden from the public. All perfectly legal, of course— unless you were a city employee like this Elliott Pilcher. The question was, what had Pilcher done for Lessek to be rewarded by the chance to invest in the waterfront development scheme? Had he provided all those city loans and tax breaks?

The next victim of Linda's scrutiny was her new boss, Art Lucenti. I read through the papers with interest, as Art had always been a hero of mine. He'd started as a Legal Services lawyer in the great anti-poverty days and had soon become known as an outspoken tenants' advocate, parlaying his popularity in Brooklyn neighborhoods into a seat on New York's City Council. From there he could be counted on to support rent control and generally act as a thorn in the side of the big real-estate interests. I, for one, had been glad to vote for him as congressman.

I wanted my vote back. Reading Linda's evidence destroyed

all that. Lucenti had been Lessek's man all the way down the line.

The first item was that Art Lucenti, like the mysterious Elliott Pilcher, was one of Lessek's limited partners, standing to make a giant profit if the waterfront deal went through. And the next item was that Art's investment had nowhere been mentioned in the sworn financial disclosure statement Art had filed before running for office. At the least, he was guilty of perjury.

That was bad enough. What was worse, at least from a moral point of view, was that all through his career as the crusading councilman, Art Lucenti's law firm had represented Todd Lessek. Linda's proof consisted of some very interesting legal papers. It seemed that an angry tenants' group had once sued Lessek, and had turned to Lucenti to represent them in court. He'd appeared on their behalf, but at the same time, the law firm that still used his name on its letterhead, that still shared an office and a phone number with him, that still doled out to him a portion of its profits, came into court for Lessek. It was as blatant a conflict of interest as a lawyer could imagine.

What I didn't know was whether the papers asking for a court investigation had ever been filed. I supposed not—it would have caused a major media explosion if they had—but if not, why not? Had the tenants' group been paid off or warned off? And if so, by whom? I jotted down the names of the plaintiffs and resolved to talk to them as soon as I could.

The last of Linda's victims, with a tiny packet of papers to her credit, was Art's wife Aida. If I'd felt saddened at learning the truth about Art, I felt doubly bad at reading Linda's notes on Aida.

Born Aida Valentin in Puerto Rico, she'd grown up in the South Bronx, worked as a secretary in a Brooklyn legal services office, and married her boss. That was the Sunday supplement version. What the papers had left out was that she had a criminal record and had once been a junkie.

At first I wondered how the papers could possibly have missed the story. It would have added considerable spice to the fluff they'd done on the "feisty but beautiful" wife of Brooklyn's "charismatic" congressman. Then I realized that the busts were either juvenile or youthful offender convictions. Sealed records.

Add the fact that drug program records are about as easy to come by as CIA documents, and it became apparent how the press had missed the boat. The question was, how much would Aida or her husband have paid to keep it that way? Publicly kicking drugs may be a good way for a fading country singer to get on talk shows, but it does less than nothing for the image of a congressman's wife.

The only strike against Aida during the campaign had been the no-show job. Everybody has them, but for Aida her position as a member of the Mayor's Committee on Minority Housing at twenty thousand a year had become a major scandal. For one thing, the ever-forgetful Art had neglected to put it on his financial statement, an oversight he hastily remedied. In Linda's file were a couple of letters from the Department of Investigation asking Aida to come in for fingerprinting and financial disclosure, normal prerequisites for any city job, but she'd resigned when the storm of controversy broke.

I stood up and took a stretch, arching my back like a cat's and unkinking the muscles I'd just realized were coiled as tight as a spring. What the hell, I wondered, was I going to do with this mess? Put my coat on, walk out onto Court Street, and march up to the Eighty-fourth Precinct? Ask for Detective Button and turn the garbage over to somebody paid to collect it? And then what? Watch while the papers ate Art and Aida Lucenti for breakfast, lunch and dinner? Catch the eleven o'clock news to get the latest on the Blackmail Secretary?

That stopped me cold. I stared out the widow at the steel-gray sky and realized that I'd been trashing Linda's reputation without any real guarantee that it would help Brad Ritchie. What I'd be giving Dawn would be a mother to be ashamed of, as well as a father behind bars.

I couldn't do it. No way could I add to Dawn's suffering for no good reason. Whatever action I took with respect to the blackmail material, I decided, had to be for the sole purpose of presenting the police with an alternative to Brad Ritchie as Linda's murderer.

It meant work. It meant questioning the blackmail victims until I had something to take to Detective Button. One quick thought: I'd start with Bellfield and the Lucentis. As Linda's employers, they were likely to show up at her funeral, where I might get a chance to talk to them with reasonable discretion.

Having a plan felt good. The helpless paralysis that had enveloped me ever since I'd sat on Dawn's bed and lied to her began to lift. I might not be able to comfort her in her loss or secure her a guardian, but maybe—just maybe—I could give her back her father.

5

What I needed was coffee. Coffee and a quiet place, far away from Kings County Criminal Court, in which to discuss Aida Valentin Lucenti with my old friend, Pat Flaherty. What I had was Part GP1 and a client named Derrick Sinclair.

"I ain't did nothin'."

I stared at him through the bars of the pen behind the courtroom. "A classic defense," I murmured, frustration turning on my sarcasm button. Hilary Quayle could have taken my correspondence course. "Is that 'I ain't did nothin', I was just the lookout'? Or, like the kid rapist I once had, is it 'I ain't did nothin', I just held her down'?"

"I told you," Derrick replied doggedly. "All I did was ask the lady for a cigarette. Since when they make that a crime?"

"How about when the guy you're with goes behind the lady and rips off her gold chain while you've got her stopped?"

"How'm I s'posed to know he gonna do that?" Derrick countered, his eyes measuring me.

"Might I suggest a little light reading?" I asked with a laugh. "Starting with your rap sheet. You and this guy Ralph Salazar have been busted twice before for the same thing. You'd better start carrying your own smokes, Derrick."

"Those cases was squashed," Derrick replied with all the confidence of a jailhouse lawyer.

"Oh, my God," I groaned. "If I had a dollar for everybody whose cases were 'squashed,' I'd . . ." I broke off, aware that I'd lost Derrick's already minimal attention.

"In the first place," I said waspishly, "nothing's 'squashed.' I'm trying to work out a deal here to cover the whole package. In the second place, 'squashed' or not, a guy who keeps getting busted in the company of a known chain-snatcher is going to have a hard time selling a jury on the idea that he just stood there with his thumb in his mouth while his buddy grabbed the chain. Do you hear what I'm saying?"

I let Derrick think about it while I dashed to the door to make sure my quarry was still waiting to be flushed. I'd done a lot of juggling to arrange an accidental meeting with Pat Flaherty and I didn't want to lose him to another courtroom.

To say the least, it had been a shock when Pat's name leaped out at me—on about the fourth reading—from Aida Valentin's application to a Phoenix House in Brooklyn. She'd listed him as a reference. It took me a minute or two to recall that before coming to Brooklyn Legal Aid, he'd been a juvenile rights lawyer in Bronx Family Court. It seemed a coincidence made in heaven—somebody who could clue me in on Aida's past and maybe pave the way for me to talk to her without scaring her half to death.

Pat stood before the bench, his humorous Irish face solemn as he spoke on behalf of his client, a guy who looked as if he'd been around the block so many times he'd worn a groove in the pavement. In the old courthouse phrase, he wore his yellow sheet on his face.

"My client, Your Honor," Flaherty boomed, "is now ready to submit himself to the discipline of a residential drug program. He's ready to—"

"Mr. Flaherty," Judge Diadona's dry voice interrupted. His lightly ironic tone was helped by the slightest of Spanish accents.

"Your client," he went on, "felt *ready* in 1982, in 1980, and in 1977. He entered drug programs in each of those years, promising each and every judge who put him there that now would be the time he would conquer his drug habit and face the world as a law-abiding citizen. May I remind you, Mr. Flaherty"—the judge was near a smile, but it was the grin of a predator about to pounce—"that in none of those cases did your client last in the program for even one month.

So kindly do not give me"—this time the 'r' had a full Spanish pronunciation " 'ready.' " The lawyers in the front row cracked up, but Flaherty looked pained, as though Judge Diadona had told a dirty joke at a funeral. That was Flaherty's strength as a criminal lawyer, I thought appreciatively, watching him work. He conveyed an air of utter sincerity, of deep concern for each of his clients, that was only partly an act. It seemed suddenly odd and touching to think of a younger Pat Flaherty using these talents on behalf of the South Bronx teenager who'd grown up to become a beautiful Aida Lucenti.

I turned and went back into the pen. "Derrick," I called softly through the bars, "what's your friend Ralph's nickname on the street?"

A puzzled frown accompanied the answer. "Speed," Derrick replied promptly.

"Oh, he's a druggie," I said innocently, "he does amphetamines."

Derrick snorted, "He ain't do no drugs. He be called Speed on 'count he *fast*."

"He's fast." I pretended to think about it. "You mean, he spots the gold, he snatches the gold, he runs with the gold—that kind of fast?"

I could picture it. The victim startled and a little alarmed by Derrick's coal-black bulk looming in front of her, then Speed's cardsharp-quick hands reaching for the gold cross, then running with the prize. It wasn't the Olympic version of "going for the gold," but what the hell, everyone who entered won something. We Buy Gold/*Compramos Oro* stores had sprung up like mushrooms in the ghetto; no one seemed to care that the gold chains they bought were invariably missing a few links.

"I ain't the one took the gold," Derrick persisted, his eyes wide with innocence. "I asked the lady for a cigarette. I ain't even touch her chain."

I sighed and walked back to the pen door. I wanted to make sure Flaherty was still in the courtroom, and I needed time to think out a strategy. Part GP1 was the last place to cop a plea before indictment; it was Derrick Sinclair's only hope of avoiding jail.

"Judge Cornelius," Judge Diadona was saying in a tone of weary exasperation, "may he be watching us from heaven, put this man on probation. But your client, Mr. Flaherty, has an atrocious sense of direction. He did not manage to find his way to Adams Street, to speak to his probation officer, once in the entire period of his probation. Can you explain that counselor?"

"My client tells me, Your Honor, that he had every intention of keeping his appointments but never received a letter to go to probation. A simple mixup, Your Honor," Pat shrugged, flashing a winning Irish smile.

"Perhaps the Probation Department *was* at fault," Judge Diadona agreed with suspicious affability. "Perhaps they *did* run out of engraved invitations." I closed the door on another laugh from the front row.

I marched back to the cage and called to the eight prisoners, "Okay, who wants to play 'People's Court'?"

"Hey, I seen that on TV," one kid cried delightedly.

"What we gotta do?" another asked, his voice wary.

"Just listen up," I answered, going into my spiel. "Two dudes are walking down the street. One dude's name is Speed. The other dude stops a lady and asks her for a cigarette. Speed goes behind the lady, grabs the chain, and runs. The other guy just happens to knock the lady down. Now the question before the jury is: Did the first dude know that Speed was going to grab the chain, or did it come as a big surprise to him?"

One kid snorted, "Huh, you shittin' me, lady?"

"'Course he knew," his friend agreed.

"What he *there* for, man," a tall kid with a pencil mustache exclaimed. "He the block."

"They be robbin' together," a dark man with sleepy methadone eyes pronounced. "They trying to get paid."

"What they offerin' you, boy?" A West Indian lilt cut into the babble. The middle-aged man with the gray-flecked dreadlocks hadn't joined my impromptu jury, but he now shared his opinion with Derrick, who stood, eyes bulging. "Whatever it is, you'd better think serious. You'd better pay heed to what your lawyer says." How fixed me with a sardonic grin. "She's one smart lady."

I bowed and smiled. "Thank you, sir," I replied, matching his courtliness. "*That* was a jury of your peers," I explained to Derrick, "*not* a jury like the one you'll actually see if you go to trial. *Those* people will be white, middle-aged, and scared to death of people who look like you. Now—what happened?"

"Me and my crimee," Derrick mumbled, "we rip the lady chain off. I block her, he snatch her."

Back in the courtroom, Pat's client was speaking for himself.

"I done turned my life around, Your Honor," he pleaded, his voice breaking. "I got a good woman now and a son I got to stay straight for." I felt a surge of sympathy, in spite of my better judgment.

"Don't you think that would be more impressive, Mr. Flaherty," Judge Diadona asked in dulcet tones, "if your client had not been arrested for assaulting the mother of his child?"

When all else fails, change your lawyer. Rule number one in the skell survival manual. Flaherty's client announced in ringing tones that he wanted a new lawyer; Pat had never visited him at Riker's Island. Judge Diadona defended Pat's skill (the only time a defense lawyer hears anything good about himself from the bench is when his client wants to dump him), but to no avail. Finally, Flaherty himself asked to be relieved, a look of weary resignation on his bearded face.

It was a confession of defeat. Exhausted and pained, Flaherty walked over and plopped his bulk next to me on the front bench.

"The very skelly are different from you and me," he sighed, as the judge announced a fifteen-minute recess.

"'Skells will break your heart,'" I replied, quoting the words Flaherty himself had used to me when I was a rookie Legal Aid lawyer learning the ropes from the old master. In those naïve days, I'd used the word *skell* to refer to anyone behind bars. Now I knew better. Now I knew the term was reserved for the utterly conscienceless, the sociopaths, the users.

Another sigh, this one longer and tireder. "What you've got," I said, trying another arrow from Flaherty's own quiver, "is the four-thirty I've-been-kicked-in-the-balls-again blues. By tomorrow," I went on brightly, "you won't even remember you client's name." As I talked to Pat, I felt a surge of warmth run through me. Since leaving the easy camaraderie of the Legal Aid Society nine months before, heart-to-heart talks with people who understood what I did for a living had been few and far between. It felt good to share the frustration again.

Flaherty turned hurt blue eyes on me. "Do you know how many phone calls I made for that guy? How many drug programs I begged before I found one that would take him? How much schmoozing I did with Probation before they'd agree to give him one more chance?"

"Pat, that skell used up every coupon in life's book of chances years ago."

"Yeah," the agreement came reluctantly, a near-grunt. We sat in silence, Pat obviously brooding, me trying to figure a way to introduce the name Aida Valentin into the conversation.

Finally, Pat spoke. "'Mother may I?'" he said. "That's the skell's-eye view of life. You want probation—just say 'Mother may I?' You want a drug program—'Mother may I?' Don't worry about the fact that you don't mean a word you're saying. Hell, these guys don't even know what words like 'sorry' and 'love' mean! Did you see"—Pat's blue eyes burned with anger—"the way that slime tried to use his own kid to get himself out of jail? A kid he probably never sees and certainly never supported, by the way. But he knows that the rest of the world—the ducks, the suckers—think kids are special, so when he's in a bind, he bleats 'my kid, my kid' and hopes he pushes someone's sympathy button." Pat, one of the world's great fathers, was clearly outraged.

"I just represented a kid," I said, pointing to the pen door, "who sees other people solely as sources of revenue. 'If it moves, grab its gold chain' sums up his view of life. But that's skells," I pointed out. "If they think you're sincere about having any values higher than self-interest, they see you as a fool, someone they can manipulate."

"Speaking of manipulation"—the blue eyes were suddenly shrewd—"what is it you want to talk to me about?"

I opened my mouth to protest, then realized denial would only make things worse. "The court officers?"

Pat nodded. "Hank told me you'd put your case off three times, waiting for me to come down for mine. So—what's up?"

"It's about an old client of yours," I began, looking around to see whether anyone was listening. Fortunately the lawyers who'd been sitting in the front now all had clients to talk to before the judge returned. Even so, I lowered my voice. "Aida Valentin Lucenti."

Pat shook his head. "She wasn't my client," he said. "I knew her, though. She was the co-defendant when I represented Nilda Vargas." The name rang a bell. Then I remembered I'd seen it on Aida's rap sheet. Flaherty continued, "But you don't want to hear about her. What's going on with Aida?"

I told him. I did better than that. Slipping my hand into my leather briefcase, I pulled out the slender packet that held Aida's criminal record and the reports from the drug program. I pointed to the box where Aida had clearly printed Pat's name as the person who'd referred her to the program.

"So even if you weren't her lawyer," I concluded, "you had some impact on her life, seeing to it she got off drugs."

There was a funny look on Pat's face as he looked at the badly Xeroxed application form. "I don't remember talking to Aida about her addiction," he said slowly. "Don't get me wrong—she was a nice kid and I'd have liked to see her get straight, but my memory is that she'd already flunked out of NACC. That," he explained, "was the old Rockefeller program."

I nodded; it took a scorecard to keep up with New York's ever-changing drug laws. The program Pat was talking about had been the fullest flowering of rehabilitation theory. When it failed, as it was programmed to do, Draconian measures replaced programs.

"Besides," Pat went on, "we were in the South Bronx. Why would I recommend a program in Brooklyn? How would I even know a program in Brooklyn?"

"Are you saying she lied when she put your name down?"

He shook his head. "I really can't remember. Maybe I gave her a list of programs and she picked that one. It was a long time ago."

"What about the rest of the stuff?" I gestured at the faded reports and evaluations from Phoenix House.

"The history's right," he said. "The stuff about her coming to New York from Puerto Rico with her junkie boyfriend. I saw him in court a couple of times and she admitted to her lawyer that she stole and tricked to keep them both in drugs."

"It's so hard to believe," I said. "She seems so together now."

"'The Beautiful Aida,'" Pat said wryly, quoting her press nickname. "She's come a long way baby, that's for sure."

"And it started here." I tapped the reports. "When she first came to the program, they sent for her school records. She'd been classified as borderline retarded, yet once she got off drugs, she finished her secretarial course at the top of her class."

Pat shook his head. "It happens a lot," he explained, "kids underevaluated due to language and cultural barriers. Not to mention the effects of drugs. You can't test too well if you're high all the time."

"This bothered me," I said, pointing to an early report. "The social worker claimed Aida wasn't honest with her about her drug use or her criminal record. I was hoping you could help me figure out which is ture—what they said or what Aida said."

"Sorry," Pat replied. "But a lot of junkies are into denial about the extent of drug use. She did well in the program later, didn't she?"

"Well?" I laughed. "She was the star. She kicked the habit and went straight as though her life depended on it. I guess in a way it did. Everything she became later she owed to that drug program."

"You want to know something?" Pat demanded, his eyes intent. "This isn't a total shock, Aida's being blackmailed."

"You mean you knew . . ."

"I knew something was wrong," Pat replied, his humorous Irish face troubled, "when I saw her at a fundraiser this fall. I've been active in the Brooklyn Independent Democrats for a few months now," he explained. I nodded, and Pat went on. "So when I saw Art and Aida at this party, I went over to say hi. Just a friendly gesture from a Park Slope poll-watcher. Or so I thought. But Aida looked at me as though she'd seen a ghost, to coin a phrase, and the next thing I knew she and Art were saying a very hasty good-bye and the word went around that she had a migraine headache."

"And you think you were the headache?"

"What else could I think? Especially if she was being blackmailed about her past and there I was, a living reminder of the old days in the Bronx. Not," he added with a sad smile, "that I'd have been so crude as to bring that up to her. But I guess Aida's a little short on trust these days."

While we both brooded about that, Judge Diadona re-took the bench. "The Nilda business," Pat murmured as if to himself. "That wouldn't do her any good either. Even if it *was* a long time ago."

I heard the name Derrick Sinclair. "Later," I whispered, then marched up to the bench to do battle. By the time I'd worked out a plea, Pat was gone.

I went from one Irishman to another. Matt Riordan was Flaherty's opposite in almost every way. Where Pat was genial, red-haired, and generous, Riordan was a driven Black Irishman who'd clawed his way to the top of the dirtiest and most dangerous segment of criminal practice. More than one of his clients had been fished out of the East River.

I caught him on a break in the trial of a court clerk accused of taking bribes. As usual in Riordan's cases, press people filled the first two rows.

I hopped up on one of the window ledges, crossing my legs. Fixing Matt with a look that I hoped would tell him I meant business, I began to talk about Ira Bellfield.

Matt shook his head. "The guy could be desperate," he said. "Word on the street is that a secret grand jury is investigating him. He's had one too many fires, and some of the tenants' groups in his buildings have gotten a lot of ink lately. Those tapes of yours could be just the clincher the DA needs."

"Thank God!" My relief was genuine; it never occurred to me to hold them back. Now that I know somebody upstairs was interested, that I wouldn't just be humored if I tried to tell the truth about Bellfield, it seemed one of my troubles was over. Just turn the tapes over to the proper authorities like a good little citizen and go about my business. Right?

Matt Riordan was not well-known as a good citizen. "Are you really that naïve?" he asked, his mouth a near-sneer.

"I'm naïve enough to want this dynamite of mine planted firmly under Ira Bellfield's chair instead of my own," I retorted. "What do *you* think I should do with them, put them in my cassette deck along with Paul Simon?"

"Maybe. That might be as good a place as any for them until you make up your mind how to use them to your best advantage. Do you really want to hand over your bargaining chips without getting anything in return?"

"What did you have in mind?"

"How about an enforceable promise to really investigate

Linda's death? Maybe even Brad's release—in return for which you'll guarantee them Ira Bellfield on toast. They'll go for it. They'll have to. Too many politicians have gotten elected on an anti-Bellfield platform not to."

"It just seems so scuzzy. Bellfield's a bad dude, okay, but why can't they nail him on their own and investigate Linda's death because they're supposed to, not because I've got them by the shorts?"

Riordan grinned. "Why can't you stop talking like a fourteen-year-old chain snatcher?"

I grinned back. "Come off it, Matt," I countered. "You know you're in this business for the same reason I am—you like the action."

"True," he acknowledged with a rueful smile. "It's like a surfer riding a wave—you can't control the force that moves you, but you *can* work it, glide along its edge, use its power to your own advantage."

"Sounds dangerous, the way you put it." My smile began to fade; there had been too many conversations lately in which I'd had the sense that Matt Riordan was heading his surfboard along giant waves too rough even for him to handle.

The court officer came into the hall to call Matt back inside.

"Think about what I said," he cautioned, his eyes serious. "The games called hardball, and if you want to survive as a criminal lawyer, you'll have to learn to play it."

"What would you do if you had the tapes?" I asked.

The famous Riordan grin split his face. "What I always do—bluff."

6

I hate open caskets. It's like watching someone become a junkie—a once-animated face is replaced by a permanent glassy stare.

I tried to tell myself I wasn't a ghoul, that I'd be at the funeral anyway, out of respect for my dead tenant. But it was no good; my eyes kept wandering from the casket to the mourners' faces. Which of them, I wondered, had she blackmailed? Which of them had hated her enough to kill?

Finally it was my turn to file past the bier. It was lined with gold satin; Linda would have approved of the way it flattered her coloring. But even the gold lining and the expert makeup job couldn't hide the tiny lines of discontent around the mouth, the crow's feet near the expressionless eyes. She had the hard permanent smile of a Barbie doll.

As I turned, I glimpsed Marcy and Dawn standing stiffly in the pew. Dawn towered over her tiny aunt; I had hardly recognized her in her tailored black suit. It was the first time I had ever seen her wearing clothes that fit. It was also the first time I had seen her hair styled. She had a grown-up air about her that went beyond clothes and hair. If, as Millay says, "childhood is the kingdom where nobody dies," then Dawn was an exile.

I turned away after a brief nod to the chief mourners. I had come less to mourn than to watch. I resumed my seat in the fourth pew and scrutinized the people filing past the coffin.

I recognized Art Lucenti at once. Everyone in Brooklyn over the age of six knew Art. His face had beamed at us from our TV screens and our front pages; even our shopping bags proclaimed: LUCENTI FOR CONGRESS. HE'S *YOUR* MAN. His politician's smile was subdued as he walked slowly up to the coffin and gazed meaningfully down at the body of his late secretary. I could already hear the six o'clock news gushing over the congressman's touching grief at his tragic loss; we had already had camera crews on Court Street canvassing neighbors who had never met Linda Ritchie for their opinions about her violent death. I knew that whatever Art said for the cameras would reflect nothing of the relief he had to be feeling.

Aida followed him, looking as demure as possible in a black Chanel suit with a white ruffled blouse. As usual, you felt she could have taken the skirt a size larger. She tried to subdue her sexy walk, but the narrow skirt and high heels created their own engineering, and she attracted every male eye in the church. Yet at the same time there was a genuine reverence in her bowed head and respectful gaze. Her expression was unreadable; between her high-fashion makeup and enormous tinted glasses, she was inscrutable as a mannequin. Once past the coffin, Art took her arm and led her past Marcy and Dawn, where he murmured a few words and received a gracious nod from Marcy. Dawn, however, stared straight ahead, refusing to acknowledge his presence. In any other context it would have been deliberate rudeness; here it could be put down to sorrow.

I was still watching the Lucentis when I heard somebody say the name "Ira." I turned to see a slight, balding man approaching the coffin. I stared in disbelief. *This* was the King Slumlord? *This* was the man whose goons and torches had terrorized whole neighborhoods? He looked like an accountant with ulcers. He looked like Maude's husband. He looked, I finally decided, like the voice on the tape.

Then I saw him peer down into the coffin. I was standing at just the right angle to see his profile. He pursed his lips ever so slightly, and I saw droplets fall into the casket. Ira Bellfield, blackmail victim, had just spit on the dead body of Linda Ritchie. Another line of Edna's came to me. "Brought to earth the arrogant brow," I recited to myself, "and the withering tongue/chastened. Do your weeping now." *Dirge* for a dead blackmailer.

What happened next I saw first as a flash of blue. It took me a moment to realize that what I was looking at were two uniformed corrections officers and, between them, handcuffed, stood Brad Ritchie.

A funeral order. It had to be. Impossible as it may seem, some lawyer had actually secured the court's permission for a man accused of his wife's murder to attend her funeral.

My only thought was for Dawn. Brad Ritchie apparently agreed. Passing the coffin without a glance, he headed straight for the first pew. The officers were hard put to keep up with his pace. Strain as I might, I could hear nothing of his conversation with Dawn. I saw his mouth work with the effort of keeping his tears back, and I saw him shake his head. Dawn reached out to him, only to have her arms virtually slapped back by one of the officers. Marcy turned sharply on him, and both officers hustled Brad away. Dawn turned a white, tearstained face in his direction, following him with her eyes. Then Dawn fell into the pew, head in hands, sobbing. Gone was her grown-up poise. Marcy stood protectively next to her niece, her hand poised over her shoulder, yet not touching the black suit jacket.

Then I saw Button. He was in the back pew, a mile of anticipation on his face. However Brad had come to the funeral, I reasoned, it was not against Button's wishes. And I thought *I* was a ghoul! Listening to Dawn's subsiding sobs, I felt a moment of pure hatred for Button. He had once done the same thing to me, treating me with little kindness after Nathan's death, just to see what my anger might produce. I'd long since forgiven him for that, recognizing the motive behind the cruelty. But this was different—he had his suspect, and it was a child he was hurting. I gave him a venomous look and got a subdued smirk in response. Button knew what he was doing all right!

After the service, people stood next to cars, deciding how to get to the gravesite. I had no car, so I waited, considering a cab. Button came up behind me. "Want a ride, Counselor?" he asked blandly.

"How could you—" I began, then stopped in mid-fury when I realized how predictable I was being.

"We can talk about it in the car," he said, as though the matter were settled. Which it was; I needed the ride, and I was determined to get a few things off my chest. I opened the passenger door to the white Audi he indicated was his.

"I can't believe you did that," I said coldly, "to a *kid*, for God's sake. What *are* you, anyway?"

The answer came as no surprise. "A cop," he snapped. "A cop with a weak case. I was hoping for a nice spontaneous graveside confession. The kind some bright lawyer can't get thrown out on a technicality."

"Yeah," I replied. "I remember how much you love lawyers." Then the words registered. "What do you mean, weak case?"

"You shysters," he began, but he grinned when he said it, "would call it circumstantial. What we have got," he explained, "is one hell of a strong motive, which as you know cuts no ice in the courtroom, supported by fingerprints found in the deceased's apartment—"

"You're kidding," I exclaimed. "Brad wasn't even supposed to know where she *lived*, let alone go inside."

"Exactly," he agreed. "And when he was first questioned,

he stuck to the story that he didn't know her address. Then he broke down and admitted that he knew, but said he'd never been there. Then he changed his story again and said he'd been past the house but never inside. When he was confronted with the fingerprint evidence, he told us he'd broken in to check on who his wife's boyfriends were but said it happened a month before the murder."

"Linda *was* broken into a couple of times," I told him.

"Yeah," Button said glumly. "We found the sixty-ones," he added, referring to the police reports. So Linda had reported the crimes; that would lend credence to Brad's story.

"And there's nothing to show when the fingerprints were made?"

"You got it. Your tenant wasn't exactly housekeeper of the year. Those prints could have been there a month—as Ritchie's lawyer will undoubtedly tell the jury—in which case he might just beat the rap. Which, in my opinion, would be a crying shame. So I brought him to the party to see if looking at his dead wife and seeing his kid might not jar loose a little truth. It still might," he shrugged. "It's not over yet."

"There's something else you ought to know," I said. I told Button everything Dawn had told me the night of the murder, about how Brad had planned a kidnap. "And another thing," I went on. "Why was Dawn sent to Marcy's that night? She only went there when Linda had a date, so who was Linda meeting? Find that out," I finished triumphantly, "and you might find another motive for murder." I didn't add, you might find Art Lucenti.

"The kid doesn't know," Button said. "I asked her. Besides, maybe she had an appointment with her ex-husband. Ever think of that?"

"If Brad so much as *thought* about visiting Linda," I countered, "she dug out her order of protection and had him arrested. Ever think of that?"

Any ideas I might have had about turning over the blackmail materials died a quick death. Button was still convinced that Brad was guilty. It would take more than speculation on my part to open his mind.

As we pulled into a small parking area in the cemetery, I saw Marcy in heated debate with an elderly woman. My heart sank. Ma Ritchie. Brad's mother. I jumped out of the car and ran to where the two women stood. It looked like trouble.

I'd run into Ma Ritchie in court a few times. Once she'd even brought a petition to get Dawn's custody transferred to her if the court wouldn't give it to Brad. "You don't understand," she sobbed into her handkerchief. "That child is my life. It's one thing for you, you've got a good job and no husband, you don't care, but I spend all week looking forward to my granddaughter's visits. And that sister of yours was going to take her away from me . . . ." She broke off in a fresh flood of tears. Marcy, standing stiffly at attention, arms folded, looked distinctly uncomfortable in the face of so much uncontrolled emotion.

"Please, Mrs. Ritchie," I murmured, "this isn't the time or the place."

Mrs. Ritchie looked up through red-rimmed eyes. "I know," she sobbed. "I just can't help it. My poor boy in jail . . ." Her voice trailed off. "Some people just don't understand a mother's heart. All I wanted was for Dawnie to spend the weekend with her grandma. Was that so much to ask?" She shot me a look of mute appeal, forgetting for the moment that as Linda's lawyer, I was the enemy.

"I told you before," Marcy replied, spacing her words in a way that spoke of controlled frustration, "she has a very important tennis match in White Plains on Saturday."

"Would it be so terrible"—again Ma Ritchie appealed to me as though I were an arbitrator—"if she missed one little tennis game?"

Even I knew that at Dawn's level, no match could be brushed aside as "one little tennis game," but I was unprepared for the controlled fury of Marcy's reply.

"Dawn *will* play that match, Mrs. Ritchie," she replied coldly. "And the court will decide how much visitation you will have in the future." Her face was implacable. I bet her Madison Avenue competition knew that look well.

"She'll be coming to live with me," Mrs. Ritchie announced, her damp eyes wary of the challenge she knew must come. "No judge could keep her from me now."

"We'll see about that," cut in a steely voice. Marcy faced the woman with determined patience. "I have de facto custody, and I think Ms. Jameson here can persuade the court to make it de jure." She turned to me. "Will my retainer," she asked, "cover the cost of a custody petition?"

It was what I'd wanted for Dawn, just not the way I'd pictured it. I nodded, hoping Marcy's icy determination wasn't all she intended bringing to the custody fight. Ma Ritchie gave a final sniff into her handkerchief and stalked away in high dudgeon.

"I'll be damned," Marcy Sheldon said, her eyes glinting, "if I'll let that woman take anything away from me."

As I watched them lower Linda Ritchie into the ground, my thoughts were of Ira Bellfield. He stood straight across from me, on the other side of the grave, his head bowed in an attitude of respectful regret. Note quite sorrow, yet certainly nothing like the triumph that had possessed him at the church, when he'd spit into the coffin. I gazed at the bald spot on his head, at the sunken cheeks blotched by the cold, at the thin fingers he blew on. I had to talk to him alone. But how could I shake my police escort? I was considering the problem when an opportune 911 call solved it for me. Muttering an apology, Button took off in a rush. I was stranded at the cemetery, but I had all the time in the world to talk to Ira Bellfield.

Time I had. What I didn't have was Bellfield. I watched in frustration as little knots of people made their way to parked cars. No Bellfield. At last, alone at the graveside, I trudged toward the parking area.

The minicams were rolling as I approached the parking lot. A solemn-faced Art Lucenti was once again expressing his "tremendous sense of loss" at the "senseless violence" that had cost him his secretary and blackmailer.

Then I noticed Aida. She leaned against the highly polished gray-and-black Fiat watching her husband charm the newspapers, her face shaded by the wide-brimmed black hat she'd worn in church, her generous mouth twisted into an amused smile. A fond mother who hated sports, I thought, might watch her eight-year-old hit a home run with just such an expression.

I walked over to her. "Mrs. Lucenti?" I pretended it was a question. "My name is Cassandra Jameson. I was Linda Ritchie's lawyer."

Aida Lucenti turned toward me, her face unreadable,

the smile gone, and I sensed a wariness in her, but the huge, tinted glasses she wore made it difficult to judge her feelings.

"Her death is a great tragedy," Aida pronounced, her slight accent like a hint of spice. "My husband will miss her a great deal."

I traveled back in time, first to yesterday's conversation with Pat Flaherty, then to the South Bronx in the early seventies. It wasn't easy to replace the high-fashion Aida Lucenti standing before me with the Aida Valentin Flaherty'd described, but I spoke at last to the South Bronx junkie, not the congressman's wife.

"Come off it, Aida," I said. "Don't give me the same bullshit your husband's handing the press. I know what Linda Ritchie was really up to, and it wasn't taking dictation."

The languid amusement vanished. Standing away from the car, muscles tensed, Aida faced me. I could smell the fear under her musky perfume, but none of it showed in her face. Tossing her head, she said, "I don't know what you're talking about." Only the sulky set of her mouth belied her words.

"Yes, you do," I replied firmly. "I'm talking about blackmail. Linda knew things about you that you wouldn't want those reporters over there to find out, and you paid her to keep them quiet. Right?"

She was a class act. No obvious panic, no whining protests. Yet she drew her breath in sharply and her face was a pale green mask. She looked as though she was going to be sick.

"How much?" she whispered through stiff lips. "How much do you want?"

Playing blackmailer for Ira Bellfield would have given me a kind of low satisfaction. With Aida, I just felt low.

"I'm not a blackmailer," I said quietly. "For one thing, I'm a friend of Pat Flaherty's."

Her face seemed to go white under her contoured makeup, but her voice was steady. "Does he know?" she asked.

I nodded. "We talked about your past. Not that there was all that much to talk about," I went on. "I mean, these days, what's a couple of drug busts?"

She forced a laugh, the color coming back to her face. "You're right," she admitted. "I'm so used to secrecy, I've blown it all out of proportion. Now that Art's won the election it would not matter so much."

"So people would turn on you," I continued, "but plenty of others would admire what you did. Kicking drugs, getting a good job—that's nothing to be ashamed of."

The gratitude in Aida's face embarrassed me, so I turned away. The television crews were packing cameras into vans, but Art Lucenti was still "on"; tossing a wisecrack to the Channel 2 reporter, blowing a kiss to the attractive Italian woman from Channel 7, he was performing for cameras that had ceased to roll. A born politician, I mused, idly picturing how rapidly the scene would change if I told these same friendly reporters what I knew about Art's financial dealings. It would be like watching a roomful of cute puppies suddenly gone rabid, tearing at human flesh. Of course I wouldn't do it, but looking at Art's beaming face—a face I'd trusted—I felt an overwhelming desire to wipe that smile away. The feeling was strengthened by memories of Dawn. Maybe her hostility toward Lucenti was nothing more than a child's resentment of her mother's lover, but somehow I suspected something deeper.

"I have to talk to your husband," I said abruptly. It didn't surprise me that my words brought panic to her face. "You won't tell him . . ." she began.

I shook my head. "No," I said, "but Linda had business with him too. I need to discuss it with him."

"Of couse," she said, but the words were mechanical. "He's leaving for Washington in a few minutes. I'm driving him to the airport. Perhaps when he gets back, a meeting can be arranged."

Suddenly, Art was with us. I found myself looking into warm brown eyes that crinkled with friendliness, my hand shaken with fervor as Aida introduced me. As he released it, Art gave my hand a little extra caress that carried a sexual tingle. No wonder, I thought, that women voters loved Art Lucenti.

"Ms. Jameson is a lawyer," Aida announced. "She would like to see you when you can spare her the time."

"Of course, of course," Art said, his voice expansive. He opened the car door for his wife, bent to enter the driver's seat, and said, "Just give my secretary a call. She'll set something up as soon as I get back from Washington."

"I'll do that, Congressman," I replied with a touch of firmness, "I'll do that."

The congressman closed the door for his wife and climbed into the car. I turned toward the direction I assumed the subway would be, then saw a familiar figure hurrying toward the lone car remaining in the lot.

"Mr. Bellfield," I called, running after him.

He turned and fixed me with a suspicious gaze. "Do I know you?" he asked.

"Maybe not," I retorted, "but I know you. I was Linda's lawyer and her landlady. I know quite a few of her little secrets." I was hoping I sounded provocative.

"Just what is it you think you know so much about?" Bellfield demanded shrilly. My provocation seemed to have been enough.

"Oh, I know about the buildings you own. The ones that burn down so often. And about the burglaries. I even know," I went on, feeling sick inside but trying for the I-own-the-world smile I'd seen Linda use and now understood, "how Linda met your wife Norma."

"You leave my wife out of this!" His high-pitched voice was a near-squeak; I could have laughed except that I knew that voice could issue orders that would be obeyed. Orders I wouldn't like.

"I can't very well do that, can I?" I asked, still smiling. "If it hadn't been for her, you would never have met Linda."

"I wish I'd never met either one of them." Ira Bellfield ran harassed fingers through his thinning hair. "Broads," he said hoarsely. "All broads are good for is trouble. First Norma, then Linda, now you." He poked a skinny finger at my chest. "But you better watch out, sweetheart. You can only push Ira Bellfield so far. Push him too far and—"

"And you end up in the Safe Haven?" I finished sweetly. But my heart was pounding; I might not get off so easily.

Bellfield had the same thought. "If you're lucky," he said, turning on his heel. The quiet tone in which he'd said the words made them seem all the more menacing.

In the subway, I consulted the map to figure out the unfamiliar way home. On the map's Riker's Island, someone had drawn a high-rise hotel and added the words *Playboy Club*. I laughed and bought my token.

My thoughts on the long subway ride home were of fire.

I could see my house consumed by flames, and my anxiety grew with every delay. Which is why when I got to Court Street and once again saw flashing lights, I nearly fainted.

7

Once again, the flames existed only in my imagination. The reality: a few bent bars on my back office window. Dorinda, who'd been pressure-cooking beans for tomorrow's burritos, had heard a noise and gone to investigate, armed with a skillet. I had to smile at the image; her pioneer forebears had probably frightened bears and Indians the same way. In any case, she'd scared the burglar, but couldn't give much of a description to me or the cops.

"It all happened so fast," she protested. I nodded. "All I saw was a pair of jeans." She shrugged. "Probably just a kid looking for dope money." She turned to the stove, where water for tea was boiling. The Morning Glory was closed, the lunch crowd long gone, but to Dorinda food meant healing, so she cooked.

"This is the third time somebody's tried to break in since I opened," Dorinda went on, popping a batch of scones into the oven. "I'm beginning to think Ezra's right. I ought to get a gun."

I was appalled. "My God," I said in awed tones, "this is it—the death of liberalism as we know it. Dorinda Blalock gets a gun."

"Why should I let some junkie steal everything I've worked so hard for?"

"Dorinda," I said patiently, "it takes you four months to decide on a *blender*. How in hell are you going to buy a gun? Besides," I went on, "I don't think this particular burglar was after your profits. My money's on Ira Bellfield. Those tapes in my office safe are dynamite as far as he's concerned."

"Who's Ira Bellfield?" Ezra Varshak asked, walking in

with his quick stride. Dorinda latest boyfriend was wearing his usual costume—jeans that looked as though they'd seen every peace march and rock festival ever held and a faded blue sweatshirt with the legend "Vulcan Science Academy" emblazoned in white letters. With his red hair and freckled face, Ezra could still pass for the seventeen-year-old sci-fi freak he'd been twenty-five years ago. Even his name, I sometimes thought, sounded like bad science fiction: "I-am-Varshak-from-the-planet-Greeb," I could hear a robot voice saying.

What was unusual about Ezra, especially for one of Dorinda's men, was that everything he touched turned to money. Take the cheap science-fiction paperbacks and magazines he'd squandered his teenage earnings on, to his mother's dismay. At the last Sci-Fi/Fantasy Convention, his collection had been assessed at over six figures. The sandalmaking business that had humiliated his father the orthopedist was now a multistate operation, grossing more than Dr. Varshak's lucrative practice. Ezra Varshak was a hippie conglomerate.

I explained to Ezra and Dorinda about the blackmail, hoping that Ezra could help me understand the financial aspects. But I knew it was a long shot; Ezra's business acumen was wholly instinctive, owing nothing to management courses. His first sandal shop had opened on St. Mark's Place in the East Village's Day-Glo heyday. It was on the parlor floor of a brownstone, and Ezra, who loved people and excitement, had put his workshop smack in the bay window so he could watch the passing parade. It was unconscious, inadvertent marketing genius. The passing parade had avidly watched him back. He became a stop on the tours of East Village scenes, a human landmark. People came in to watch him hammer leather and left with a pair of his sandals on their feet. The sandals, ugly but comfortable, became a sixties symbol, yet Ezra was too smart to be left behind when more attention to fashion returned. He added lines of boots and shoes, sold handmade bags and briefcases, and introduced vests, skirts, and pants in soft suede. He had shops in all the best suburban malls—each with the workbench in the window—and was now negotiating leases in the Midwest.

Dorinda poured tea and put a huge plate of hot scones on the table. By the time the cups were drained and the plates empty even of crumbs, I had finished the story.

"Why Bellfield?" Ezra demanded. "Why not one of the others?"

"Are you kidding? He commits burglary every day of the week—or at least has it done, which is the same thing. If you'd heard those tapes—"

"Take it easy, Cass. I'm not the guy's defense lawyer." Ezra smiled and I relaxed. "But you just got through telling us you called *all* the blackmail victims yesterday and made appointments to see them this week. So anybody could have put two and two together and gotten nervous."

"Hey, I'm not a fool," I protested. "I didn't call these people and say, 'Let's talk blackmail.' I have *some* sense." But I was uneasily aware that this was sheer defensiveness; I had gotten myself in deeper than I'd planned, and I was beginning to wonder whether I wanted Linda's murderer caught this badly.

Dorinda's voice held no accusation, but her question was, as usual, uncomfortably penetrating. "Did you mention Linda?"

"Of course," I snapped. "The calls made no sense otherwise."

"Sure, Cass," she said soothingly. "But don't you see, that's all it would take. Especially if the person called looked in the phone book and found that your office is in the same building where Linda lived."

"Oh, God," I groaned, the reality closing in on me. "What you're saying is that it's not finished—that whoever tried to break in this afternoon will try again until they find what they're looking for."

I got two nods. "You'd better find a safe place for that stuff, Cass," Ezra warned. "A safe deposit box, maybe. And Cass," he added, his face serious, "you'd better let these people know you don't have the stuff anymore."

I thought about safe places while Dorinda cleared up and she and Ezra bickered good-naturedly about the Morning Glory. My mind was only half on their conversation, but the sound of human voices cheered me. I wasn't ready to go back to an empty office or apartment—especially with an uneasy dread that they wouldn't be empty enough.

"Take-out," Ezra pronounced, leaning back in his chair with an authoritative air. "Remember in *The Graduate* when that guy says to Dustin Hoffman, 'I've got just one word for you: *plastics*?" It was a rhetorical question and Dorinda, her hands in the suds, knew it.

"Well, the word for the eighties is *take-out*. I can see it." Ezra's face took on the faintly spaced-out look it got when he contemplated profit margins. "All these singles coming home to lonely apartments. Two-career families where nobody has time to make dinner. They're tired of eating out, tired of staying dressed from work. They want to relax in front of the TV, but they don't want McDonald's, the don't want Wendy's. They're used to eating well. What do they want?"

Dorinda gave me a grin, so we both joined in the inevitable answer: "Take-out!" we shouted in unison, then laughed. I'd been here before, but it took my mind off bent bars and blackmail.

"The dishes you already serve here are perfect," Ezra said with enthusiasm. "Curried vegetables, great soups, all kinds of ethnic foods. Just add a couple of quiches—"

"No quiche," Dorinda replied, her tone adamant. "I refuse to be trendy. This is a working-class luncheonette, not a yuppie hangout. No quiche, no butcher block, no kiwi fruit."

"Who said anything about kiwi fruit? I *did* suggest you could cut down on the alfalfa sprouts, but what the hell, it was only a thought. But as for the idea that this place is working class—" Ezra was getting hot under the collar, his face reddening. "First of all, very few workers eat lunch in Cobble Hill. Second, the ones that do grab a hamburger or Kentucky Fried; they *don't* eat vegetarian. You can serve all the stuffed cabbage and black bread in the world, babe, but this is not a blue-collar lunch spot. Besides, we were talking about take-out. So don't serve quiche here, just sell it to go."

"Ez, I'm already getting up at five A.M. to open for breakfast at seven. Then it's lunch and an occasional afternoon snacker. We close at three-thirty and I spend the rest of the afternoon and evening cooking and baking for the next day. When do I make this take-out and how late do I have to be open to sell it?"

"Good questions," I put in. It was funny to see Dorinda, my least practical friend, turning into a businesswoman before my eyes. With, it must be said, Ezra's help.

Of course, Ezra had answers. Of course, Dorinda didn't

like them. Of course, the argument ended in the usual friendly stalemate.

Finally, Dorinda's cooking was done, and we stepped out of the restaurant together. As Ezra kissed me good-bye, he whispered, "Cass, I've got one word for you, too: burglar alarm."

"Why is sex always so much better when you're on trial?" Matt Riordan's famous courtroom voice was lazy as he murmured the question in my ear. We both knew the answer, so I replied with a quick hug instead of words. The adrenaline that had carried him through the long, rough court day and the brutal press conference that followed had propelled him into bed. Our lovemaking had been as intense as his cross-examination—and just about as tender. I understood. I try cases, too.

A muffled snore woke me from a light doze. I raised myself on one elbow and turned to see Matt, exhausted from his long day of performing for court and camera, thoroughly asleep.

Reminded of the scene in *Gaudy Night* in which Harriet Vane's sympathy is aroused by a sleeping Lord Peter, I smiled at my slumbering lover. Sleep had taken years from him; gray-flecked black hair, tousled like a toddler's, fell across his brow. One hairy arm was flung protectively over his head, as if to ward off a blow. It was, I realized, the only time I'd ever seen Matt Riordan vulnerable.

And yet, vulnerable he was, and growing more so every day. His entire professional life had been spent on a tightrope, with clear lines of demarcation between what he would and would not do for his clients. Now the lines were beginning to blur. Already the press slyly insinuated that hiring Matt Riordan for the defense was itself a confession of guilt. He'd been held in contempt during his last trial, and before that a federal judge had publicly questioned his ethics. There were new worry lines around the shrewd blue eyes, and it was taking two or three more glasses of whiskey to relax him after a day on trial.

The tightrope on which he'd always performed was swaying now. I'd tried to talk to him, to share my fears for his future, but Matt Riordan, who'd always prided himself on working without a net, had only laughed.

Now, watching him sleep away the tension, I found myself wishing I'd pushed the conversation harder, made Matt listen. The feeling was irrational; I knew from experience that no one made Matt Riordan do what he didn't want to do. And so I sighed and pulled the covers up to his chin. Then I slipped out of bed and went for my coat.

I went home to Brooklyn. There wasn't much to smile at in my thoughts, so I spared an inner laugh for the graffiti in the Bergen Street station: *In God we trust, in transit we bomb*.

At home, I quickly undressed and sat down to finish the latest Arthur Lyons. It was great, as usual, but the words began to blur before my eyes. Sitting in the glare of a single lamp, a comforter wrapped around me, I thought at first that the real mystery that had entered my life was dwarfing the fiction, but then I found my thoughts wandering.

Nathan. I felt a sharp pang of loss as I remembered my dead lover. I'd buried my grief in work, realizing for the first time the fierce joy I took in practicing law on my own, without the safety net of Legal Aid. I had a moment's pride, thinking how proud of me Nathan would have been.

My house. It was more than a building that devoured my cash—it was a responsibility bigger than any I'd ever known. In a way, it represented all my hopes for the future. It *was* my future—my office, my home, my business. I'd feared for its life before I'd ever heard the name Ira Bellfield. All my anxieties about leaving my job and starting out on my own seemed to center on that one four-story building. I'd visualized it in ashes, or burglarized, or, most humiliating of all, foreclosed on, several times a day for the last six months. The fact that my fears had coalesced into a horribly realistic prospect was something even Sigmund Freud couldn't have anticipated.

Riordan. He was attractive. He was dangerous. He was also in danger, yet he made it clear he wanted no help from me or anyone.

Being alone. Proud as I was of my ability to handle my caseload, my responsibilities as a homeowner, there were times I wanted to share the burden, to feel someone else's shoulder pushing along with mine. For all Matt Riordan and I could understand each other, we were irrevocably separate, our paths wholly distinct.

Being needed. By Matt Riordan, by Dawn Ritchie, by someone. When in hell had *that* become important to me?

8

It was your basic New York City government building, old and drafty, but efforts had been made. The walls were white, the woodwork fire-engine red. The lobby was lined with lithographs of famous fires being fought from horse-drawn engines, while horrified citizens in Victorian dress looked on. There was a glass partition with FDNY and a fireman's hat emblazoned in red. I knocked, went in, asked for Fire Marshal Duncan Pitt.

I don't know why his being black surprised me. So Linda was an equal opportunity blackmailer. Or maybe, having known Button, as honest a cop as ever wore blue, I unconsciously considered corruption a white man's disease. I tried not to let my surprise show as I sat in the wood chair, one of two in his tiny office. It was purely a working environment; every inch of the scarred desk was covered with reports. I wondered idly how many were honest and how many were doctored.

The phone rang. As Pitt answered it, I took stock of him, trying to get a clue as to how best to conduct what I suspected would be a very difficult interview.

Pitt was a big man, balding, with a salt-and-pepper mustache and full lips. He had a tough drill sergeant's face and a voice to match. Yet the cut of his uniform, the perfectly trimmed hair, the almost exaggerated precision of his speech gave me a sense of a man who cared greatly for appearances.

The only personal touch in the drab office was photographs. On the desk, pushed aside by papers, were graduation pictures of a boy and a girl, both with even-toothed smiles that probably cost a pretty penny in orthodontists' fees. I hoped I wasn't going to hear Pitt use them as an excuse for what he'd done.

On the wall, there were the standard political photos I'd seen a hundred times in judges' chambers all over the city. Photo opportunities with the candidate of the moment, displayed to demonstrate the politicial clout of the person doing the displaying. But the person shaking hands with Shirley Chisholm, Andrew Young, and Jesse Jackson wasn't Pitt, but a light-skinned woman whose broad, buck-toothed smile seemed familiar. If she was the mother of the graduates, I thought, I was right about the orthodontics.

"Well, Counselor," Pitt began in an expansive tone that seemed to have nothing to hide, "what can I do for you?"

"I represent a young man named Tito Fernandez," I began crisply. "He's charged with arson, second-degree. You filled out the fire marshal's report." I put my briefcase on my lap, opened it with a snap, and pulled out the report I'd gotten from the DA's office. "As you can see," I went on, showing it to him as though I were putting it into evidence in court, "it has your signature on it."

He didn't take it. His face wore the bland smile of a bureaucrat about to hide behind the rules. "You really ought to know I can't discuss a pending case," he said smoothly. "You can ask me anything you like in court, but before that . . ." He raised his palms in a gesture that was meant to express rueful apology. His face, however betrayed his satisfaction.

"Oh, I have plenty of questions to ask in court," I answered brightly. "I just wonder whether you really want to wait to hear them—and whether you really want them asked in such a public forum." I gazed at Pitt with what I hoped was a wealth of meaning.

"Some people," Pitt replied, his voice hard underneath the ruminative tone, "might consider that a threat. But I don't think a smart lawyer would threaten a public official in his own office." He shook his head. "It would be a very foolish thing to do, wouldn't it? So if that's what you're doing, Ms. Jameson"—his eyes were as hard as his voice—"I think you'd better leave before things get out of hand."

"Things are already out of hand, Mr. Pitt," I countered, my voice remarkably steady even if my hands weren't, which is why they got the job of holding onto my briefcase as though it were a life preserver. "They started getting out of hand when you started taking those manila envelopes from Ira Bellfield."

I literally held my breath waiting for my bluff to be called. All Pitt had to do was throw me out—or worse, file a complaint against me with the bar association. What I was doing hadn't been covered in my legal ethics class.

"That's a pretty serious allegation," Pitt replied, giving the word every one of its syllables. His face had lost none of its bland assurance. "I wonder," he went on, his voice silky, "what could have put such a far-fetched notion into your head.",

I had won. The calm didn't matter. The smoothness was a defense. What was important was that he had neither denied the charge nor picked up the phone. He hadn't laughed either. He was playing for time, trying to find out just how much I had. My move: to convince him I had more than I really did.

"Ira Bellfield has a lot of fires," I said conversationally. "Of course, you'll say that he owns a lot of buildings and that some of them are in bad neighborhoods and that some of his tenants aren't sober all the time, so it's no wonder he has fires. But there are a couple of reports in here"—I tapped the briefcase significantly—"that could make you look really bad in court." What I didn't mention was the astronomical odds against my actually being able to introduce into evidence at Tito's trial fire marshal's reports from unrelated fires. "Irrelevant, incompetent, and immaterial" about summed it up. My heart thumped, and I remembered an argument I'd forgotten to use against Riordan when he'd suggested running the bluff. I hated poker.

"Take 1309 Bedford Avenue," I continued when the silence convinced me he wasn't going to rush into guilty explanations. "You call it a gas leak fire. Would you be interested to learn that the Brooklyn Union Gas Company cut off service for nonpayment the week before the fire?"

"People in the ghetto," Pitt answered with a crocodile smile, "have been known to supply their own gas when the regular service runs out. It's a dangerous practice." He shook his head mournfully, but the twinkle in his eye told me he liked poker a hell of a lot more than I did—and probably played it better. "These poor tenants learned that the hard way."

"What about 2718 Herkimer?" I shot back. "Do most fires started by winos have two points of origin and use accelerants? Doesn't that pattern say 'torch' loud and clear? And yet you blame the fire on the drunk who was sleeping it off in a vacant apartment."

"Cheap whiskey makes a pretty good accelerant." Pitt snapped the words in a way that made me feel as though my hand might contain enough cards after all.

"But that's not the biggie, is it?" I asked, airily waving away my hard-won points. "The real problem with these reports is that by the thirteenth fire somebody should have realized that these buildings were owned by the same man. All the phony holding companies in the world couldn't have shielded him from a *real* investigation—but that's just what these fires never got. And nobody bothered to notify the insurance companies, either, so they just paid and paid. Even the fires you did label 'suspicious' were blamed on people who couldn't fight back. I suppose," I went on, real indignation beginning to seep through the act, "it never occurred to you that innocent people like my client, who happens to be a deaf kid, could get hurt by your covering up for Bellfield?"

"This is all very interesting," Pitt said suavely, "but it's all speculation, isn't it? Which you know as well as I do. So if that's all you have to say . . ."

So much for poker. With an inward sigh I took out the hardball so highly recommended by Matt Riordan.

"I'm not just Tito Fernandez's lawyer," I announced. "I also represented Linda Ritchie. If there was nothing wrong with those reports," I asked sweetly, "why did you pay her to keep quiet about them?"

Pitt's brown eyes, which had seemed almost amused, now took on the hard blankness of obsidian. "I should have known," he said wearily. "I should have fucking known."

"You did pay her?" I made it a question, my voice softer than I'd intended. Winning may be everything, but it isn't always fun.

He nodded, then cleared his throat. "Had to," he said flatly. "Not much choice about it. The lady wasn't one to leave room for doubts about what she'd do to me if I didn't."

My turn to nod. "And you hated her for it," I said. "The question is, did you hate her badly enough to kill her?"

"Shit, I thought her old man done took care of that for me," he snorted. The smooth façade had cracked a bit, and I could see the streetwise ghetto kid peeking out from behind the urbane civil servant.

"Maybe, maybe not," I replied enigmatically. "But don't you think the cops might be interested in where you were the night she was killed if they knew she was blackmailing you?"

"Maybe so," he agreed warily, "but you're not the cops. Am I to assume you are in the same line of work as your late client?" The bland bureaucrat was back with a vengeance; I found myself looking at the same smooth façade that had already bounced my best shots back at me.

I shook my head. Amazingly, the suggestion made me feel dirty, though I'd tried my best to sell just that picture of myself to Ira Bellfield. "I really do represent Tito Fernandez," I explained, "and I have my doubts about whether Brad Ritchie killed his wife. You weren't her only victim, you know."

"I know. People like that seldom stop with one. Which was one reason," he said with the unnatural calm I was beginning to associate with lying, "that she didn't really bother me all that much."

"Oh, you enjoyed paying blackmail?"

"No," he admitted with a smile I was supposed to find ruefully charming. "But I accepted it. A man in my position"—again he spread his palms—"it was a little like paying taxes." He shrugged.

"A cost of doing business?" My sarcasm wasn't working, and I had to admit that falling back on it was an admission of weakness. No matter what weapon I pulled out, he had a better one to parry me with. Now instead of poker, we were fencing—and he was D'Artagnan.

"Exactly," he beamed. "Hell," he went on, "how self-righteous could I be? Stood to reason somebody was bound to come along and do me like I was doing. Way the world works. Everybody takes a cut, one way or the other. I took mine, and Linda took hers."

"Nothing personal?"

"Nothing personal." The crocodile teeth gleamed in the

black face. The angry street kid I'd glimpsed for a moment wouldn't have paid Linda without a fight, but he was buried now, and I knew I had no more weapons to force him out again. The question was, had Linda had those weapons?

There was nowhere to go but home. I rose to leave, not missing the gleam of triumph in the black eyes as Pitt stood up behind his desk.

Then my memory came up with a name for the smiling lady in the political photographs. "Dory Anderson Pitt," I said slowly. "Just elected to the school board from Starrett City." I wheeled on Pitt with a triumphant smile. "Does your wife know about the manila envelopes?"

Pitt sank slowly into his chair like a deflating hot-air balloon. His face crumpled, the complacent calm replaced by a defeat so utter that my victory seemed a shabby thing indeed. The stakes of my little game seemed suddenly too rich for my blood; against all my better judgment, I began to feel sympathy.

"You gonna tell her, bitch? You gonna break that woman's heart like Linda said she was gonna do? What good you think that'll do, huh? Make you feel righteous?"

"Was that what got to you, Mr. Pitt? It wasn't the money, was it? You didn't lie about that, the money you would have paid without anger, but the threat to tell your wife—that got you. Did it get you enough to kill her?"

"Hell, yes!" Pitt replied, slamming his fist on the desk. "What did the life of that bloodsucking bitch matter to me next to Dory's happiness? I'd have wasted her in a minute, if I could have been sure to get away with it. If only she'd taken the money and been happy," he went on. "But she wasn't like that. She was always poking and prying, looking for some way to hurt. She didn't like it that I just paid up every week with no complaints. She liked pain. She liked hurting, so one day she does the same thing you did, looks at the pictures, and says, 'Does your wife know?' All innocence and sweet magnolias." He looked into the distance, as though he could see the scene before his face. "Like a damned fool, I panicked. I should have said, 'Hell, girl, whose idea you think it was?' But I didn't. I let her know how bad the idea of Dory's knowing got to me and from then on I didn't have a moment's peace. She called all hours, asking to talk to Dory, sometimes getting Dory on the phone and then hanging up. Letting on like she was going to tell her and then making me beg her not to. She liked me to crawl."

"If you were so ashamed of what you were doing, why did you do it in the first place?"

Pitt sighed. His sigh was for the man he was before Bellfield, the man Dory Anderson married, the man those two high-school graduates thought their father was.

"I was one of three black rookies in my class," he began. "One of us died in a supermarket fire, the other quit the department 'cause he couldn't stand the harassment; and I made fire marshal. Not the first black man to hold the job, but one of very few in those days. Man"—he shook his head—"the graft I saw. Seemed to me like everybody I knew was on somebody's pad. The indifference came from the top down. I remember as a nappy-haired kid trying to get up some interest in SRO fires. You know," he explained, "those single-room-occupancy hotels for men on welfare. The attitude came down, 'Who cares, they're just bums.' But then when it was a money fire, you'd find that influential people didn't want the true reason for the fire known, so the report would read 'insufficient evidence.'" He gave the words all possible syllables, well spaced out for emphasis. "It was discouraging as hell. And all the time there were lazy, dumb, honky shits getting promoted over my head. Finally, in comes this affirmative-action bullshit and dumb *black* shits are moving up and white guys left behind are looking at me and nodding their heads like they *knew* I wasn't promoted on merit."

"So you started taking Bellfield's money."

"Hell, girl, everybody's taking somebody's money. I just woke up and smelled the coffee."

"Your wife never asked you where the extra money came from?"

"She never asked me what it feels like to go into a burning tenement and carry out what looks like a burnt-up pot roast, only it ain't a piece of meat, it's a baby," he said, his voice as thick as the smoke from an oil fire. "She never asked me what it's like watching another firefighter fall through a burning floorboard or how it feels when neighborhood kids throw rocks at me while I'm putting out a fire. Man has to do," he explained, his palms up a the now-familiar gesture, "a *lot* of things he can't be telling his woman about. Way it *is*," he said, in a tone I might have called pleading.

"Did you kill Linda?" I don't know why I expected a straight answer, but there was something in Pitt that, while I couldn't call it integrity, had a certain strength.

"No," he said quietly. "You have no grounds for believing me, but here's one reason you might consider it." His smile was genuinely rueful this time. "If I'd have done away with that bitch, I'd have damned sure done it before the election."

I must have frowned. "Your wife's election?"

"Sure," he answered. "That was Linda's big threat—to make my crime public just before voting day and destroy Dory's chances. Once the election was over, it wasn't as important. She knew that. That's why she really kept the pressure up right then and kind of backed off in December. Tell you the truth, I kind of got the feeling she wasn't as interested in me after that, as though maybe she had some fresh blood to suck."

"A new victim?" I thought of the Lucentis. The election argument, if it held up, might apply to them too, but there was the move to Washington. It seemed a safe bet that Linda had gotten the job through blackmail, and maybe she'd been concentrating on Art instead of her other victims.

"But wait a minute," I said, thinking aloud. "Even if your wife is on the school board, wouldn't she still be hurt if it came out that you took bribes?"

"It would hurt her personally," he admitted, "and the news media would be all over her. But she really couldn't be removed from office for something I'd done, whereas before the election, a lot of people would just have changed their votes and there'd be nothing she could do about it. No," he said, shaking his head. "If Linda had really wanted to destroy Dory, she'd have gone public before the second week in November."

"And if you'd thought she was going to do that?"

"I'd have killed her," he said simply. "Then. Not now."

9

The orange cube, I reminded myself as I stepped out of the Fulton Street subway station into a surging flood of humanity. I was meeting Elliott Pilcher, the mystery civil servant, at an orange cube in front of a black glass office building on Broadway. He'd whispered the directions over the phone with the hushed anticipation of a practiced conspirator.

I plunged into the chaotic flow of traffic like a pioneer fording a spring-swollen river, and reviewed what I knew about Elliott Pilcher. As I crossed Nassau Street going toward Broadway, I came face-to-face with just how little that was. Hell, I recalled, I still didn't know where he worked, let alone what he'd done for Todd Lessek to earn his limited partnership in the waterfront deal. I cursed the phone company for promoting direct lines; I'd expected Elliott's phone to be answered by a helpful secretary who would announce the name of the agency as a matter of routine.

I turned south on Broadway and saw the cube in a people-filled plaza in front one of those faceless black-box office buildings that seem to be taking over Manhattan. It was a popular meeting-place; at least twenty people stood by the cube and scanned the crowd, searching for their lunch dates. I tried to guess which one was Pilcher, then decided I was too early. The uneasy feeling that I didn't have enough information to run a decent bluff began to grow on me. The one thing I could be sure of, I thought wryly, was that wherever Elliott Pilcher worked, it was nowhere near the black-clad building with the orange cube.

Bellfield burned buildings. Pitt covered up. Todd Lessek bought the burned-out hulks and turned them into co-ops with boutiques where the butcher shop used to be. What did Pilcher do? Lessek, I knew, had gotten city-backed loans and tax incentives for his renovations. It seemed likely that Pilcher made sure that the public trough was open whenever Lessek cared to drink from it, in which case he probably worked for HPD, the city's umbrella housing agency. But was "probably" going to be good enough? Wasn't my best bet to stay as silent as possible and let Pilcher think I knew more than I did?

"Funny"—a voice in my ear punctured my thoughts— "you don't *look* like a blackmailer." The tone was faintly aggrieved, a near-whine. I turned and saw a pudgy, oatmeal-faced man with colorless eyes behind thick glasses, mousy, thinning hair, and a sulky expression about the mouth. On the other hand, I decided, nobody looks his best when he's being blackmailed.

"Elliott Pilcher, I presume," I said affably. "I don't suppose you want to talk here. Where shall we eat?"

He grimaced. "Much as I hate the thought of breaking bread with you," he intoned, "I suppose I ought to eat something. There's a dairy restaurant up this way." He turned on his heel and plunged into the crowd, walking swiftly in the direction of City Hall, leaving me to follow as best I could.

The place was called the Dairy Planet, which gave me what I assumed would be the only laugh of the lunch hour. Inside it were aluminum-clad walls and traditional Jewish dishes—as if Molly Goldberg had been the cook aboard "Star Trek"'s *Enterprise*.

If you ask me, too many people have seen the scene in *Five Easy Pieces* where Jack Nicholson dumps his lunch on the floor because the waitress won't serve him what he wants. Elliott had obviously enjoyed that part.

". . . and some iced coffee." He completed his order and folded the huge menu with a flourish.

"It's January," the elderly waitress answered in a Bronx accent that could cut glass.

"I didn't ask you for the time," Elliott replied with exaggerated patience, "I asked you for iced coffee."

"We don't serve iced coffee in the winter," the waitress replied. "We don't have it made up."

"Let me make this easy for you," Elliott persisted, going into his Nicholson impersonation. "You have coffee, right? And I presume you have ice as well? Good. Then a glass—you *have* glasses? Put the ice into the glass and pour coffee over it. Then bring it to me. Is that too hard for you, or do you think you can handle it?"

The waitress pursed her lips but said nothing. I had the feeling she knew Elliott would make maximum trouble for her if she said another word. I would have liked to apologize, but I settled for giving my own order. Blintzes, red, white, and blue (cherry, cheese, and blueberry); a trip to the moon on gossamer wings.

"You know," I said when the waitress left, "all you're going to get is coffee-flavored water. The hot coffee will melt the ice and weaken the coffee. That's all she was trying to tell you, that there was no coffee already cooled."

"But I *wanted* iced coffee," Elliott replied petulantly. "I don't like stupid people telling me what I can't have." The stubborn look on his face reduced him to babyhood; I wondered if he would have held his breath had the conversation lasted another ten seconds.

"What makes you think she's stupid?" Having no handle on Elliott the employee, I decided to try for one on Elliott the person.

He glanced disdainfully at the waitress, who was hauling a heavy tray to a table of Orthodox Jewish businessmen. "She works here, doesn't she?" he sniggered. "Hardly a job for a mental giant."

"Intelligence is very important to you, then?" I asked noncommittally.

Elliott smirked. "When I was eight years old," he said, "I realized that I was smarter than everybody I knew— including my parents."

And you haven't met anybody since? I thought it; I didn't say it. Goading Elliott wasn't the game plan at this point. I had him pegged now; Mama's bright little boy all grown up and unable to accept the fact that a lot of people in the world had also been their mama's bright little boys and girls. He still wanted to show the grown-ups he could tie shoes all by himself. He still wanted the gold star and the big red A on top of his paper. It was a good bet that working for the City of New York as a faceless bureaucrat had not been the height of his ambition.

"With your brains," I said, hoping the soap wasn't too obviously soft, "I'm surprised you stay in the public sector. There must be a lot more money in private enterprise for someone like you."

"Oh, I've thought about it," he said airily. "But there are advantages to working for the government."

"I'm sure there are. Especially," I added dryly, "if you're working for Lessek at the same time."

I got a smug smile. "If those idiots I work with ever knew," he gloated. "They think I'm a loser like them, putting in my time, kissing the boss's ass, just waiting for my gold watch and pension. . . . If they knew," he chuckled, savoring the thought.

"If they knew, you'd be canned," I cut in. "Which is why you killed Linda," I said, finishing my onion roll.

"A lot of good it would have done me if I had," Elliott retorted sourly. "The blackmailer is dead; long live the blackmailer."

I had come to lunch fully intending to disabuse Elliott of the notion that I was Linda's successor; now was not the time. "Face it, Elliott," I said, "there *are* people smarter than you. I'm one of them. Linda was another."

"Linda?" Elliott almost squeaked the name. "Smart? That little gum-snapping high-school dropout! That *sec*retary! That mental as well as physical midget—"

"That 'mental midget' had you dancing on her string like a puppet, Elliott," I pointed out. "What do you call that, stupid? She gave the orders and you obeyed. She called the tune and you—"

"Just because she had something on me, that makes her intelligent?"

"Elliott," I asked softly, teasingly, "how did she know?"

I let him consider that proposition as the waitress deposited our lunch on the table. I couldn't look at her, still conscious of Elliott's tantrum, but he wasn't embarrassed to ask for more apple sauce for his potato pancakes. We ate in silence; even the oppressive atmosphere at our table couldn't dull my enjoyment of the heavenly blintzes. As I sipped my second cup of coffee, I said, "At the risk of repeating myself, Elliott, just how *did* little old dumb high-school dropout Linda Ritchie get the goods on brilliant Elliott Pilcher?"

"Listening at keyholes, probably," he sneered. "How smart do you have to be for that?"

"In other words, you don't know. Elliott"—again I went into a soft, insinuating tone—"don't you think someone with *real* brains would have found out how she knew? Don't you think a really clever man would have figured a way to get Linda off his back? It hardly takes a genius to pay up week after week, does it?"

"I had plans," he replied truculently. "I had ideas."

"Of course you did, Elliott," I said in a soothing voice, calculated to drive him up the wall. "I'm sure you could have done something very smart—but only *after* you'd found the blackmail papers. Am I right?"

He nodded.

"Otherwise, she'd be dead, but you'd be in hot water."

"Right," he agreed. "And then fate stepped in and made it all unnecessary."

"You mean, someone killed her."

"I mean, her husband killed her."

I shook my head, a teacher despairing of a pupil she'd thought was finally showing some brains. "No, Elliott, you don't really believe that nonsense, do you? The police just arrested him as a smokescreen while they investigate the blackmail angle."

Elliott thought about it. His petulant face was screwed up with the effort. But he wasn't as dumb as I'd hoped. He put his finger on the problem right away.

"If the police know all this," Elliott said suspiciously, "why haven't they been to see me?"

"They will, Elliott, they will," I said confidently. "But you have nothing to lose by answering my question. Who killed Linda? I'm convinced her death was motivated by the blackmail, so which of her other victims got mad enough to do the job? If not you, how about your boss? How about Lessek?"

"Let me tell you something, Miss Smartass." Elliott pointed a shaking finger at me. "I don't believe your phony story for a minute. If the cops knew what you said they knew, they'd be all over me. You're pulling some cheap little hustle on your own, and I know it. But hear one thing, lady, you play this little game with Mr. Lessek and you'll be sorry."

"Oh?" I raised my eyebrows. "Will he do to me what he did to Linda?"

"He's got ways of taking care of business," Elliott bragged. He was like the fat kid at camp who taunts the others and then hides behind his best friend—the camp bully. I suddenly had a strong desire to meet Todd Lessek face-to-face. The prospect even reconciled me to paying the check after Elliott walked out, ostentatiously leaving me with it.

I stopped in a plant store on the way back to the office. I bought a giant hanging fuchsia for Vince and Jenny Marchese, who were buying a co-op on Amity Street. I'd have to schedule my visit to Lessek around the formalities. I smiled at the thought; somehow I didn't recall Philip Marlowe postponing an investigation in order to do a closing.

10

When I saw the red Ferrari, I knew I was in the right place. Amid the gray warehouses and deserted streets of Brooklyn's waterfront, it shone like a rose. A neon sign, flashing "Lessek is here!"

I looked up. The warehouse was a cast-iron beauty, all spindly columns and newly cleaned window panes. Perched on top of the building like a flashcube sat a little widow's walk. Todd Lessek, King of the Waterfront, had appropriated it for his headquarters, and raved to the newspapers about his spectacular skyline view of Manhattan. What he'd failed to add was that at street level all you saw were other warehouses—and, of course, Lessek's Ferrari.

The elevator was still the creaking, clanking freight job that had hauled sewing machines up to the small businesses that used to occupy the premises. I'd seen their faded logos in the lobby—Royal Baseball Cap Company, Pearl Ribbons and Trimmings, Del-Mar Sportswear. I wondered idly what had become of them, and of the people they'd employed for so many years.

The building itself might have been put up in the 1880s, but Todd Lessek's office was strictly 1980s. The elevator doors opened to reveal a high-tech paradise, with office supplies lined up neatly on open shelves, streamlined chrome chairs, black desk accessories; even the staplers had won design awards. The only thing of beauty was the panorama, visible on three sides, of Lower Manhattan, the bridges, and, finally, the Empire State and Chrysler buildings. When I could tear my eyes away, I had to admit I'd finally seen a justification for the aridity of high-tech. It was the only possible backdrop for that incredible view.

There was something artificial about the place. It was like a movie set; the slim, glossy secretaries who bustled around bearing computer printouts were too perfect; the shrilling phones too insistent upon conveying an impression of high-powered real-estate deals conducted at breakneck speed. The young men who sat in shirtsleeves, phones cocked at an angle under their chins as they stirred coffee and doodled on notepads, were pure Central Casting. After a while, I got tired of watching the movie and drifted over to the lone wall, where a wash drawing of Lessek's dream development occupied most of the available wall space.

I identified the building I was in by its flashcube penthouse. It was evidently destined to become a shopping mall, with prestige stores, boutiques, and specialty shops. Next door, the windowless brick warehouse I'd passed on the way would emerge, suitably windowed, as a luxury co-op. The low-rise buildings nearer the river would house the sports complex. In the picture, well-dressed people walked along tree-lined streets (the secret of growing trees in cobblestones was not revealed) into the renovated warehouses. Colorful banners proclaimed the fanciful names Lessek had given the buildings. It was South Street Seaport by way of Faneuil Hall with a touch of Akron's Quaker Square thrown in. A shopping mall for people who hate shopping malls.

"Fantastic, isn't it?" A voice as deep and rich as a David's cookie sounded behind me. I turned to see Todd Lessek beaming at his proposed baby. "And it'll be a reality by 1990—I guarantee it."

I decided against explaining that I wasn't a potential investor; I got the feeling everyone from the garbage collector on up got the sales pitch. Lessek ushered me through the movie set to an oversized slab of ebony laid over heavy chrome struts. The effect was of an extremely elegant sawhorse. Lessek waved me to a chrome-and-velvet chair, and I sat down.

"I'm not quite sure I understand," he began smoothly, "just what it is you want, Ms. Jameson."

"Well, you know," I answered conversationally, "I'm not sure I would have come if it hadn't been for Elliott Pilcher's mentioning your name." I sat back to watch Lessek's reaction to a name I was certain he didn't want coupled with his.

What I got was a slight puckering of the tanned forehead, a raising of the bush eyebrows. "Pilcher, Pilcher," he murmured. "I meet so many people," he said with a deprecating smile that reminded me of Tom Selleck, "and I'm ashamed to confess my memory for names is atrocious. It's a terrible handicap for someone in my business. Just where"—he added the slightest touch of shrewdness narrowing his eyes—"did you come across this—Pilcher?"

"Never mind that, Mr. Lessek," I said crisply. "What's really interesting about Pilcher is that when I had lunch with him and tried to ask him a few simple questions, he started threatening me, telling me all about what this friend of his would do to me if I didn't lay off. His words," I added with an apologetic smile.

"And what does that have to do with me?"

"You," I replied, watching him carefully, "were the friend."

His laughter sounded almost genuine. "This Pilcher must have quite an imagination. I hope yours is a little less fanciful. You can get in a lot of trouble, believing everything you hear."

"That's why I came here," I said. "To see for myself."

"Did those questions you were asking," he began, leaning back in his chair like one of the Central Casting minions, "have anything to do with the fact that you were Linda Ritchie's lawyer?"

"I should have known Elliott would make a complete report to his boss as soon as he left me," I responded, hoping I sounded cooler than I was. I'd come expecting to put Lessek on the spot, not watch him do the same to me.

"Oh, come now," he answered, sounding genuinely annoyed. "Do you think I depend on the likes of Elliott to tell me what's going on? I knew who you were from day one. What I don't know is what you hope to gain by running around questioning everybody. If you want to pick up where Linda left off just name your price and let me get back to work. I've got a multibillion-dollar project here." The tone was affable in a superficial way, but there was a bite underneath that let me know he was serious. It was time to get down to cases.

"I can't help the timing," I shot back. "I'm sure if she'd

known it would inconvenience you, Linda would have gotten herself murdered some other time, but—"

"Don't be a smartass," Lessek snapped. "There's no connection between me and Linda, so it doesn't matter when she was killed. It's not my problem."

"Then what am I doing here?"

"God knows," he answered simply. "You could be angling for a piece of the action. Lots of people want a piece of me right now. Or you could be putting on a little squeeze, like some of the sleazo politicians who just remembered I gotta have this variance and that license before I can go ahead, and it just so happens they know a lawyer who can get it for me. Their brother-in-law. Or maybe you want to stop the project—or at least hold it up long enough to get some cheap publicity by taking a whack at me. Sometimes I feel like an elephant covered by a swarm of ants. And I'm getting sick and tired of it. Linda Ritchie was nothing to me alive and she's even less to me dead. I don't know Elliott Pilcher except to say hello to on the street. Is that for God's sake the end of this conversation?" Lessek's utter weariness was touching; he was Robert Redford all but beaten by his enemies yet gallant to the end. It was a shame to spoil the scene.

"If you don't know Elliott Pilcher," I asked softly, "then why is he listed as one of your limited partners? Do you always let mere acquaintances in on the ground floor of your biggest deals?"

"Did the little creep tell you that himself, or do you have other sources?"

"Linda told me."

"No, she didn't. That little bitch never told anybody anything she didn't have to tell. So don't try to sell me that one."

"Okay. I found some papers after her death."

He nodded. "That I can buy. What did those papers have to say about me?"

"Why should I tell you?"

"Because I want to know. And because there are some things you want to know. And I don't see why I should tell you anything when I don't know what you already have. What I've seen so far," he said brusquely, "doesn't amount to a hill of shit."

"I know you're paying off Elliott Pilcher. That's bribery."

"Prove it. All you've told me is that you've seen Elliott's name listed as limited partner."

"That's pretty suggestive. Enough for Elliott to face some pretty tough questions."

"That's his problem."

"You're a swell guy to work for, aren't you?" I was doing it again, falling back on sarcasm when real weapons had failed. I sighed inwardly and put my cards on the table, face up, hoping to God they amounted to something.

"Okay. You've done a lot of renovations in this city. Buying empty hulks—most of them made empty by Ira Bellfield's gestapo tactics. Then you've obtained low-interest loans, gotten tax breaks and zoning variances—all from the city and all whenever you needed them, no questions asked. You paid Art Lucenti for legal work when he was on the city council, even though he wasn't supposed to represent clients before city agencies." I caught the faint smile and amended crossly, "Oh, I forgot, that's *his* problem, right?"

The smile got broader. "Right. And before you continue your little diatribe, Ms. Jameson, let me tell you a few facts of life in the big city. You accuse me of buying buildings emptied by Ira Bellfield. Guilty. I'm what they call a 'second-generation' owner. The first generation—thats Bellfield—are the slumlords, the ones who milk a building for profit without giving adequate services or putting anything back in. They're the ones who do all the things the liberal newspapers cry about, the fires, the burglaries, the strong-arm stuff. It's terrible, what they do," he said mockingly, "but the important thing here is that *I* don't do it. I just buy from those who do. I pick up what's left when they're finished."

"At a good price."

"Of course." He ignored the sarcasm. "That's how I can afford to stay in business. And what I do is upgrade the neighborhood, rehab the buildings, bring back the business."

"At only four times the old rent, too," I marveled.

"Since when is profit a dirty word?"

"What about the loans and tax breaks? Who do you have to pay off?"

His answering grin told me I'd just said something very amusing—and very stupid. The trouble was I didn't know what.

"You don't do real estate, do you?" he asked. "Do the words *as of right* mean anything to you?"

I frowned. "I'm not sure," I replied lamely.

"I thought as much. In order to avoid the possibility of the very suggestion you're making," he explained with maddening patience, "the law specifically provides that *every* owner of *every* building meeting certain specifications is entitled to low-interest loans and tax abatements in order to do repairs. These are granted *as of right*, which means, one; I don't have to pay anybody anything to get them, and, two, I'm entitled to them even if I'm Attila the Hun, which, by the way, I'm not. So, Ms. Jameson, my suggestion to you is that before you come bursting into a man's office accusing him of crimes, you do a little homework so that you know what you're talking about. It might," he added with a sneer, "prevent you from making a fool of yourself."

My face reddened; my exit from Lessek's office, followed by his gloating laugh, was no triumph. But I didn't feel like a fool. I'd lost a big pot, but I hadn't really had the cards. Next time, I promised, I'd deal myself a better hand. I got out of the building as fast as I could and stood on the cobblestones drinking in the frigid river breeze as though it were fresh water after a polluted swim.

I was so involved with my own thoughts that I failed to notice the footsteps that must have sounded on the cobblestones. The first thing I knew, a man wearing only a raincoat against the cruel wind stood before me, blocking my path. He was hatless; his ears looked on the verge of frostbite. His hands were jammed into his coat pockets, and his voice was a rasp.

"You work for that bum." It was less than a statement, but not quite a question. Recalling the high-fashion look of Lessek's female staff, I felt vaguely complimented. I was about to deny the truth of the assumption, when the man pulled a raw, red hand from his pocket and thrust a dirty envelope at me. "Give him this from me," he urged. There was an unblinking intensity, a hint of fanaticism, about the man that was beginning to bother me. I looked around; not a soul on the waterfront. Not surprising, with a wind-chill of minus nine.

"You're making a mistake," I said quietly. It was the same calming tone I used with crazy people in the pens in

Criminal Court. "I don't work for Lessek; I was just seeing him on business."

"Don't give me that." He shoved the envelope into my midriff. "I'm tired of getting the runaround from you people. I got a right to get my message to Lessek, and I'm not going to be stopped. Not this time."

"Who's stopping—" I began, ready to explain to the man just how paranoid he sounded, when suddenly, out of the shadows between the two warehouses, stepped two burly young men.

"You again," one of them said, raking over the old man with contemptuous eyes. The man in the raincoat, though a head shorter and thirty years older than the bruisers, returned their contempt. "Go ahead," he offered, with a wave of his chapped hand, "get rough. Show me how tough you are. Break my nose like you did the first time."

"Don't tempt me, Pop," one of the musclemen snarled, stepping forward. The other, who had been frowning at me since he arrived on the scene, held out a restraining hand. He inclined his head toward me and shook it. "Mr. Lessek don't want no trouble," he remarked. Not with a witness around, I amended mentally.

"Look," the smart one said smoothly, spreading his hands covered with fur-lined leather gloves, "we don't want a fuss here. Mr. Lessek's a busy man and he can't see you right now, so why don't you and this young lady just go on about your business, okay?"

The little man had come to the same conclusion I had: The bruisers didn't want to be seen by a witness roughing up an old man. He decided being roughed up in front of a witness was exactly what he did want. "You gonna make me?" he taunted, his voice shrill. "You gonna rough me up? Come on, then," he offered, beginning to dance like a boxer, "come on."

"Aw, go away," the belligerent bruiser said with disgust. "Just get outa my sight, that's all."

The clever one turned to me with an apologetic smile. "Mr. Lessek's made a few enemies. We gotta see to it that he's not harassed when he goes in and out of the building."

"Yeah," his partner chimed in, "you ought to seen what this here lunatic's done to Mr. Lessek. Carryin' signs, passin' out crazy flyers, all about how Mr. Lessek killed his business."

"How awful." I shook my head in mock dismay. "Exercising his First Amendment rights," I commiserated. "And on public property, too."

"What about creosote?" the belligerent guard challenged. "You call that First Amendment rights, spreading creosote all over the sidewalk?"

"Not to mention the eggs," his buddy added. "You like egg-throwing, don't you, Pop?"

The man in the raincoat was still dancing, still inviting a fight, but with less energy as he realized he wasn't going to get it.

"Look, Pop," said the clever guard with what was supposed to be affectionate exasperation, "you remember what the judge told you when you got busted and had to go to court. If we so much as see you on this sidewalk, it's a violation of the court order and we can have you put in jail. Now, I don't want to be a hardnose here, so I'm not gonna do that—provided you get away from the building right now. Okay?"

It was the voice of sweet reason. An honest businessman was being hassled by an obvious wacko and the guard was being a lot nicer about it than he had to be. Why didn't I buy it? Was it just because Lessek had pinned my ears back and I wanted to believe the worst about him, or was it because I sensed that if I weren't there, those two thugs would have made hamburger out of a freezing old man and liked it?

The old man knew it, too. Puffing ominously, he stopped moving and said, "Okay. You win. You can buy more judges than I can. But"—he pointed a shaking finger at the guards, who were smiling at him with amused contempt—"I'll be back."

"I'll bet you will," one of them murmured as we turned and walked away from the waterfront, the wind whipping at us as we rounded the corner to start up the hill. We were almost at Henry Street when my companion said, "Abe Schine. Royal Baseball Cap Company."

"I saw your logo in the lobby," I replied. "I'm Cassandra Jameson. I'd like to ask you about Lessek. Would you like some coffee?"

The coffee shop was so overheated, the windows steamed. I usually hate that, but after the numbing cold of the waterfront, it felt wonderful. It must have felt even better to poor

Abe, who blew on his raw hands and held his hot cup with both hands when it came. I waited for him to warm up enough to let the story unfold.

"People don't wear baseball caps like they used to," Abe Schine began. "Once upon a time, inna fifties, you had your Dodgers, your Giants, your Yanks—alla kids wanted caps. Plus," he added proudly, "we made 'em for the players too. Official baseball caps, with hand-sewn insignias. I had twenny girls workin' for me in those days. Sewing machines clackin' all day, phones ringin' from orders comin' in. Music to my ears."

"What happened?"

He shrugged. "Dodgers went off to California. Fellas started watchin' football. Only trouble with football—no caps. How you gonna tell what team somebody's for without he's wearin' a cap? Answer me that. I'm down to ten girls, then eight. Two salesmen. We're just barely hanging' on—but we're still in there pitching, you should pardon the expression. Then"—his voice lowered and he leaned forward—"along comes this *momser* Lessek. Wants to buy us out—that's what he says at first. Help us relocate. Queens, the Island, New Jersey—wherever. Which I'm not in favor of at all. I'm a Brooklyn boy all my life, what do I know from the Island? My girls are all old now, they can't commute all the way to Jersey. One of my salemen's got terminal cancer. He shouldn't be working at all, but what the hell, retirement'll kill him so I let him come into work, write up some orders—he's gonna take the E train to Queens? Does Lessek care? Hell, no! He wants me out, come hell or high water, and he don't let nothing stand in his way."

The old man was trembling from cold and the intensity of his feelings. "Drink some coffee," I urged. "It'll warm you up." He gulped a mouthful, and I motioned to the waitress to warm his cup. He didn't notice.

"First, it was the heat," he said after a pause. "It was July, and we'd have steam hissin' outa the radiators. I had no air conditioning; we never needed it. Just open the windows and the breeze off the river cools you off. But that don't help when you're being baked alive, so I had to shut down for two weeks, send all the girls home. We got behind in the orders. I was just catching up, had a whole shipment of caps ready to go out, when the flood happened. I couldn't believe it. My biggest order, ruined. Lessek said it was a burst pipe, called it 'an act of God.'" He shook his head. "I didn't believe it. Not when the only damage in the building was to *my* cartons of finished goods.

"It was the end," he finished sadly. "I begged my customers for more time, I begged the banks to tide me over with a loan, but everybody was deaf all of a sudden. They had money in their ears, that's why. Lessek's money. It was in alla papers, how great the new development was gonna be, how it was gonna create new jobs." Schine's eyes wavered between tears and hot anger. "What about the old jobs? What about the old businesses? Answer me that!" Abe's voice choked. "I was the last. Pearl sold out. So did Manny Helpern and Al Wong. They still got businesses. All I got is hate. You know what that *momser* told the television when he finally got into my place?" Abe's face was distorted with rage, and his hands gripped the cup as though it were a lifeline. "He stood there in his Italian suit and blow-dried hair and looked at where my sewing machines used to be and said, 'We're going to transform this dump into something the city can be proud of.'" A tear hovered at the edge of one rheumy eye. "Dump! Forty years of my life and he calls it a dump!"

"So that's why you go to his office?"

He nodded, suddenly shamefaced. "Hell, you think I like spreading creosote, throwing eggs? A man my age, he should be in Florida, warm in the sun, not freezing his ass off and making a fool out of himself. Oh, yeah," he said, giving me a shrewd glance over the top of his coffee cup. "I know I'm a fool to think Lessek cares whether I'm picketing his place or not. Even the eggs don't really bother him. He's got the dough—he just buys another suit, that's all."

Abe Schine looked down at his cracked red hands. "A man should have dignity when he gets to my age. But that Lessek—" His voice broke and the tears began to fall. "He stole my business, he stole my pension I had ready for my old age, and he stole my dignity. I got nothin' left, nothin'."

11

As I watched Dawn twisting her lips, gnawing at them like a small animal trying to free itself from a trap, I had a strong sense of déjà vu. We had come full circle, Dawn and I, back to Family Court, back to the issue of her custody.

There the similarity to the last court appearance ended. Where Linda had sat, artifically prim and childlike, Marcy now projected her power image—black pin-striped suit, royal blue blouse, discreet gold jewelry. She was impeccable, not a hair out of place, as complacent as a spring breeze. She radiated confidence, ignoring her rival with an ostentation that bordered on contempt, as though afraid simple politeness would put her one down in the power game.

I was conscious of a sinking feeling. Marcy was too sure of herself, too utterly certain that there could be no contest between her and Ma Ritchie for Dawn's custody. While I was all for the power of positive thinking among my clients, I had the feeling Marcy had taken Dr. Peale's advice a bit too literally. Just because Brad's mother was a silly woman didn't mean she could be discounted. Viola Ritchie was a grandmother—a gray-haired, churchgoing, cookies-and-milk grandma—and that was more likely than a Ralph Lauren blouse to impress a Family Court judge. It was Norman Rockwell versus crabmeat quiche, and I doubted Bettinger was a quiche man.

We started with a homily on Linda's tragic death. Heads were appropriately bowed. Then Judge Bettinger assured Mrs. Ritchie that her son's arrest for the murder would in no way prejudice her application for custody. The fact that Ma Ritchie failed to leap to her son's defense was a tribute to her laywer, who had clearly coached his client.

When Bettinger asked me for an update on Dawn's living situation, I described in glowing detail her bedroom in Marcy's East Side co-op. I told him that although Dawn was continuing in her old school for the present, Marcy was looking into private schools. Let Ma Ritchie top that, I thought with satisfaction.

She did. Private rooms, she implied with a sniff, were a dime a dozen. Dawn could have one in Bensonhurst with her. As for private schools, St. Anselm's had been good enough for Brad and was right across the street. The clincher was that she had already talked to her boss at the supermarket about cutting down her hours at the checkout counter so she could be home when Dawn came in from school. Milk, I thought ruefully, and cookies.

I sighed inwardly as Bettinger turned to Marcy and asked how many hours a week she put in at her office. It was the question I'd been dreading. In retrospect, my midnight session with Linda now seemed like child's play, a mere rehearsal for dealing with her sister. Marcy cocked her head to one side and then, as though trying to impress the company president, replied with a shrug, "Oh, somewhere between sixty and seventy-five, I guess." She smiled a power smile. "You can't run your own business," she explained patiently, "on forty hours a week."

I groaned inwardly, hoping my dismay didn't show on my face. I felt the way I had when poor crazy Juanita Flumer had jumped up in the middle of her child abuse hearing and announced to the judge in ringing Old Testament tones that she intended to follow Abraham's example and sacrifice her children to the Lord. End of hearing. Today's disaster, while hardly that conclusive, was bad enough.

"Well, what did you expect me to do?" Marcy challenged, hands on her hips. "Lie?" We were outside the courtroom but not quite out of earshot of Ma Ritchie's lawyer, whose expression was a mixture of triumph and sympathy.

"Keep your voice down," I muttered. "And if you really have to work that much, maybe you should reconsider this whole thing. Not only won't it wash with the court," I pointed out, "but it's not fair to Dawn." Dawn's visit to the ladies' room made plain speaking possible.

Marcy's jaw clamped shut. I tried another approach. "Look," I suggested, "why not think of this as a public-relations campaign?"

My client looked startled but receptive. I pressed my luck. "You've got a selling job to do in there," I pointed out, waving a hand at the closed courtroom doors. "You've got to sell Marcy Sheldon as the best possible guardian for Dawn. You're not going to do it by stressing how hard you work. It's the wrong pitch for this particular market."

Marcy liked it. I could tell by the relaxed lines of her thin face, the receptive gleam in her brown eyes. I had struck the right note. I only hoped my words would pay off in more than a superficial change in strategy.

I turned to see Dawn coming down the corridor. As she reached her grandmother, Mrs. Ritchie held out her arms for a hug. Dawn hesitated a moment, then allowed herself to be enfolded into the embrace. For a moment, she seemed to disappear into Mrs. Ritchie's voluminous wool coat.

Watching, I wondered, not for the first time, how the winner-take-all adversary system could in fairness be applied to Family Court. Much as I felt Dawn needed her aunt's stable, realistic support for her career goals, it seemed to me there ought to be room for milk and cookies too.

Marcy hadn't noticed the exchange. Busily writing in a leather-bound notebook, she seemed wholly absorbed. I reminded her of the adjourned date, then I brought up another item that was on my mind. I'd done some thinking since my visit to Todd Lessek. I was still convinced he was one of Linda's blackmail victims, but I had to admit I didn't know what he'd done. One thing I did know was that Linda, the real-estate professional, would never have made the mistake I'd made, thinking Lessek bribed his way into city funds he was entitled to as of right. Conclusion: Somewhere there was a second envelope of blackmail material, and it contained the real goods on Lessek. I wanted it. I wanted to be able to go back to that flashcube penthouse of his and confront him with something that wouldn't make him laugh, something he'd have to take seriously.

"Marcy," I began, "did Linda ever give you any papers to keep for her? A manila envelope, maybe?"

"You mean," she asked, a frown appearing on her well-made-up features, "something to do with the estate? Insurance policies?"

"I'm not exactly sure," I said with truth, if not candor, "I just think there's something that ought to be with her other papers but isn't. I thought of you," I went on, a little lamely, "because it's something she wouldn't have trusted to just anyone."

"Then she wouldn't have trusted me," came the decisive reply. If the reflection hurt, she didn't show it. "She wasn't a truster, Linda. Especially of other women."

I nodded; I'd seen that myself when I'd offered to store her valuables in my safe after her first break-in. She hadn't said in so many words that she thought I'd snoop, but I sensed her suspicion when she declined the offer.

"Was there anybody she might have trusted?" I asked. It was a long shot, but there was no one else for me to ask. If I came up empty with Marcy, it was dead-end city.

The answer was a long time coming. Marcy seemed distracted, focused on something else. I got the impression the answer had been clear to her all along, but that she didn't want to admit it.

"Harry," she said at last, distaste in her voice. "Linda's father. Mine too, but Linda was Daddy's girl. Linda worshiped him—God knows why. He's never been anything but a—" she broke off, biting her lip. "She might have given something to him."

"Do you think you could ask him about it?" I tried to suppress the eagerness I felt. The dead end had opened up unexpected pathways. "That is, if you see him."

"I really don't like to ask him for anything," Marcy said, but then she relented. "I take Dawn to see him sometimes. I could mention it."

"Thanks," I said, wondering how I was going to tell Marcy the truth about her sister's "insurance policies."

It was only noon; I decided on a quick foray across Adams Street to the Supreme Court. My chances of getting my case called were not large, but I could check in with the clerks and reassure my clients. I was zipping up my down coat when a social worker I knew slightly ran up to me. She was out of breath, but looked triumphant.

"You're still here!" she said brightly. "Thank goodness;
we need you in Part 7 right away."

I frowned. "I don't have anything in that part."

"Oh, I know that," she said, almost grabbing my sleeve
in her eagerness to keep me in the building, "but there's a
case the judge would like to assign you to, and she asked me
to see if I could find you." She fixed me with warm brown
eyes that pleaded like a puppy's. Her shirt hair was honey-
blond, and her voice had a sprightly touch of the South. I'd
seen her in court before, but where? And who was sitting in
Part 7?

I put two and two together and came up with Glenda
Shute. Why else would the social worker say "the judge"
instead of using a name? Usually when a judge calls in a favor,
it's because he or she has done something for you along the
way, but that wasn't the kind of arithmetic Glenda Shute
understood. She knew damned well I wasn't about to come
running at the sound of her name.

"Are you sure," I asked warily, "that Judge Shute asked
for me, Miss—"

"Dechter," the social worker replied, putting out a friendly hand. She had a good handshake. "Mickey Dechter."

I frowned. "I remember now," I said, "the Morrissey
case. The PINS petition. You backed me up when I told
Shute the mother only wanted the kid declared a 'person in
need of supervision' because the common-law husband didn't
want the kid around anymore."

She nodded, a conspiratorial grin flashing across her
face. "You and the judge sure went at it."

"And now, having had second thoughts, Judge Shute
wants to call me into her courtroom to apologize?"

"Not exactly—"

"Has she run out of court officers to do her personal
errands?" I asked. I was beginning to get into this. "Does she
want me to pick her kids up at school for her?"

I got a wry smile and a shake of the head.

"Then why *does* Ralph Shute's princess daughter want
me in her courtroom?"

Mickey Dechter hung her head. "She doesn't," the social
worker confessed. "I do. All the judge needs is a woman
lawyer for this respondent who insists on being represented

by a woman. But I think the mother needs more than that. I think she needs somebody who'll really do a job for her, not just get on the railroad."

"What kind of a case are we talking about?" I was afraid I already knew the answer to that, and I was right.

"Permanent neglect," came the reply. "The child welfare agency wants to put her five kids up for adoption, and they're trying to terminate her rights."

"Sounds delightful," I said without enthusiasm. "I'm supposed to become a fifth lawyer she fires? I'm supposed to let myself be jerked round by Glenda, the wicked witch of Brooklyn? I'm supposed to voluntarily get myself up to my ass in social workers? No offense," I added. But even as I spoke, my down coat was unzipping itself and my knit hat was shoving itself into a pocket and I was following the social worker through the labyrinth of hallways to Part 7.

My better judgment was right. I regretted my rash act as soon as I saw my client. Arnette Pearson wore at least ten political buttons, each proclaiming a more militant proposition than the last. She also wore the belligerent expression of someone who's been fighting so many systems for so long, she has trouble distinguishing friend from foe. Or maybe everyone was a foe until they proved themselves otherwise. Which meant that was my first job—to demonstrate to my own client that I was on her side.

It was a pleasure. I decided, out of the many ways I could accomplish this, to do it by picking a fight with the judge. It was two birds with one stone—show Arnette I was with her all the way, and show Glenda I wasn't here to do her any favors.

When I'd won my minor point, I stepped outside to talk to my new client. Judge Shute had grudgingly granted me a ten-minute recess, but I knew her well enough to know that she'd be on the phone politicking for a good twenty.

"Hey, you were all right in there," Arnette Pearson said, in a tone that sounded rough-edged. It could have been a whiskey voice or a heroin voice, but her eyes were full of judgment. She was weighing and measuring; so far I was all right, but her wary stance told me I was still on probation.

She was small but solid. Her voice was deep, her words articulate, her face a weathered black mask. She wore what appeared to be a karate outfit, all in black, and her hair was arranged in the shoulder-length dreadlock style made popular by Whoopi Goldberg. She was a scary sight, and I bet Glenda Shute had already decided in one glance that she was no fit mother for her five kids.

"Tell me about your kids," I began conversationally. Her quick frown told me she wasn't up for a chat. I switched to business. "How did they get into foster care in the first place?"

"It was my mother's fault," Arnette replied defensively. "I left the kids with her for a while so I could get myself together, you dig. So I could think about my options, whether to go to school or get me a gig or what. When I came back, they was gone." She shook her head, her wild-looking hair bobbing as though it had a life of its own.

"This was all five kids?"

"Not then. The first time it was only three—Tanika, Jomo, and Kamisha. The court gave me custody as soon as I came back that time. Then I had the twins, Kwame and Kwaku. Everything was cool for a while; they father was with me, you dig. But then he went south with his new woman, and I got restless again, so I left the kids with Mama and went to Philly with this dude I knew. When I came back, they was in foster care *again*. Damn!" She exploded, hitting the wall with her fist. Her face was distorted with rage; I was glad the other side wasn't there to witness her anger. "I was so mad at the woman, I done give her a black eye. What she mean puttin' *my* kids in foster homes?"

"What did she tell you about it?"

"She *said* she was too sick to keep 'em," Arnette replied with narrow, suspicious eyes. "What kind of grandmamma gets too sick to care for her grandbabies? She did it to spite me, on account of she never like Jerome—that's the dude I be with, you dig. She just gettin' back at me for goin' off with him. That's all they was behind her puttin' the kids in foster care, is all."

There were a lot of things I could have said to that, but

the time was ripe for none of them. I wasn't sure, looking at my client's intransigent, outthrust jaw, that it ever would be.

"Then the social workers done started in on me," she went on, "like the sittin' in judgment, callin' me a bad mother. They sayin' I 'fail to plan.' Damn social-work bullshit is all that is. How'm I gonna plan when welfare won't give me the money for a bigger apartment without I got the kids home with me, and they won't give me the kids unless I got a place to keep 'em?"

"That's a problem, all right," I agreed.

"*Thank* you," she answered with satisfaction. "I don't know why them high-toned bitches at the agency can't see that, but it's true. True as I stand here. All I wanted was to take my kids home with me, but every time I went to that agency, all I got was more bullshit. I got so tired behind that, I stopped goin'. They was puttin' me through too many changes. Next thing I know, I was in court and they talkin' about permanent neglect and takin' my kids away forever. Now I can't even visit no more. Fuckin' bullshit social workers!"

There wasn't a tear anywhere near her eyes or her voice, and yet, somehow, the pain came through clearly. Her anger was palpable, but so was the sense of loss. "Do you want me to try to get your visitation rights back?" I asked.

"Damn straight," came the reply. "And that's just for starters, you dig."

Back in the courtroom, I noted that the Hon. Glenda was engaged in conversation with the agency's lawyer, another dress-for-success type who could have passed for an oversized Marcy Sheldon. I bet forty-hour workweeks were unknown to her too. She smiled a lipsticked smile and promised me full access to Arnette's copious records any time I cared to come to her office in Lower Manhattan. I thanked her and took her card. It was all very ladylike, and I hated to turn it into a street brawl, but as the great Mao said, a revolution is not a tea party. And for Arnette to have the slightest chance of winning her case, at least a revolution would be necessary.

I started right in on the visitation issue, painting to the court a picture of my client as a bereaved mother, deprived finally of the only solace she had since she had been unable to meet the agency's requirements for regaining custody. My touching portrait might have been helped by my client's looking less like somebody you wouldn't want to meet in a dark alley, but it was good for openers.

The agency lawyer's tone was more-in-sorrow-than-anger as she outlined to the court the reasons why Arnette's visits had been stopped. First there had been the time she showed up high. Then the time Jerome had accompanied her—armed with a loaded pistol. The words "disruptive," "argumentative," "disturbing influence on the children" began to creep into the conversation. One one memorable occasion, Arnette had punched a social worker during a visit. As if all that weren't enough, she finished with a clincher. "After each of her visits, Your Honor," she purred, "one of the twins, Kwame, invariably wets his bed."

"He always *had* that problem," Arnette muttered. "It ain't *my* fault he still doin' it."

"How old is he?" I whispered.

"Be nine next birthday."

A topic better left undiscussed, I decided, and went back to the generalized platitudes about a mother's rights. I tried to point out the strain Arnette had been under during the visits, and the fact that she wasn't responsible for what Jerome brought to the agency. I knew none of it would impress Glenda; she and the agency lawyer were probably meeting for lunch after the court day, but I wanted Arnette to see me in there slugging.

The agency lawyer surprised me by pointing to several lengthy time periods—the longest fifteen months—during which Arnette didn't visit at all. "So much," the lawyer concluded with a tartness that also surprised me, "for this mother's burning need to see her children."

End of argument. An adjourned date was set, but no change in visitation was granted. It didn't mean the war was over, but it was a larger battle than I really wanted, or could afford, to lose.

Outside in the hall, I had a more antagonistic opponent to face. My client stood, feet apart, looking for all the world like a karate expert about to slice a board in two. Her mouth was set and her eyes burned. She wanted an explanation, and she wanted it fast.

She wasn't going to get it. We had to settle a few things

between us, and one of them was that I wasn't afraid of her and I wasn't taking her orders any more than I was taking Glenda's. I had to shift the emphasis from my failure to get visitation to her failure to tell me the whole story.

"Well, that was a lot of fun," I said sarcastically. "I always love getting bad news from the other side first. Especially in front of the judge. It makes my job so much easier."

"What you talkin' about?"

"I'm talking about why you didn't visit for fifteen months! Do you think it looks good to tell the judge how much you care about your kids when you didn't even bother to see them for over a year?"

She opened her mouth to retort, but I cut her off. "And don't give me any bullshit about how they put you through changes. I know what they do, but anybody who really wants their kids puts up with it. At least they get to see their kids. They don't just walk away."

"Easy for you to say," she said sullenly. "You don't be sittin' there havin' them look at you like dirt. You don't be in the office lookin' at your own kids watchin' you like you was a stranger. With them so-call foster mothers right in the room and one of them be callin' to *my* child, 'Come to Mama.' Ain't nobody say to *my* baby 'Come to Mama' except me, you dig. That's why I hit that lady that time. It just hurt me so bad to see Kwaku callin' somebody else Mama like he done. He don't know no better, but that social-worker bitch did."

"And that's why you stopped visiting?"

She ducked her head and something like shame crossed her face.

"I didn't mean to hit her," she said. "I just got so crazy. I was afraid I might freak out again, and don't know what I'd do, you dig?"

I nodded. "I see your point," I said. The truth was, the way she described the visitation shocked me. In an office, with the foster mother present. No wonder Kwame had wet the bed—torn between two "mothers," each urging him to favor her over the other.

Arnette looked up, determination and anger back in their accustomed places on her face. "Talk's cheap, lawyer," she said. "Next time, I want to see some action, you dig."

She turned and walked away, her dreadlocks bouncing, her stride masculine and intimidating.

For once I wasn't alone as I watched a client walk toward the courthouse elevators. I sensed Mickey Dechter's presence before either of us said a word.

"Some wonderful case you got me into," I grumbled, looking at her out of the corner of my eye.

She shrugged. "Hey, you know how it is," she answered in a mock-tough tone. Then she grinned. "It's a tough business," we both said at once, and then shared the laugh that followed.

12

IT'S NEVER TOO LATE TO HAVE A HAPPY CHILDHOOD. The words were in green, lettered in a calligraphic style I'd never seen before. Drawings of kids at play surrounded the words—kids jumping rope, kids swinging on trees, tossing colored balls, playing with a cocker spaniel. They were Lois Lenski–style drawings, very open and sweet but not cloying.

Just as I was deciding I liked the poster a lot, I thought of Dawn. Never too late to have a happy childhood? When you're passed from a self-centered mother to cold-fish aunt? When the alternatives are a smothering grandmother or a spoiled-brat father? I turned away; it was a nice picture, but that was all.

It would have been hard to imagine a less likely place to track down the murky past of Art Lucenti and Todd Lessek than the Friday's Child Day-Care Center. In the middle of the big room a group of toddlers sat wide-eyed as a bright-faced young black woman told a story with puppets. In the corner, two young men were changing diapers. In the other corner, babies too young for the story were crawling on blankets, watched by a middle-aged woman who cooed at them encouragingly.

When the diapering was done, one of the men came over. He was tall, with a thin face and lank blond hair, worn in a pony tail. "Hi," he said, extending his hand. "I'm Chris Alter. Do you have a child you want to place here?"

It was a natural question, but it flustered me anyway. "No," I replied, too quickly. "I'm not even married." The absurdity of the remark struck us both at the same time. We smiled and he said, "Neither are the mothers of some of these kids. But I get the feeling you're here about something else."

I nodded, then glanced around the child-filled room. "Is there somewhere we can talk?"

"Sure," he said. "My office." He led me into a tiny cubicle off the main room. Desk, two chairs, rusting metal gooseneck lamp. Very spartan, except for the wall posters, which were elaborate, fanciful renderings of classic children's book illustrations. Twisted trees, pre-Raphaelite fairies with long curly hair, and a wonderful *Alice in Wonderland* caterpillar.

He caught me looking at the posters. "Arthur Rackham," he explained. "From the Green Tiger Press in California. My lady's an artist; she gave me those when we moved in here."

"She did the drawing in the other room?"

"Yeah. It's great, isn't it?"

"It's pretty," I replied. "It's not true, but it's pretty."

His eyebrows went up, but he said nothing. Just sat back and waited for me to go on. He would have made a good shrink—or a good lawyer.

"For some people it *is* too late to have a happy childhood. What about abused kids, molested kids, kids whose parents are dead—not all kids' problems can be solved by an hour or two playing with a puppy." I didn't know why my voice was taking on a hard vehement edge it sometimes got in court, why it suddenly seemed so important to convince Chris Alter of the rightness of my position. Some obscure honor demanded that he acknowledge the limits of his profession.

"Nobody said," he replied gently, "that all kids have the same kind of happy childhood, or even that you have to be a child to have one. An adult who learns to play, to free the child within, to love without restrictions—that person is giving herself the happy childhood she couldn't get from her own parents."

His use of the feminine pronouns was interesting, to say the least. "You mean," I said warily, "that I'm taking the sign too literally?"

"Maybe." He smiled the kind of sweet innocent smile I hadn't seen on an adult face since the days of flower power. "Although I suspect you have a particular child in mind. In which case, all I can say is I have seen abused, neglected, bereaved kids who can be helped to happiness. All it takes is a little extra love along the way."

Welcome to Walton's Mountain, my mind retorted. That "little extra love" was just what Dawn wasn't getting from anyone. But I hadn't come to talk about Dawn and I was sorry I'd started the topic. I changed the subject.

"Why Friday's Child?" I hoped my tone was as light as I'd intended it to be. "What's wrong with Monday's or Tuesday's?"

He smiled as though the question was the bantering one it might have been if I'd asked it before we'd had the other conversation. "Monday's child is only 'fair of face,'" he replied. "Friday's child is the one we're trying to encourage— 'loving and giving.'"

I hadn't changed the subject as far as I thought I had. "A noble sentiment," I muttered, unable to shake the mood of cynicism that caused me to take a shot at anything Chris Alter said. I hoped getting down to business would dispel some of it, but considering the nature of my business, it wasn't likely.

"You used to occupy space in a different building, didn't you?" I asked. "One owned by Ira Bellfield?"

"Yes," he answered, wariness tightening his face, closing it off just a fraction. I was interested; apparently Alter wasn't as childlike as he seemed at first blush.

"I'd like to ask you some questions about what happened between you and Art Lucenti over that building," I began. "I promise it won't go any further. I'm doing some investigation into a different matter entirely, and I need a little background."

"What makes you think I know anything you'd be interested in?" The wariness was on the front burner now. Apparently a happy childhood didn't necessarily preclude a cautious adult—or maybe Chris Alter's dealings with the real-estate crowd had taken its toll of his innocence.

"I've seen the court papers, Chris," I said quietly. "The ones you never filed, charging Art Lucenti with a conflict of interest."

"Oh God." Wariness had turned to what seemed to be utter despair. I wasn't sure why, but I liked the lanky, ponytailed man well enough to feel a pang of guilt. "Look, I don't know how you got those papers, but *please*—"

"I *said*," I interrupted firmly, "that it wouldn't go any further and I meant it. I just want to talk to you off the record about what happened before you had those papers drawn up. I promise not to make trouble for you."

He wasn't convinced. I could see it in his face, as shut off as an abandoned building with tin in the windows to prevent vandalism. I might not be asked to leave, but I'd get nothing but panicky denials unless I tried something drastic.

"The thing is," I began, trying not to sound as desperate as I felt, "a woman's been murdered. Her husband's in jail for the murder. The only person who believes in his innocence is their daughter."

The long, tense face relaxed. "You're not from them?" he asked. "You're not a reporter or anything like that?" I didn't say any more. I didn't exactly want to mislead him into thinking I represented Brad, but I knew the truth was too complicated to serve my purpose. And the word *blackmail* might start a panic I couldn't quell.

"And the child? She was the one who was in your thoughts when you saw our sign, wasn't she? The one you hope it's not too late for?"

I nodded, uncomfortably aware that I was using Dawn. But it *was* her cause I was fighting for, and she *had* been in my thoughts, so I decided my subconscious wouldn't lie to me and pressed on.

"It seems," I said carefully, "that other people had a motive to kill her mother—who was, by the way, Art Lucenti's secretary."

"Heavy stuff," he said seriously. "I heard it on the news." He looked at Alice's caterpillar as though seeking advice, and then turned to me, decision in his ascetic face. "Okay. What do you want to know?"

"When you first moved into the other building, it was Ira Bellfield's?"

"Yeah. Slum city. We had a real hassle getting city approval for the day-care center, what with all the problems. Exposed wires, leaky pipes, falling plaster—you name it, we had it. We were up to our ears in Health Department inspectors, but finally we got certified. Most of our workers lived in the building. We started as a cooperative to help each other out with our own kids, and finally ended up as the biggest facility in the neighborhood. But the building itself was falling apart. We were constantly on rent strike in those days."

"Who was your lawyer?"

His answering grin told me I'd asked the right question. "Art Lucenti, of course. He was a Legal Services lawyer. Man, you should have seen the show he used to put on in court." He shook his head, admiration in his face. "He'd walk up to the bench, carrying about fifty folders, and start haranguing the judge about the heat, and the plumbing, and talk about how one of the kids got hit by falling plaster. Once he brought a rat to court. Dead, of course, in a Bloomingdale's shopping bag. That was the part that got me," he chuckled. "The Bloomie's bag. Here's the judge thinking Art brought his new shoes to court, and all of a sudden, he opens the bag, takes out the shoe box, takes off the top, and there's this big old hairy dead rat. The judge closed the courtroom and left for the day."

"What happened to the case?" I was intrigued. Art sounded like the kind of lawyer I'd have been proud to know. I wondered what had changed him into somebody whose Bloomie's bags contained nothing more than Gucci shoes.

"Well, we held on to the rent," Chris said with a laugh. "That was the name of the game. Keeping the rent in escrow. Not giving it to Bellfield until real repairs were done, and not giving it to the court either. Art kept our money for us that day. That's not all, either. We had rent-strike meetings every month, and Art organized picketing in front of Bellfield's office. We were on television six times," he said proudly. "Once, we all got on a bus and went out to Bellfield's house to picket."

"He must have loved that," I murmured.

Chris grimaced. "It was a fiasco. He lived in Seagate and we couldn't get past the guards."

"I suppose a slumlord *would* live in a heavily protected private enclave," I said absently. What bothered me was the suspicion that Art must have known where Bellfield lived before putting his clients on the bus. In which case, he'd been more interested in putting on a show of militancy than in actually being an effective advocate. And that was *before* he'd worked for Lessek.

"We thought we'd finally won," Chris Alter went on, "when Bellfield walked away. We ran the building ourselves for about a year. Paid for oil, had some repairs done. Then the next thing we knew, this Todd Lessek guy had bought the building. We had a party on the roof, we were so happy." He shook his head. "How naïve can you get? We actually thought Lessek would fix up the building and let us all stay there."

"What did he do?"

"First thing he did was ask us to leave. Politely, offering relocation money. Some tenants took it and left." He shrugged nonjudgmentally. "Some of us didn't. A day-care center's not so easy to move. We finally had all the city licenses and approvals, so we decided to tough it out and hope for the best.

"He sent in a new super. A real animal. Next thing we know the boiler's busted—not just down, but out for the rest of the winter. Didn't take long for the Health Department to find out either. We had electric heaters set up all over the center, but they didn't care. They slapped fines on us every time we were the slightest bit below code standard, whether it was Lessek's fault or ours."

Alter sighed and clasped his hands behind his head. "Then the pipes burst and water overflowed throughout the building. Toilets backed up. We started getting hit by burglars— well, to be fair, we always did, but it was like five minutes after you left to go to the supermarket, they were breaking in 'cause they knew you were gone. How did they know? The super told them. Great, huh?"

"What did you do about it?"

"What could we do?" He snorted. "Cops thought we were paranoid, so we called our lawyer. Art was in private practice by then, nice little storefront office in the neighbor-

hood. 'Course we didn't know it's not his only office, that he
also had his name on the door of a fancy firm on Court Street."

"He was happy to represent you?" I asked. "He never
said anything about a conflict of interest?"

"Hell, no. In that neighborhood, Art was a saint. Old
Italian ladies who never voted in their lives couldn't wait to
get in the booth and pull the lever for good old Art. He was
already on the City Council making speeches about tenants'
rights, so he welcomed us with open arms and talked about
how we were his clients in the old days and he won't let us
down now. We felt great. We invited him to the next roof
party—and our roof parties were justly famous, let me tell
you. He said don't worry about a thing and he went into court
to ask for an Article 7-A administrator."

"What's that?"

"Someone the court appoints to run the building," he
explained. "Someone who collects the rent and makes sure it
goes toward the building, not into the landlord's pocket."

"Lucenti appeared in court on the case?"

"Amid some publicity in the local paper," he said. "We
didn't know a city councilman's not supposed to appear before
city agencies, or represent clients who might have an interest
in city laws he votes on. That was dumb enough. But what
we were really burned about was finding out that the fancy
law firm in the Heights that carried his name on the door
represented Lessek."

"You think that's why you lost in court?"

"We lost because Lucenti never wanted us to win. All that
rhetoric . . ." Chris shook his head sadly. "All that bullshit about
tenants' rights and neighborhood loyalty. He was on Lessek's payroll and we never knew it. That roof party turned into a wake—
but we still had Lucenti there. We toasted good old Art and told
him not to feel bad, it wasn't his fault. Man, were we taken."

"When did you find out the truth?"

"Believe it or not, when Lessek's lawyers sent us a
notice on their stationery—and there was Art's name, listed
as 'Of Counsel.' Whatever that means."

I nodded; what it meant was trouble for Art Lucenti.

"So what did you do?"

"Talked to another lawyer. One we could trust. He told
us all about the conflict-of-interest thing and drew up the
papers to take it to court. I was so mad I just wanted to ruin

Art, spread it all over the newspapers what he'd done. But the lawyer convinced us that wouldn't get us our space back. We'd have a better chance if we could show the court that we never really had counsel in the Article 7-A proceedings because Art was really on the other side."

"It would have been picked up by the media either way," I pointed out. "One thing I want to know is, why wasn't it?"

Chris ducked his head, and his thin face reddened. He mumbled something I didn't catch. I was about to ask him to repeat it, but then I realized I didn't have to. The space the Friday's Child Day-Care Center now occupied was large, well-finished, and clearly beyond its means.

"Lessek owns this building." I said it flatly.

"Yes."

"I understand." Cynicism back in full force.

"No, you don't." The embarrassment was gone, replaced by genuine indignation. "My job is helping kids, not fighting crooked politicians. I'll do whatever it takes to get my kids what they need—and if that means getting in bed with Lessek and Lucenti, then that's what I'll do. Look out there."

I looked. The kids had formed a band and were marching in step around the room. Some had solemn, intent faces as they concentrated on playing their instruments. One little black girl with yellow barrettes on her tiny braids squealed with delight as she banged her tambourine. The triangle player had a plastic brace on one leg, and brought up the rear with a quickstep trot that didn't show on his beaming face.

"They don't care about Lessek or Lucenti or conflicts of interest and neither do I."

"I understand," I repeated. This time I meant it.

13

The sign for *fire:* the hands move up and down, fingers wiggling frantically, like licking flames. The sign for *lawyer:*

the L-sign held up against an open palm (representing a lawbook), then the sign for *person* added on. The sign for *bad:* the right hand at the mouth, then forcefully thrust downward, as though throwing away rotten food. That was the sign the boys made when Ira Bellfield turned the corner and headed, straining against the gusty wind, toward the burned-out building.

I had a copy of the court order in my pocket, just in case. There was no doubt of my legal right to be there, looking at and photographing the arson site, but I knew Bellfield would hold me to every technicality in the book. He'd made that clear already, the way he'd tried to convince the court to refuse my application for access to the building. His strenuous opposition had only made me hungrier to see for myself what it was he was trying to hide.

Ira Bellfield walked straight up to me, ignoring the eight or so Unknown Homicides, who stood in a sullen, wary group around me. His petulant face was set in a mask of distaste. A hat covered his balding head, the kind of hat private eyes used to wear with dash and style. Bellfield's hat had neither, since he wore it square on his head, clamped on like a lid. He gave me a distinctly unfriendly look from under its gray brim.

"Let's get this over with," he said in his nasal, slightly aggrieved whine. "I got things I gotta do."

I was sure he did, things like arranging burglaries and commissioning fires. But I had already promised myself that Linda's murder wasn't on the agenda today. I was here as Tito Fernandez's lawyer, and I owed it to my client to let nothing interfere with a thorough investigation of the crime scene. If only the back of my mind didn't contain the tantalizing, treacherous thought that by proving Bellfield guilty of Linda's murder, I'd be clearing Tito as well. I shoved the thought ruthlessly aside and said calmly, "I can't start until my investigator gets here."

Bellfield snorted. "I shoulda known a broad couldn't do something like this on her own. So you need a big strong man to come and hold your hand?"

I caught sight of two things that cut off my heated retort.

One was a huge oxlike man with a hammer in his hand who stood on the edge of the building, eyes fixed on Bellfield. From what the boys had told me, I decided he had to be the building super, a part-time wrestler who worked out in one of the front rooms. Evidently Bellfield was the one who felt the need of a strong man to hold his hand.

The other person who caught my eye was Angie, my investigator. She was coming down the street at a fast clip, the press camera swinging at her side. Her mass of dark curly hair was windblown, and her bootheels clicked on the broken pavement.

"The only reason I even need an investigator," I explained to Bellfield, "is that I'd rather not become a witness in this case. If I took the pictures, I'd have to take the stand." I was annoyed at myself for needing to explain, but I wanted Bellfield to know I wasn't afraid to be there. The problem was, glancing uneasily at Gorgeous George idly swinging his hammer, that it wasn't entirely true. I *was* afraid of what Ira Bellfield could do, or have done, to me.

"If you'll excuse me, Mr. Bellfield," I said, reverting to a coldly professional tone, "I'd like to consult with my clients and my investigator. In private."

He gave me a smirk as he turned and walked toward the huge super, who stood immobile, looking like a robot in a science-fiction movie. I suspected Bellfield of having a remote control box in his pocket, and I pictured him pushing buttons, causing the massive torso to lurch forward in huge, awkward strides.

With Bellfield gone, the atmosphere lightened considerably. Using Frankie as interpreter, I introduced Angie to the boys. She produced delighted grins by greeting them in sign. "You learn a little of everything," she explained with a smile, "in the cops." Angie was a retired Housing policewoman who'd incurred bad back damage in a fall down some concrete steps, a fall engineered by a startled burglar. She was on disability but did some investigative work for the panel that assigns lawyers to the poor. "I can say hello in Vietnamese and Arabic, too," she added proudly. "In addition to the more conventional languages."

"I don't know what language you'd need to talk to that super of Bellfield's," I remarked. "How's your gorilla?"

"Let's see the police and fire reports," Angie said with a laugh.

I dug into my Channel 13 tote bag, having left my new leather briefcase home, along with my three-piece suits. Professional image is well and good in its place, which is not climbing over charred timbers in an abandoned building. I pulled out a sheaf of papers. Police reports, fire marshal's reports, interviews with witnesses—all pointing the finger at the Unknown Homicides in general and Tito in particular.

"The fire started in Tito's apartment," I said. "His mattress was doused with kerosene and lit up like a bonfire." Angie nodded. "But there was also, according to these reports, a pool of kerosene in front of Tito's room. In fact," I went on, "Tito's story is that he slipped in the puddle on the way to his room and that's how the stuff was all over him when the cops arrived. Of course, the DA says 'a likely story,' but the fire marshal's report does confirm the puddle's existence. Not conclusive either way, but I'd like to see where the puddle was."

"And where everyone says they were when the fire started?" Angie asked. I agreed, then turned to Frankie so he could let my client in on the discussion.

Given the shabby nature of the building they had called home, the Unknown Homicides seemed inordinately eager to show it off, laughing and pointing at the melted windows as though they couldn't wait to get inside the soot-streaked walls. I decided finally that it was the visual nature of the investigation that appealed to them. So far the case had consisted of words laboriously translated, abstract. Now for the first time it was concrete, something everyone could see, something in which they could participate equally.

I waved at Bellfield, and he started forward, accompanied by the wrestler. I suppressed a smile as I noted Bellfield's hand in his pocket—fingering a little black box with buttons, no doubt.

"You finally ready?" he whined. "You sure been taking your sweet time."

"Listen," I pointed out, "you don't have to be here. You can go do whatever it is you have to do. Get a cup of coffee, whatever."

"Listen, lady," he snarled, "you're gonna be inside my building, I'm gonna be there. I don't let nobody mess around behind my back. Understand?"

I understood, all right. What I wasn't sure of was whether I was understanding more than was really being said. We turned and went into the building in a silent, incongruous parade. Bellfield and the wrestler led the way, while Angie and I followed and the boys, subdued by Bellfield's presence, brought up the rear.

It still smelled of fire, an acrid, ugly smell that emanated from torn walls, charred beams, bits of burned mattress. Apparently no effort at cleaning up had been made. Which meant that maybe I'd get a better idea of what had really happened that hot August night that seemed so remote in frozen January.

The ground floor was a rabbit warren of rooms. Once a longshoremen's boarding house, the building had become, in New York parlance, an SRO. Single-room occupancy, rented out to the poorest and most isolated men in the city—the winos, the junkies, the wackos, and the Unknown Homicides. The rooms were cheap, and enough of the boys had lived there to turn the place into an unofficial clubhouse, much to the annoyance of Bellfield's wrestler, who even now stood glaring at the boys as though they had insulted his manhood. Was it possible, I asked myself, watching his hostile glances, that he had lit the fire himself, not on Bellfield's orders, but for his own purposes—to drive out and discredit Tito and his friends? It was an idea I couldn't ignore. It would be a mistake to get so caught up in the case against Bellfield that I missed other lines of defense that could help Tito in front of a jury. Once again, I gave myself a sharp reminder to think like Tito Fernandez's lawyer and not Linda Ritchie's avenger.

We stopped at Tito's room. He pointed to it excitedly and tapped his chest to denote possession. The door had been removed; I looked inside. The mattress was a black lump, one or two springs sticking out to identify what it had been. The walls were black, and water had ruined whatever fire hadn't. A sooty plaster saint lay in a corner, one arm broken off; a green votive candle lay nearby.

"Saint Jude," Frankie translated Tito's fingerspelling.

"Tito say he prayin' to Saint Jude alla time. Patron saint of the impossible, that's Saint Jude."

Behind me I heard a guttural voice. "Goddamn spics and their superstitions. Candle prolly started the fire inna first place."

I turned to Frankie and in a voice only slightly louder than usual told him to tell Tito to keep up the prayers even without his statue. Tito smiled at me and made the promise. What the hell, I thought, to soothe my atheistic conscience, it couldn't hurt.

"Okay, Tito," I said, "show me what you did that night. Where you came from, what you saw. You'll have to get out of his way, Mr. Bellfield," I said, motioning him to stand behind me. I wasn't crazy about my clients' telling their story in front of the enemy, but Bellfield did have a right to be in his own building, so I made the best of it.

Tito pointed to the front stairway, walked up it about three steps, and then, putting on a face that registered panic, he rushed down and started toward the door of his room. Stopping abruptly, he pointed at the concrete floor and spelled something out to Frankie.

"The puddle of kerosene," I guessed. Frankie nodded.

Tito mimed slipping in the puddle. He had gotten up and was about to dash into his room when the same guttural voice said, "There wasn't no puddle. He's lyin'. The little dummy's lyin' to save his ass."

All eyes turned to Gorgeous George. Even the Homicides, who couldn't hear him, sensed he had challenged Tito's version of events. I willed myself not to look at Angie lest some hint of triumph cross my face. Evidently the burly super didn't know that the puddle was more than a figment of Tito's imagination; it had been seen and noted by the fire department itself. The super was looking at Bellfield expectantly, like an obedient dog who'd just earned himself a juicy bone.

"When were you in this hallway, Mr.—" I tried to keep my tone neutral, but Bellfield wasn't as stupid as I'd hoped. Before his employee could answer, he broke in. "Hey, you got no right to ask my man questions," he protested. "You got a court order says you can look at the building. Okay, take a good look. But this man's got nothing to say to you." He glared at me and at the wrestler, daring either of us to continue. I stared back defiantly, but finally I gave in, knowing that once the order had been given, I could expect nothing more from the massive super; his master had muzzled him once and for all.

I turned back to Tito. "After you fell in the puddle, what happened?" What I saw was a replay of what the boys had already told me in court—the door flung open, the flames beating Tito back, the retreat out of the building, where he was seen, captured, and held for the police by Gorgeous George. Angie took pictures of the room, of the hallway where the puddle had been, and of the front stairway, while Bellfield made exasperated noises.

When we were finished, the boys led us upstairs to where they had been when they first noticed the fire. We walked down a dark, narrow hallway to a room in the back. It had been relatively untouched by flames, but was unoccupied, Bellfield having used the fire as an excuse to empty the whole building.

Even without fire damage, the room was no place I'd have cared to call home. The peeling paint had been put on so long ago, it had to be the deadly lead-based stuff outlawed a good ten years ago. Part of a naked bulb hung from a cord in the middle of the ceiling; I guessed the bulb had filled with water from the firemen's hoses, then cracked and fallen of its own weight. The remaining filament dangled from the socket like a translucent spider.

There was no closet in the bare room; I noticed two stout hooks on the wall and imagined all of Julio's clothes draped over them in a huge layered bunch. The last time I had seen anything like that was in a photograph in Jacob Riis's classic *How the Other Half Lives*. Apparently, in Bellfield's building, the other half still lived the same way. Yet Julio pointed delightedly at the window facing the courtyard, paved with cracked cement, through which now-bare trees poked spindly branches. And he smiled at the tattered, water-damaged Clash poster on one wall. I guess my surprise showed in my face, for Frankie explained, "He can feel the vibrations."

Remembering the group's raucous sound, I smiled. "I'll bet he can."

"Okay," I said briskly, "who was where?" There was some good-natured shoving among the boys as they arranged themselves into the group that had been in Julio's room and the group that had come running from further down the hall. There were gestures of dismissal and contempt when someone had it wrong, but finally it was settled to the satisfaction of the majority. Again the story was much as I'd heard it in court, but it made a difference to see the boys together, as seven of them headed down the back stairs to safety, while Tito ran against the crowd to the front stairway to check on his room. A few more pictures and we were finished.

Back on the sidewalk, I thanked Angie warmly and told her I wanted the pictures rushed. She agreed and dashed off, with a quick wave as she reached the corner. I was ready to say good-bye to the boys and head home, when Tito suddenly began making agitated gestures toward the building. Frankie told me there was something important Tito wanted to show me. I turned to follow him inside, when a groan from Bellfield stopped me.

"You're jerkin' me around here, lady," he complained. "I told you, I got things to do, and you're bustin' my chops."

"I already told you," I replied tartly, "you don't have to stay."

"Just make it quick," he said, glancing at his watch. "I got a phone call to make." He headed toward a phone booth as I followed Tito and Frankie to the building.

At first, in the dim light, I had no idea what Tito was pointing at, but when my eyes adjusted to the dimness I saw rusty inoperative sprinkler heads in the hall ceiling. I nodded at my client and made a note to check it out. I wished I had Angie to take photos, but it was certainly a violation Bellfield should have had repaired before the fire.

I was making a note in my file, oblivious to my surroundings, when I felt myself grabbed from behind and dragged. I flailed around, dropping my file folder, too paralyzed to scream. As I saw Frankie and Tito walking out of the building assuming I was behind them, I realized that screaming wouldn't help.

I was pushed into a room, falling so that my knees skinned the concrete floor. The door slammed, and I heard a key rasp in the lock.

If I'd had any doubts about who had dragged me here, they were banished with one look around the room. It was a makeshift gym, with chest developers and jump ropes attached to the walls, weights ranging in size from little hand jobs to enormous circus-style dumbbells, a rowing machine and a stationary bicycle. It was a one-man Stillman's gym, a ghetto Jack LaLanne's. It could belong only to Gorgeous George. The sole decorations were bodybuilding posters so exquisitely photographed as to raise serious doubts about the gorilla's sexual preferences.

I couldn't believe what had happened. I stood a moment, catching my breath and trying to put the whole thing in perspective. Ira Bellfield was no fool; he wasn't about to let me come to harm, when it was well known where I was. It could only mean trouble, and he had enough of that already without having to explain dead lawyers turning up in his buildings. Beside, how did he know my death would solve his problems? For all he knew, I'd done what everyone does in books, sent the incriminating contents to my lawyer in an envelope to be opened upon my death. I hadn't in fact done anything so melodramatic, but it was beginning to sound like a good idea.

At any rate, I decided, taking off my coat and sitting on the stationary bicycle, there was no sense in panicking. Gorgeous George had probably acted on the same kind of stupid impulse that had led him to lie about the kerosene puddle, and Bellfield would probably have his hide for it and then run into the building, eager to release me and offering profuse apologies. Insincere, but profuse. No need to panic at all, I told myself, idly beginning to pedal the bike.

Then I smelled smoke.

14

I panicked.

Jumping off the exercise bike, I dashed to the door and began pounding as hard as I could. Against the hollow steel, my blows fell like thundering timpani crashes at the end of a rousing symphony. My hands felt like raw hamburger, my voice sounded cracked and witchlike, but the door gave not an inch.

Exhausted, I turned and saw smoke seeping through the walls. I could already feel its harshness in my throat, but the sight got me crazy. I ran to the window. Barred, of course, with good thick bars that would give a crowbar-wielding burglar pause. Like Julio's window upstairs, this one faced the rear courtyard; I could see only a sliver of the alleyway that led to the street.

Screaming would do no good, I reminded myself. The building was empty except for the makeshift gym, and my research had told me the surrounding buildings had also been emptied, Bellfield-style, by fire and harassment. The only people who cared if I lived or died couldn't hear me; those who could didn't care. No, screaming would be stupid.

I screamed anyway. Running back to the exercise bike, I grabbed a hand-weight and threw it at the window. The gesture and the satisfying tinkle of glass that followed gave me new energy. I ran to the window and screamed my guts out. As the smell of smoke grew strong, screams subsided into sobs of frustration and fear.

I knew only one thing—I wanted to be out of this place as much as I'd ever wanted anything in my life. Never before claustrophobic, I hung on those bars and gulped air from that window as though my life depended on it.

After what seemed an eternity, panic began to ebb. I still smelled the smoke and now heard an ominous crackle to go with it, but I had some control of myself. I forced my rubber legs to walk to a small sink in the corner of the room. I ran water, first dashing some onto my flushed face, and then dousing my white shirt in it. Thank goodness, I thought wryly, for fashion—the oversized white shirt I'd tossed on over my turtleneck would make a perfect mask. Holding the wet shirt to my mouth, I began to explore the room, hoping against hope that the gorilla had left a spare key. Coughing and gasping, I walked to where the smoke was strongest, wanting to get it over with quickly. It was the wall with the jump ropes. I started in one corner and methodically searched the dull gray surface for a key-hook. Halfway across, I had to run back to the sink to re-wet the shirt. The air was stifling, worse than the oppressive heat that hits New York in August.

I ran back and finished that wall, my shaking hands roaming the surface I could barely see, my streaming eyes searching for any place a key might be hidden. I checked under the bike and the rowing machine for magnetic key-holders.

Seven trips to the sink later, I'd done all the walls and was reaching the door. My hands were spastic as I reached up above the jamb in the place a lot of householders leave their spares. My hopes were waning, and yet my mind refused to accept the inevitable. I was on the verge of doing what I'd done as a kid, promising the God I no longer believed in a virtuous life if only He'd get me out of this one. I even gave a passing thought to Tito's favorite saint—the one who specialized in the impossible. I laughed harshly at myself as I realized what I was doing: plea-bargaining.

No key. I sank to the ground where I stood, my legs folding under me like a secondhand bridge table. My wet shirt was drying out from the heat, filling with the acrid smell of smoke and denying me the tiny taste of oxygen I'd been getting. The sink would help; the window, away from the engulfing smoke, would help even more. I could scream again, I thought in despair, knowing how futile the act would be. I could search again, knowing I'd already done a thorough job. I could—

I didn't care. I sat in front of the door hoping death would come quickly, realizing the sink, the window, were only temporary respites. The smoke would eventually invade my lungs wherever I was, whatever I did, and I would die. Then the flames would lick at my extremities, nibble and gouge me to death with fiery teeth, and I would end up as what Duncan Pitt had called a roast. A piece of charred meat.

I heard whimpering. I looked around wildly, then realized it was me. I hated myself at that moment, hated my weakness. I sobbed aloud, pounded and kicked the door. I think I screamed out the words that had made me a lawyer at the age of four: *It's not fair!* I threw myself against the door in a paroxysm of rage, the kind of tantrum toddlers throw in the supermarket, then sat spent and staring.

It was time to get up. I did it mechanically, wearily, yet with a deep and utter calm. I walked to the window, leaned out as far as I could, and took long yoga breaths. I tried to hold the air in as long as I could, but I was stopped by racking coughs. I brought up acrid black sputum and spat it into the courtyard, then inhaled again and again, gradually replacing the smoke with life-giving freshness. The cold air felt good to my sweaty, tear-streaked face, and I finally woke up enough to wipe my running nose with my now-dry shirt. I was almost alive again.

Alive enough to realize I wasn't whimpering or kicking anymore. Alive enough to think. Sound was out. The hearing people within earshot had put me where I was. The people who could help me couldn't hear. What *could* they do? They could, I decided, see. What I had to do was give them something to see.

I bent down and picked up the weight I'd used to break the window. It had hit a bar and fallen back inside the room. It was a small hand-weight; probably Gorgeous George lifted it with his pinky. But to me it was heavy. And I had to hurl it out the window, across the courtyard, through the alley, and out into the street. This from the girl chosen last for every softball game Chagrin Falls, Ohio, ever had.

I swung back my arm, trying not to notice the immediate protest lodged by stiff shoulder muscles. I flung the weight, holding my breath involuntarily. It got about halfway across the courtyard, landing with a dull thud even the hearing wouldn't have noticed. The second weight I threw went almost to the alley. I was getting better. The third hit the opposite wall, chipping a brick. The fourth was the last one I felt I could throw with any success, and I stood in indecision, hating to let it go, when I suddenly had a flash of inspiration. The jump ropes! I ran to the wall, through the black cloud of smoke, ripped the ropes off the wall in one motion, then ran back to the window, gulping more air and spitting out smoke. When I was reasonably recovered, I pulled the handles off the ropes and tied them together with hands steadier than I thought possible.

I threw without hesitation, my aim good enough this time to send the weight into the alley itself. I had to smile

with pride. That pitch could have evened a lot of scores
back in Chagrin Falls. I grinned as I pulled the weight
back in and prepared to try again.

I had my arm raised when I saw it. A movement at first,
it soon resolved itself into a sleeve, and then a jacket—a
jacket with the colors of the Unknown Homicides on the
back!

The boy was facing the street, away from me. I had to
force down the shout that wouldn't be heard. Summoning up
everything I had, I flung the weight into the courtyard, into
the alley, where it landed just short of the boy. Anyone else
would have turned to look at the source of the unexpected
sound, but the boy just stood.

It was back to prayers again. I was afraid to haul the
weight in, afraid my next try wouldn't get that far. All the boy
had to do was turn around and look down. I begged him to do
it. The sight of one of George's weights attached to a rope
would have to lead to an investigative walk into the courtyard, where he'd see me waving frantically in the window.
My mind screamed what I knew it would be futile to cry
aloud.

The boy in the alley walked away as quickly and silently
as he had come. I saw red, then black, before my eyes as I
hung, defeated, in the window.

At first, I didn't even hear the noise, but then, restored
to my senses, it sounded as loud and welcome as any sound
I'd ever heard. It was the rasp of a key turning in the lock on
the steel door.

Frantic, I ran for the door, my breath coming in sobs and
coughs; when the door opened, I rushed through it—and
flung myself into the arms of Ira Bellfield.

It was like a scene from a romance novel. I buried my
head in his coat and sobbed with relief, my fingers kneading
his back. His arms were around me, holding me up, and his
voice whispered soothingly, "It's okay now. The fire's out.
Don't cry." It was a touching moment, except for one thing—I
was still convinced it was Ira who'd tried to kill me in the first
place.

We hobbled out of the building together. My legs
were still too wobbly to support me on their own. I
wanted to sit down, but the cold, broken pavement in
front of the building didn't appeal to me. "I'm taking you

to my car," Ira said in my ear. "You'll be out of the wind there, anyway." I didn't protest as he opened the door of a black Mercedes and gently lowered me into the passenger seat. I leaned back against the leather upholstery and closed my eyes. I was no longer crying, but tears coursed down my cheeks.

A touch on my shoulder startled me. I jumped, then turned to see Tito, looking anxious, holding my now-grimy down coat. I mustered a smile and let him tuck it around me like a blanket. I was trying to reassure him that I was all right, and finding it pretty hard going without Frankie the interpreter, when Bellfield came back, followed by the rest of the Homicides. He handed me a Styrofoam cup. "Coffee," he explained. "I thought you'd like something to drink." I tore off the lid and sucked thirstily at the deli coffee Bellfield had brought. It was overmilked, oversugared, and utterly wonderful.

"It was just a couple of mattresses set on fire," Bellfield said, gesturing toward the building. "Turk put the fire out with an extinguisher he keeps in the basement. Coulda been kids." He gave me an appraising look, then added, "Anyway, no harm done. Thank God for that."

"You thank God," I snapped, my voice an ugly and unexpected croak. "Kids, my ass. Somebody locked me in that room—and the only person I know has a key is that gorilla of yours. Turk, is it? What's his last name?" I glared at Bellfield. "I'll need it for the police report."

I wasn't sure what reaction I expected, but what I got surprised me. "Let's not be hasty, here, Miss Jameson," he said in a smooth, confident tone. "If the police get into this, they could hear evidence that could cut both ways."

"What's that supposed to mean?"

"Those boys of yours"—Bellfield gestured at the Homicides, who were watching us intently but without comprehension— "have already been charged with arson once."

"Why would any of them want to hurt me?" I responded with scorn. "I'm on their side, and they know it."

Bellfield shrugged. "Some people are crazy about fires," he said. "They don't care who they hurt as long as they get to see the pretty flames. Or maybe," he went on, "it was an accident. Maybe somebody tossed a match in the wrong place, and being deaf, didn't hear the flames start to crackle. Could be a lot of explanations. 'Course," he went on, giving me a piercingly shrewd glance from under the gray hatbrim, "it's up to the fire marshal to decide what really happened."

The fire marshal. Duncan Pitt. My heart sank, and the anger that had led me to threaten Bellfield with the police evaporated. Pitt would write in his report whatever Bellfield told him to write. Turk wouldn't be mentioned at all, and if anyone got the blame, it would be the Unknown Homicides. Maybe someday, the whole mess would be straightened out, but in the meantime, I'd be a complaining witness against my own client. It would be the end of my representation of Tito Fernandez.

Suspicions creased my forehead. I turned away, ostensibly to finish my coffee and dispose of the cup in Bellfield's plastic litter bag, but really to think. Had that been the reason for the fire—to trap me into filing a complaint and removing me as Tito's lawyer once he turned out to be the person charged? If so, why was Bellfield telling me his plans before the trap was sprung?

It made no sense, and yet, clearly, he had placed me in danger. Equally clearly, he had rescued me from the danger. Conclusion: He wanted me scared, not dead. I turned from the inside of the car toward Bellfield's face. It wore the same mildly solicitous expression he'd worn before, but the eyes seemed implacable, cold, calculating. I shuddered, a great racking shiver that traveled through my body and made the coat jump off my shoulders. If Bellfield wanted me scared, I admitted sourly, he'd achieved his purpose.

"You know," he said conversationally, "it's just as well they can't hear. Some things you and I ought to talk about that maybe it's better they don't hear."

I had to clamp my lips shut to keep my teeth from chattering. It made for clipped answers. "Like what?"

"It doesn't have to be this way." He shook his head sadly. "All this court business. You and me on opposite sides."

I couldn't think of a two-word answer, so I just sat, trying to look receptive. In truth, I was curious as hell to see where this was leading.

"All I wanted," he went on, "was to find out who torched my building. I thought it was your boy. Maybe"—he spread his hands and smiled ingratiatingly—"maybe I was wrong.

Maybe Turk got the wrong idea. He's a good super, Turk, but a pretty dim bulb, if you know what I mean. Plus, he hates your boys like poison, calls 'em dummies. He was always on my case to get 'em outa the building."

"I know," I said. Clenched teeth made the answer sound snappy, so I went on. "So what?"

"So maybe he jumped to conclusions when he seen your boy inna hallway there. Maybe your kid did get the kerosene on him from slipping in a puddle. Who knows? I wasn't there that night, all I know is what I get from Turk. And if he was wrong, or just saying something to get your kid locked up, well, it'd be a real shame for a kid like that to do time for something he didn't do, wouldn't it?"

I was having a hard time accepting Ira Bellfield, the voice on the tape, as a passionate advocate for the rights of deaf defendants. What, I wondered, did he really want?

"I don't know much about the law," Bellfield went on, "so let me ask you something. What would happen in court if there wasn't enough evidence against your boy? If, say, one of the witnesses didn't show up in court? Or told the DA his memory wasn't too good? They'd throw the case out of court, right?"

"It depends," I answered. I was playing for time. This was the kind of conversation lawyers are taught to be very careful about. One wrong word and I was up to my ears in collusion. The bar association could get very interested. "My advice," I said slowly and deliberately, in case the conversation was being recorded, "would be for that witness to come to court and tell the truth."

Bellfield nodded his approval, whether of my advice or of my discretion, I wasn't sure. "But sometimes," he said insinuatingly, "it's hard to say what the truth is. It could be one thing one day and another thing tomorrow. It all depends."

"On what?" My teeth had stopped chattering, but terse answers had become a habit.

"On which side of the bread the butter's on," he replied. "On whether or not certain people stay out of other people's business." He leaned forward, close enough that I could smell his aftershave. "I would advise certain people to do just that. You see where poking your nose into things got you today. It could happen again, lady, and maybe if it did, I wouldn't be around to help you out of it. Got me?"

I got him, all right. Stepping out of the car, I pulled on my coat with hands that shook and walked away without a word. The Homicides surrounded me, fingers flying, eager to learn what they'd missed. I wanted distance between me and Bellfield, so I kept walking until we were around the corner. Then Frankie stepped in front of me. "Talk," he ordered, in his eerie voice, "tell us. We have a right to know."

I sighed. It was true. They did have a right to know. But could I tell them that I could get Tito off the hook if only I'd agree to suppress evidence about Ira Bellfield? Their answer would have to be that Tito should be saved at all costs, regardless of what that meant to Bellfield's past and future victims. And as Tito's lawyer, wasn't that supposed to be my perspective too? Was I in a conflict of interest between living Tito Fernandez and dead Linda Ritchie? If I was, then one of them would have to go.

It didn't bother me in the least, I realized, that Bellfield would use perjured testimony to release Tito. Since the case against him had been a frame from the beginning, I couldn't let myself get hung up on the means of opening the trap.

"It could be," I began carefully, "that some new evidence that could help Tito might turn up. We can't count on it," I went on, raising my voice instinctively as the boys began a laughing, back-slapping celebration. Realizing that loudness wasn't the answer, I grabbed Frankie's sleeve. "Tell them not to get their hopes up," I said. "It might not turn out that way." But it was too late; good news was so rare that they had to enjoy it. Even as Frankie solemnly promised, his grin split his face wide open. He and Tito exchanged open-palm slaps and the boys headed down the street. I realized for the first time that they walked with the same rhythmic beat, the same air of walking to internal rock music, that characterized Hearing ghetto kids.

Watching them, I realized I couldn't just reject Bellfield's proposition. For all I knew, he'd punish Tito if I did, coming up with even more phony evidence against him. I owed it to Tito to figure another way out. I thought long and hard as I watched them head for the subway. Tito versus Linda—and Dawn.

In the station, I saw further evidence that the Unknown

Homicides had made themselves part of the neighborhood. Under the vivid spray-painted hate slogans *Death to the Jews* and *Death to the Arabs,* someone had scrawled, *Death to the Hearing.*

15

"Taste," Dorinda urged, holding out a small dish of something tomatoey. I slurped up a spoonful and rolled it around my tongue. Not ratatouille, and not the vegetable stew she'd stopped serving because it was too bland. Whatever this stuff was, blandness was not one of its problems. The taste was familiar, but . . .

"Goulash!" I exclaimed. "Hungarian goulash without meat! Dorinda, you're a genius. This stuff has some serious paprika in it."

Dorinda beamed. "Yeah. I picked it up the other day at the spice market on Reade Street."

"This is perfect," I went on. "Noodles or rice?"

"A choice. Whole-wheat noodles or brown rice."

I groaned. "Dorinda, do yourself a favor. Brown rice if you must, but make it egg noodles. The broad kind, with plenty of butter. Forget cholesterol for once."

Dorinda wrinkled her forehead in thought. "With poppy seeds?"

"Okay, with poppy seeds. What's on the side?"

"A red cabbage and apple salad and black bread."

"Sounds great. Save some for me. I'm afraid I'll miss lunch tomorrow. I'm starting trial."

"Which case?" I was pleased to note that even though the noon rush was on, since hiring a third waitress, Dorinda had a minute to talk.

"Terrell Hopkins. The kid with the grandmother."

"Good luck. Are you ordering now or waiting for someone?"

"Waiting," I replied, then added, "here she comes now."

The door opened and Mickey Dechter came in, looking around for me. I waved her over. Her face was red from the windy walk down Court Street. Although the Morning Glory was a long way to travel from Brooklyn Family Court for lunch in January, she'd agreed to meet me here, knowing how dangerous it would be for us to be seen together too close to the court. We were supposed to be on opposite sides.

"Nice place," she said, settling her coat behind her and looking around. "Real homey. I like that." The slight Southern accent I'd noticed before came through loud and clear.

"Where are you from?" I asked. It was a question my flat Midwestern A's had let me in for a good deal.

"You wouldn't recognize the name," she replied. "It's just a one-horse town just outside of Knoxville." She pronounced it "Knoxvl," and lifted her voice in a near-question at the end of the phrase.

"What brought you to New York?" I asked, then softened the inquisitory style by remarking, "I'm from Ohio myself. A one-horse town near Cleveland. I came to the city to go to law school."

"I came with my ex-husband. We met at UT—the University of Tennessee?" Her trick of lifting her voice at the end of statements had me nodding when no answer was required.

"He was in the business college and I was in the school of social work. We met in an industrial psych class. Next thing I knew, we were pinned, and back then in Tennessee, pinned was prett' near engaged."

"So you decided to go all the way?"

The grin she gave me showed she was no pure-minded Southern princess. "Honey, we'd already *done* that in the back of Hal's 'sixty-three Valiant."

I laughed. The new waitress came over to take our order. As a regular, I knew what I wanted. "I'll take the pasta e fagioli," I said, "with house dressing on the salad."

"Well, I'll be! I haven't seen this item on the menu since I left the Smokies. I didn't know you Yankees even knew about bean soup and cornbread. I'll have that, and to hell with my diet!"

"Good choice. Dorinda puts bits of corn in the cornbread and serves it hot. Don't expect ham in the soup, though. She's a total vegetarian. Anything that tastes like meat is probably a smoked soybean bit." I was aware that I was

talking about everything except what we'd come here for, but
I was unwilling to push my companion. She could be risking
her job by talking to me about Arnette Pearson. Still, I
decided, someone had to begin, or we'd spend the whole
lunch on small talk.

"That's some difficult case you got me into," I remarked.

"I know." Mickey's voice was rueful and her big brown
eyes were concerned. "I got to thinking later about whether
I'd done the right thing, asking you to get involved and all.
But," she said, looking straight at me, "I reckon I did. That
woman needs help and so do those kids, and, like it or not,
this is their last chance of getting it."

I nodded my agreement. "Once the court decides she's
an unfit mother, she'll have no more visitation rights—or any
rights. But—forgive me for asking, and it doesn't really affect
my ability to represent her—but is that really so bad for the
kids? Wouldn't it be better for them to have permanent
adoptive homes, like the agency wants, instead of spending
years shuttled from one foster home to another, waiting for
Arnette to get herself together enough to take them back?
Because you and I both know that's a long way away, if ever."

"That all depends," Mickey answered, in a voice several
shades colder, "on which kids you're talking about. The
twins, Kwame and Kwaku? Two cute little boys, identical
twins, came to foster care as toddlers, spent the last six years
with the same couple, who are all set to adopt? Hell, yes,
they'll be fine without their real mother. They hardly know
her as it is. But," she went on, the warm brown eyes
somehow accusing, "it's a different story for the three older
ones. One, they know their mama better. They'll miss her if
they don't see her every so often. Two, they're not going to
be adopted, I don't care what the agency lawyer says. Jomo's
in trouble in school, Tanika's run away from four different
foster homes, and Kamisha's got a lot of hostility against her
mother that she needs to work out. They've all three been
bounced around different homes, usually split up, and terminating Arnette's parental rights won't make a damned bit of
difference except to cut them off from the only person in the
world who cares about them. Your client's a whole lot less
than the perfect mother, but she's all the mother those three
kids have got."

The waitress came back, bringing hot, fragrant foods. I

concentrated on eating while I thought about what Mickey had said. Only after we'd finished and coffee had been ordered, did I move the conversation back to business.

"So what do we do," I asked, "to keep the court from ruling in favor of the agency? Judge Shute seemed pretty tight with the agency lawyer, and you know how she feels about me. So I'm not going to win this one on personality. As to the law—"

"As to the law, there are some cases saying the agency has to show what efforts they made to keep the natural family together. I can guarantee that when you see those agency records, there'll be nothing in there to show they did a damned thing to help Arnette Pearson to reclaim her kids."

I was impressed. I wasn't sure what I'd expected from Mickey Dechter, but my prior dealings with social workers hadn't led me to believe they knew much law. Vague theories and hand-wringing had been my usual experience.

"I'll do the legal research," I promised. "And I'll get the records the agency lawyer promised me. Will you help me decipher them and figure out places where they could have done more for Arnette but didn't?"

"Sure," she agreed, sipping her coffee.

"May I ask a question?" I asked it anyway. "Why? Your department is officially on the side of the agency here, pushing for the termination. Why are you helping me help Arnette?"

"Because I've been there," she answered simply. "I was a foster child back in Maryville." She pronounced it "Maryvl."

I was probably staring, but she went on as though unaware of my shocked reaction. "There were three of us, my older sister Loretta, me, and my baby sister Holly Ann. Our mother wasn't bad, just crazy, and Daddy drank too much. So we lived with all kinds of foster mamas. They weren't all bad, some of them were downright kindly, but I never felt I belonged. One place I stayed, the lady used to feed her own kids first and then us foster kids." She snorted with a laugh that held no humor. "Not only did they get portions twice as large as we did, but when we were done eating, she'd lock up all the food so's we couldn't take more'n our share. But the worst part"—she gave me a direct look with her intense brown eyes—"was how they only talked to Loretta about Mama. And Loretta hated my mama, hated her so bad and so deep that she told Miss Hotchkiss she never wanted to see Mama again. And that's all that old witch needed to hear." Mickey's eyes filmed, but her voice remained steady. "Never mind that I loved Mama and that Holly Ann and I needed her. All they cared about was that Loretta refused to visit Mama, so none of us could."

"And you feel the Pearson kids are going the same way?" I asked. "Because it's good for the twins, the other three will lose their mother?"

"And each other," she added vehemently. "Once the twins are adopted, that mother isn't going to be any too pleased to see the older ones coming around, especially with the trouble they get into. There were three years there when the only time I saw Holly Ann was at a special camp for foster kids. We got to stay two weeks and ever' night, even though it was against the rules, Holly Ann would creep over to my bed and tuck herself under the covers. I'd have to wake her up at the crack of dawn and tell her to scoot on over to her own bed before the other kids woke up, or they'd tell on us and we'd be moved to different cabins."

My thought was, how could it be against the rules for two sisters to sleep together? Then I recalled Arnette's account of the agency visits, with the children torn between two mothers. When agency policy was placed above human kindness, it seemed any cruelty was possible.

There was a lot I wanted to say to Mickey Dechter, but before I could open my mouth, she was putting on her coat. "Just look at that snow!" she exclaimed. "I really have to run." I suspected the snow had less to do with her sudden departure than the realization that she had spoken too freely to a stranger.

I walked up to court slowly, letting the big flakes melt on my face, savoring the tingle. I couldn't rid my mind of the image of two small blond girls huddled in one camp bed, afraid someone would see—and part them.

"The prosecution is ready for trial, Your Honor."

"Defense ready," I answered. No matter how ready I was, my heart quickened a little as I said those words. The roller-coaster ride from jury selection to verdict was about to begin, and I tensed up just as I had when I was a kid, waiting for the Blue Streak at Cedar Point to grind up the hill for the big descent.

"Both sides ready," the judge called to his clerk. "Send for a trial part."

I gave Terrell Hopkins a reassuring smile and walked back to the first row. I was surprised to see him looking distinctly worried. Maybe it was because his grandmother had left court early for a doctor's appointment. I hoped nothing serious was wrong with her. Aside from my admiration for the old lady, I didn't want Terrell's mind distracted from the trial.

We drew Part 14. Judge Murray Segal. A good man for a plea, but not my favorite trial judge. I like to ask my own questions, run my own defense. Judge Segal was one of those jurists who felt that any period of time in which he wasn't talking was dead air. On the plus side, he wasn't about to begin anything at four P.M. We'd schmooze a bit, set the agenda for the rest of the week, and go home. I'd have plenty of time to start preparing Terrell for the ordeal.

When the housekeeping chores were done, I went up to the pens to talk to my client. I liked to give a pep talk, to acquaint my defendants with courtroom procedures and protocol. Seldom had I seen anyone in more need of a pep talk than Terrell Hopkins.

"Listen," he said, drumming his fingers on the table. He was jerking his knee as well. I'd never seen him so jumpy. "Listen, I got to ask you somethin'."

"Is something wrong with your grandmother?" I asked gently. "Is that what's on your mind?"

No answer. My client's eyes were fixed on the iron door in back of me. His body swayed to unheard music while his fingers relentlessly bopped out the beat on the metal table between us.

"Terrell!" I said sharply. "Will you pay attention? This is your fucking life we're talking about here."

He stopped. He went as still as I could have wished, fixing me with his brown eyes. Then he asked his question. "Can I still get that flea bargain?"

I was stunned. Yet, on swift reflection, I realized I shouldn't have been. Terrell had never really wanted a trial. What he had hoped for was a miracle. Now that he knew for certain one wasn't coming down the pike, he was ready to face reality.

"I'm not sure," I answered truthfully. "The problem is that the time to plead guilty is before you get moved to trial. You were offered a plea to rob two with a sentence of one and one-half to four years in jail. Now we're in a trial part, and you may not be offered the deal. You may have to plead to rob one at two-to-six. And even that's if I get Judge Segal in a good mood tomorrow. But"—I gazed directly into Terrell's unnaturally still face—"are you sure that's what you want?"

"I'm sure."

"Have you told your grandmother?"

"Not yet. I`be callin' her tonight, I'll let her know."

"Next question: Why?"

"'Cause I'm *tired* of comin' to court behind this shit," he replied. "I want to get it *over* with."

"Is that what you're going to tell your grandmother?"

I didn't catch the mumbled answer, so I asked him to repeat it. "Ain't none of your business what I tells her."

"Goddamn it, Terrell!" I banged my hand on the metal table and had the satisfaction of seeing him flinch. "Don't lie to me, don't lie to your grandmother, and above all, don't lie to yourself! You want the plea, fine, I'll bust my hump to get it for you. But don't tell me you're copping out because you're tired of coming to court. You want the plea because you know you're going to blow trial and the reason you're going to blow it is that you stole the coat."

My mind flashed from Terrell's sullen face to his grandmother's hopeful one. "You want that poor woman to cry herself to sleep every night thinking of her grandson who's upstate for something he didn't do? When all the time you know you *did* do it and you're afraid to admit it to her. She loves you, Terrell, and she's not going to stop loving you because you made a mistake. Not if you tell her about it honestly and ask her to forgive you." I switched to a gentler tone of voice. "Look, think it over tonight. Call your grandmother. I know it'll be hard to tell her the truth, but I know one thing, Terrell. Once you've done that, really faced it, hard as it is, and gone through with it, you won't be a kid anymore. You'll be a man, because it takes a man to stand up and say he made a mistake."

*   *   *

Stepping out of the courthouse, I entered a fairyland. Snow blanketed everything, and though the cars on Court Street honked their annoyance, and people who'd forgotten their boots hopped gingerly over the snow mounds piling up at the curb, I strode into the blizzard with a smile on my face. I'd been waiting for this.

I walked over to Clinton Street, to where rows of stately brownstones stood, the snow on the window ledges and door frames creating what seemed like endless blocks of gingerbread houses. Most of the buildings had elaborately curlicued cast-iron fences, which collected snow rapidly. What a picture, I thought exultantly. What a fabulous series of black-and-white shots I could take! Each fence had a distinct design and the row itself, repeating a single theme of orderly brownstone beauty, would make a stunning wide-angle shot. I stood and framed shots, people slipping on the ice and lugging groceries passing me by, snowflakes on my eyelashes, until I finally realized something. It was too damned dark to take photographs.

I was in the middle of cooking—well, defrosting—dinner when the phone rang. It was Marcy Sheldon. She got right to the point.

"That envelope you asked me about?" I nodded into the phone, but Marcy wasn't waiting for an answer. "I'm at Harry's house in Midwood. He has something Linda gave him to keep. Could I bring it by later on my way home?"

"Sure," I said. "Anytime tonight." I was numb; while I'd deduced the existence of a second envelope, a part of me had never expected to see it.

I hung up the phone and went to take my frozen entrée out of the oven. For about the hundredth time, I found myself wishing Dorinda would listen to Ezra and start selling take-out. On the other hand, I decided, looking at my boeuf bourguignon, Dorinda was already turning me into an involuntary vegetarian. The only time I saw meat anymore was when I spooned it out of little tin trays.

The hot meal, the evening news on TV, my comfortable chair, didn't relax me as they usually did. Maybe it was the thought that Terrell Hopkins might choose trial after all that kept me tense. Or maybe it was the realization that Marcy Sheldon, no-nonsense businesswoman, wasn't just going to hand over the precious envelope and go away. She was going to demand to know what was in it. And I wasn't looking forward to telling her.

16

The doorbell rang. I buzzed in my visitor, then put a kettle on to boil. Tea was already in the pot, and two mugs stood on the table, flanked by milk, sugar, honey and a plate of lemon slices. As a hostess I'm no Dorinda, but I could rise to an occasion, such as entertaining one of my few paying clients.

I needed an extra cup. I should have known, I realized, recalling that Marcy had said she saw her father only because he wanted contact with Dawn. But still I was unprepared for the tall, awkward figure in my doorway. I froze for a moment, wondering how she felt at being in the house where her mother had died. Then I wondered how Marcy and I could discuss blackmail with Dawn present. I was so disconcerted I forgot my manners, and Dawn stood immobile, unwilling even to loosen her scarf or take off her knit hat without permission.

Recovering quickly, I said, "Here, let me take your coat. It's a new one, isn't it?"

"Aunt Marcy bought it for me," Dawn replied. "She's parking the car. She said to tell you she'd be right up."

"Nice colors," I commented. The peach scarf-and-hat set definitely warmed Dawn's skin tone, and the fawn-colored down coat made her look far more grown-up than the baby-pink jacket her mother had foisted on her. I began to feel a little better about Marcy's chances of obtaining custody. Surely the court had to give points for such subtleties as helping an adolescent girl make the most of her looks.

"I'm making tea," I said. "Do you drink it, or should I fix you some cocoa? Or would you like a soda?"

"Cocoa, please," Dawn replied. I motioned her to the table, then went to the cupboard for the chocolate mix and an extra mug.

I was about to ask Dawn how things were going at school,

when I remembered my Great-Aunt Hester. She'd asked questions like that when I was a kid, and I'd hated it. Instead, I asked bluntly, "Have you seen your father?"

Dawn nodded, her eyes wary. "Aunt Marcy didn't want me to go," she explained, "but I had to." She paused and looked away, her face half-hidden by her honey-colored hair. "You have to wait outside," she whispered, "in a long line."

I nodded. I'd passed the mournful procession often on my way into the Brooklyn House of Detention. Lawyers go in by a special entrance and are whisked in and out; families aren't.

"Then they search you. I had to leave my purse in a locker. In case I was trying to help him break out," she added scornfully. "Like if I had a gun or something."

"They do the same to me," I commented. "It doesn't mean anything." Then I had a thought. "Would you, if you could? Break your father out?"

"Yes!" came the impassioned reply. Leaning forward across the table, her eyes intent, Dawn said, "I *know* he's innocent. I *know* Daddy didn't kill Mom. So why should he have to be in jail for something he didn't do?" She fixed me with what I felt to be an accusatory gaze. "Isn't there any new evidence?" she asked. "Every time that cop talks to me, I know he thinks Daddy's guilty."

"There could be," I began, against my better judgment, "some new developments. I can't talk much about it, but—"

"Did you talk to Congressman Lucenti?" Dawn interrupted. Her face was flushed with eagerness; I got the uneasy feeling she was expecting a lot more than I was prepared to deliver.

"I can't," I explained. "He's in Washington. I'll have to wait till he gets back."

Dawn's face fell. "But he . . ." she began, then stopped as if afraid to say too much. "He might know something about who killed Mom," she finished lamely.

The raucous buzz of the doorbell startled me so that I jumped. Only then did I notice I'd boiled away nearly all of the water. I refilled the tea kettle and ran for the buzzer. While I waited for Marcy to walk up the flights of stairs, I said to Dawn, "I'm working on something that might help. But," I cautioned, "don't expect miracles."

One look at Dawn's face, radiant with hope, told me that my Great-Aunt Hester had been a whiz with kids compared to me. I'd have done a lot better to stick to seventh-grade math as a topic for discussion. A miracle was the least of Dawn's expectations, and I was the self-proclaimed miracle worker.

Marcy sailed in, her fur-trimmed coat already open. I took it from her and hung it up as she joined Dawn at the table. ". . . took me forever to find a parking space," she was saying. "Everybody in this neighborhood must own a car."

"Everybody but me," I agreed cheerfully, pouring the tea. I put out a plate of cookies as well. They were the last of my Christmas cookies, brought back from Ohio in a tin. It's a New York Christmas ritual, as stylized as a potlatch. From Manhattan and parts of Brooklyn, the children of the Midwest send presents bought at the Museum of Modern Art. From Omaha and Iowa and Ohio come back nutty ginger cookies, frosted animals with silver balls for eyes, pfeffernusse and all the other tastes and colors of childhood. I glanced at Dawn as I set out the plate, hoping to give her a tiny taste of the warm family life I'd known as a child.

Conversation was light, deliberately kept that way, I decided, by Marcy Sheldon. I was beginning to realize that just as my defense orientation was instinctive, her public-relations talent stemmed from a deep need to put the best face on things, to manage, edit, and, ultimately, control perceptions of reality. She'd done it with Detective Button, subtly turning Linda's murder from sordid to tragic. I wondered how she'd handle Linda's blackmail, and Dawn's reaction to the truth about her mother.

I didn't have to worry. After we'd finished our tea and cookies, Marcy said to her niece, "Dawn, honey, Cass and I have to talk business for a while. Will you stay up here and watch TV while we go downstairs?"

Dawn nodded, her big eyes solemn. She probably assumed our business was her custody. I didn't disabuse her. I turned on the television, handed her the TV listings, and showed her how to change channels. Marcy picked up her hot-pink briefcase and we walked down the stairs to my office.

It was cold. I'd turned off the radiators. But it wasn't nearly as cold as Marcy Sheldon's voice, cutting across the gloom like skate blades on ice.

"What the hell is going on?" she demanded. "What is in this envelope? And don't give me another song and dance about insurance!"

"What makes you think it's not insurance?" I shot back. "You didn't open it, or you'd know what's in it. So what makes you think it's not a piece of the rock?" What I really wanted to know was whether or not Marcy had any reason to suspect her sister's activities before she got the envelope from her father.

The answer was swift and laden with bitterness. "Harry," she said. I'd switched on a light or two by now, and I saw the curl of her lip, the unmistakable contempt.

I sat behind my desk, motioning her to take the client's chair. She remained standing, then turned suddenly and asked, "What's your father like?"

"Picture Dan Daily without the dancing," I replied.

She laughed. It was not a pleasant sound. "Harry's more like Frank Burns on 'M*A*S*H'. Old ferret-face. Some wonderful image to look up to, right? He's not capable of doing anything straight. Even the place he lives is illegal—what they call an illegal three."

I nodded my understanding. Owners of houses approved as two-family often rented out the basement for a few extra bucks. I'd seen the cases arising out of the arrangement in Civil Court arbitrations. The whole situation was a lawsuit waiting to happen.

"So when I asked Harry if Linda ever left any papers with him, I got the envelope but I also got a lot of hints and innuendos." She paused and looked at me directly. "I don't think he knew very much. Linda was too secretive for that, even with him. But whatever was going on wasn't straight. That much I could tell from Harry's attitude."

"Your father's done time?"

She sighed. "Some. He's a gambler and a con artist, in a penny-ante sort of way. He always had some get-rich-quick scheme going when I was a kid. It was either boom or bust with Harry. When it was bust, he used to hit my mother out of frustration and anger. When it was boom, he spent the money on good times and other women, leaving Mom and me alone."

Something was missing from this recitation. "Where was Linda?" I asked.

"She was born when I was ten," Marcy replied. "I was an accident, the reason my parents had to get married. Linda was the love child, the one conceived during one of Harry's boom times. She was his little princess, and he was her knight in shining armor. After she was born, whenever he was flush," Marcy recalled, her eyes far away, "he'd buy her dolls bigger than she was. When she was eight, he bought her a real diamond necklace. Just a little pendant, but it was more jewelry than Mom and I ever saw. Linda wore it everywhere and told everyone it meant her daddy loved her best. She was right." Marcy's tone was matter-of-fact; if there was any bitterness left, it was a dim echo of what she must have felt as a child. "Harry and I never got along. I was too busy hating him for what he'd done to Mom, but Linda was cute and cuddly and nonjudgmental. She didn't care where the money for her dolls came from or that it might have been better spent on food and school clothes. She loved them—and she loved Harry for giving them to her."

"How did that make you feel?"

"By that time, I knew him for the worthless loser he is," she pronounced. "All I wanted was out. Scholarships, jobs—I left Brooklyn behind at eighteen and never looked back."

"Not even to see your mom?" I asked softly. "Or your baby sister?"

"What's in the envelope, Cass?" Marcy demanded, her voice hard. "Enough with the family history, okay? Just tell me what's going on."

I told her.

"It can't be true," she whispered. It wasn't an assertion; it was a prayer.

"It's true," I replied, looking straight at her. Marcy's eyes looked sunken, her face drawn. "You know it's true."

She was still. No more protests, no more denials. At first the immobility was shock, but then I began to see the wheels turning as she assimilated the news, working at fitting it into her game plan. Once I saw that, I could have predicted her next question.

"Have you told anyone?"

"Always the public-relations lady," I laughed, only half-kidding.

Her eyes blazed. "You try spending your childhood covering up," she challenged. Her hands, with their blood-red nails, clenched and unclenched. "Telling the neighbors your mom got her black eye running into a door. Telling your teacher your dad's on a business trip when he's really serving six months on Riker's Island. Pretending to everybody that your family is nice and normal like theirs when you *know* deep down that it's not, that it's sick for a man to buy a diamond for an eight-year-old and call her his little sweet-heart when we're on welfare half the time." She stopped suddenly, breathing heavily and beginning to look ashamed. Even now, it cost too much to tell the truth. Even now, the family secrets had to be protected.

"I'm sorry," I said, and meant it. I could understand Marcy's coldness now, her need to control. Perhaps I could understand Linda too. Perhaps the blackmail and the teasing had been a way to recapture that eight-year-old's feeling of being Daddy's favorite, showered with expensive presents. I recalled the lines of a blues song I'd heard: "You know a man is born to love a woman, to work and slave to pay her debts." The words summed up a lot about Linda Ritchie—and now, hearing her sister talk, I had some insight into how she'd gotten the way she was.

"I haven't told the police," I said, bringing the conversation back to a businesslike plane. Marcy sighed her relief.

"But . . ." I began. She looked up sharply, her eyes narrowing. "I *have* talked to some of Linda's blackmail victims. In fact, I've met them all by now."

"Why? What good do you think that's going to do?" Marcy's voice rose, edged with hysteria, tinged with denial.

"What good? Marcy, Brad Ritchie's in jail, but he's not the only person with a motive to kill Linda. In fact, after talking to some of these people, I don't even think he's in the top five."

"Brad?" Marcy's tone was one of utter disbelief. "You mean you're stirring up this ugly mess just so that worthless piece of trash can go free?"

"Marcy," I began patiently, "he might be innocent. There might be more to this whole thing than either one of us knows. And the man *is* Dawn's father." I fixed her with a deliberate stare and added softly, "Not yours."

"Meaning?" Her voice was a challenge.

"Meaning maybe Brad reminds you of Harry and that's why you've decided he's expendable. But think about it. Dawn loves him, and if he didn't kill Linda, he should be free."

"The police think he's guilty."

"The police," I reminded her with a touch of acid, "don't know one thing about Linda's little hobby. Of course," I went on, "I could always tell them and then we'd *both* know whether it made any difference to Brad's position. Is that what you want?"

"No!" The answer came swiftly and decisively. Marcy sighed and added, "I don't know what to say. The whole thing is so sordid. I never suspected, but..."

"But?"

"I had to wonder. She had more money than I would have expected, knowing how little she got from Brad. And she was a great one for hints, Linda, she got that from Harry. She'd show me a new outfit or a piece of gold jewelry and she'd kind of lead me to believe it was a present from a man. I thought they were boyfriends, but now—I wonder if she wasn't telling me about blackmail instead."

"And what if," I said slowly, watching her face, "one of them got tired of playing Daddy Harry to her Little Princess and stabbed her to death? Left her bleeding body in my upstairs apartment? You want him walking around free just to preserve the family name?"

Marcy shuddered. "Okay, Cass, you win. Go ahead, open the envelope. Ask questions. Go to the police if you have to. Just..." She paused and gave me a direct look with eyes that were so like Linda's. "Just be careful."

She opened her pink briefcase, took out a sealed manila envelope, put it on my desk, and turned to go. "Dawn and I can let ourselves out," she said, closing the door behind her.

I stood at the window, watching them go. Marcy stepped briskly along the street in her high-heeled boots, refusing to take notice of the ice underfoot. I'd shoveled, but the melted snow had refrozen after nightfall, leaving a thin, treacherous sheet. Dawn picked her way along, head bowed, examining the sidewalk as she followed her aunt to their car. I watched the peach-colored knit hat, lit like a beacon by the streetlamps, until I couldn't see it any more.

I sighed, wondering if my newfound insight into Marcy's character was going to help me with Dawn's custody. I could understand her aloofness now, could see the childhood hurts it stemmed from. But the fact remained, she wasn't giving Dawn what she needed. I could understand why not, but could I, in all conscience, ask a judge to give her custody anyway? I needed to talk to someone; oddly enough, the person who came to mind was my new friend Mickey Dechter, the Family Court social worker. I'd sensed a deep concern for people beneath the pain of her own childhood experiences, and I thought that if anyone could help me help Dawn, she could. But did I dare to ask?

I went back to the desk and slit open the envelope. Giving the papers inside a cursory glance, I felt like a crystal-ball reader. Everything pertained to Todd Lessek. Old holding-company incorporation papers listing Todd Lessek as one of the officers of the corporation. The addresses were unfamiliar at first, until I opened my safe and checked them against buildings known to belong to Ira Bellfield. They were the same premises.

Rooting through the rest of the stack, I came upon a piece of paper that made all the rest unnecessary. Cumulative evidence, as we say in the trade. It was a partnership agreement, executed in 1976, between Ira Bellfield and Todd Lessek. In addition, there were checks made out to Lessek from the various holding companies, and an endorsement showing Lessek as guarantor of several Bellfield mortgages.

Todd Lessek had described himself to me as a "second-generation" landlord, but these papers put him right smack in the first generation—among the owners who burned and looted their own buildings. In fact, in a strictly financial sense, Todd Lessek *was* Ira Bellfield.

And Elliott Pilcher knew it. Finally I understood where Pilcher worked and why his silence was so important to Todd Lessek. Lessek needed city approval on the waterfront deal, city approval and city money. Before he could get it, he would have to be thoroughly vetted by the city's Department of Investigation. They were supposed to check him out from grade school to yesterday, examining under a microscope every financial transaction involving more than fifteen bucks. Then they'd made a recommendation to the City Council. They'd checked and rechecked and finally declared Lessek clean as a whistle. The DOI's man in charge: Elliott Pilcher.

I decided, looking at the papers with a smile on my face, that it was time for another visit to Brooklyn's picturesque waterfront area. The one that was probably *not* going to be developed by Todd Lessek.

17

I'm the world's worst pool player. I've been told this on many occasions, by people who ought to know. And yet, once in a great while, when I've had just the right amount of alcohol and the jukebox is knocking out just the right rhythms, I can run all the balls off the table without even thinking about it. It's like Zen and the art of pool; everything comes together in a way that has nothing to do with my conscious mind.

I was feeling that same rush, that same sense of infinite possibilities, as I stood before Judge Segal's bench. I was on a strange high, with not-quite-heard music sounding in my ears, feeling for all the world like Paul Newman in *The Hustler*, ready to take on Minnesota Fats.

I wasn't sure what it was that put the beat in my head, the bounce in my step. Maybe it was the prospect of finally getting Terrell Hopkins and his grandmother squared away. Or maybe it was the thought of wiping the smirk off Todd Lessek's face that had me jumping. I was primed for action, ready for anything, feeling reckless and powerful.

"Three-to-nine, Counselor," Judge Segal intoned in his ponderous voice.

It was a bad break; I'd been hoping for two-to-six. But I refused to show disappointment; the game was a long way from over.

"Judge," I said expansively, just a touch of pleading thrown in, "this is Brooklyn."

"I *do* know what borough I'm sitting in, Ms. Jameson," the Hon. Murray replied with a twinkle. "That's why they made me a judge."

"I just don't want you to start remembering you were a Queens DA, Your Honor," I explained. "My kid's got enough to worry about without that."

"Counselor," Judge Segal said with a patient smile, "if this case were on in Queens, I'd have made it four-to-twelve."

I returned a rueful grin; I had to admit, the judge was a fair pool player himself.

The district attorney picked up a cue, applied a little chalk, and decided to join the game.

"My office," he began in a high voice that contrasted sharply with Segal's full bass, "offered a plea to rob two in the complex. Ms. Jameson's client could have had one-and-one-half-to-four, but he turned down the offer. Seven times!" His voice rose to a near-squeak of indignation. I suppressed my giggle when I recalled that courthouse rumor had him winning his last ten cases in a row.

"So now," Judge Segal finished, "the district attorney is no longer offering the rob two. Your client must plead to the entire indictment, or go to trial. And I see no reason to promise a minimum sentence in a case where a gun was recovered. Ms. Jameson, what is your client's pleasure? Plea or trial?"

It wasn't looking good. The other two players were sinking ivory balls like crazy, while I just stood and watched. I had to turn things around.

I was saved by the bell. Only it wasn't a bell, but the white light that served as a bell on the courtroom phone. While the judge talked in a stage whisper, I glanced over at Terrell. He was dressed for trial, in a maroon shirt and gray pants. New sneakers. His grandmother had finally realized she could give him clothing only at the prison, not in court. His indifferent slouch was gone; he leaned forward in his chair, his eyes wide, intent, and frightened. I flashed him a reassuring smile. The match wasn't over yet; I hadn't picked up my cue.

The one thing that worried me was Hattie. She wasn't there. I hoped she was all right. Terrell had plenty to worry about as it was.

Back to the game. Time to put a little spin on the ball. "It seems to me," I said in a reasonable tone, "that there are two considerations here. The DA"—I turned to ADA Haskell— "appears to think my client's playing fast and loose with the system."

"Well, what would you call turning down an offer seven times and then trying to snatch it back on the eve of trial?" the shrill voice challenged.

"I'd call it fear."

Haskell snorted. "Come on, Cass. Your kid's been around the block."

"Not really," I countered. "He got probation last year and before that he had a couple of juvenile busts. He's not in a gang. He's not the worst kid you'll ever see."

"What about the gun?" Judge Segal cut in. "I, for one, find it hard to give a minimum sentence to someone who pulls a gun on another individual."

Minnesota Fats had just missed his first ball. Trouble was, he didn't know it yet.

I picked up the cue, leaned over, and looked long and hard at the way the balls were laid out. Then I took my shot. "Unloaded," I said, turning to the DA for confirmation.

It came reluctantly, but it came. "It was unloaded when the police recovered it," Haskell admitted, "but who knows what it was when your kid pulled it out of his waistband and held it on Duane Rogers."

Red ball in the side pocket. "Did your cops recover any bullets?" I countered. The trouble with this question was that I didn't know the answer, but I figured if there had been bullets, I'd have heard about them by now, so I took the chance.

"No," Haskell conceded with bad grace, "but he had plenty of time to get rid of them."

"If he'd done that," I pointed out, "why didn't he get rid of the gun, too?"

Now a blue ball followed the red into the pocket. It looked as though my run was starting in earnest.

"Mr. Haskell," the judge boomed, "in view of what Ms. Jameson has told us, I'm inclined to come down to the minimum of two-to-six. Is your office still firm on the rob one or would you consider reoffering the rob two?"

"Absolutely not!" Haskell squeaked, his chin thrust out. "We can't let people play games with the system," he explained in a more normal voice. "Why should my office give him the same break now—after I've put witnesses on alert and prepared the case for trial—that he would have gotten on his first appearance in Supreme Court? If he'd taken the plea then, he'd have saved the system time and money. Now—he's just jerking us around."

"Counselor?" Judge Segal seemed to think the game was tennis; he shifted his attention from Haskell to me as though watching a ball bounce back and forth. It was an attitude that matched the hand-printed motto he kept on his bench: *A likely story*. It was up to me to smack Haskell's lob over the net—or into it. I hoped I'd be as good in my court as Dawn Ritchie was in hers.

"You're right," I said stoutly. "Terrell Hopkins *could* have copped that plea in his first appearance in Supreme, and that's exactly what I as his lawyer advised him to do. But you're wrong about why he didn't. He's not jerking the system around; believe me, he doesn't *care* about the system. What he *does* care about is his grandmother. She's not here yet, but she's been in court every time the case was on, despite poor health. The trouble was, Terrell didn't want to admit his guilt to her. He's finally realized he has no other choice. It's a hard thing for him to do, so it took him a long time to come to the decision to take the plea. That's why he turned it down seven times—not because he's playing games."

Something in the judge's face shifted subtly from wariness to understanding. For the first time, he looked at Terrell Hopkins and saw a person instead of a defendant. I felt a rush of elation, the same feeling I'd had on those magic nights when all the colored balls did just what I wanted them to do.

Judge Segal gave me a rueful smile. "Counselor," he begged, "stop bleeding all over my bench." Then he turned his attention to the DA.

"Well, Mr. Haskell," the judge asked, "does this change your view? I have to admit, I don't see the big difference between one-and-one-half-to-four and two-to-six. Either a little jail time will straighten this boy out or it won't—and six extra months upstate won't be the clincher."

The DA had strict instructions not to come down, however, so the judge and DA left to reason with the DA's supervisor on the chamber's phone. I walked back to the defense table and sat down next to Terrell.

"What happenin'?" he wanted to know, his eyes wide with apprehension.

"We're doing all right," I answered. "The judge wants to give you a break, but he has to convince the DA's office. I think we're in good shape, though. The only thing I want to say is be sure to answer all the judge's questions, Terrell. Tell the whole truth about the gun, the coat, everything. Okay?"

He nodded vigorously. "I done thought a lot about what you said yesterday," he said softly. He wouldn't look at me,

but the words were clear and firm. "About not lyin' to myself
and all. About bein' a man. I'm ready to do what I gotta do.
That's all I'm ready."

The jukebox sounds in my head exploded in a shriek of
dissonant glory. This time I'd really cleared the table. Not
only because I'd turned three-to-nine into one-and-one-half-
to-four, but because something I'd said had the power to
penetrate Terrell's thick wall of indifference. I felt as good, as
much a winner, as I did when I heard those glorious words,
"We find the defendant not guilty."

We took the plea. Terrell stood tall and told the truth.
No lies, no posturing. Inside my head, the mellow sounds of
my mental jukebox put a glow in my eyes as I pictured my
imaginary pool table. Even the eight-ball had fallen into a
pocket.

My Zen-and-the-art-of-pool high carried me down the
Henry Street hill toward the waterfront. The pale winter sun
was low in the sky; I'd had a lot to do before I could get free
to meet Lessek. I stepped around patches of dirt-blackened
snow with a bouncy step that matched the music in my head.
This time when Lessek and I faced off, I knew I wouldn't be
retreating in blushing embarrassment. This time I'd make
him talk.

I passed Dorinda's house, noting that the fancy restaurants that used the Brooklyn Bridge and the New York
skyline as a decorative backdrop were setting up for dinner. I
could see waiters placing intricately folded peach napkins at
each place. Near the River Cafe—actually a barge floating on
the East River—spindly trees decked with Christmas lights
tried—and failed—to compete with the majesty of the Great
Bridge.

Once around the corner, I was back in warehouse city.
No decorated trees here; no trees period. Just cobblestones
and dirty brick buildings without windows. Of course, if
Lessek had his way, the whole waterfront would be gaily lit,
full of fashionable people arriving by cab to expensive restaurants. The area would be shorn of its gritty reality, and of
Dorinda and her artist friends.

I turned another corner, walked under the huge suspen-
sion bridge, then along the water to Lessek's warehouse. As I
approached, I noticed something strange. Instead of empty

streets, their stark grayness broken only by a single red Ferrari, I saw a knot of people—and a police car.

My mind flashed back to the night I saw Linda's body carried down my front steps. My heart began to race. Could Lessek be dead? Killed by the same person who murdered Linda? Had Ira Bellfield gotten fed up with playing Todd Lessek's back-street boy, taking the rap as a slumlord while Lessek drove his sports car to places like the River Cafe? Or had Elliott Pilcher been found out and fired, then taken his revenge on Todd Lessek for offering him what he'd been only too willing to take?

I realized suddenly that the answer was simpler than that. Who had been displaced and humiliated by Todd Lessek? Who had been driven nearly insane by the desire to hurt back? Who spent day after frozen, weary day trudging in front of the building, waiting for a confrontation with the man who'd ruined him? Abe Schine. My mind repeated the name as I ran along, my boots clattering on the cobblestones. Once I slid on the ice and narrowly missed falling, but my pace didn't slow. What if this time, when Abe Schine stepped out of the shadows, he'd been armed not with eggs or creosote, but bullets?

I reached the edge of the small crowd just as the ambulance careened into the street, sirens howling and lights flashing. Stepping through the crowd, I tried to catch a glimpse of the figure under the blanket. I heard a couple of remarks about pushy broads and ghouls who like to watch accidents, but I didn't care. I looked at the head as the figure was carried by, and only gradually realized that I was seeing not Lessek's tight curls, but a bald pate with liver spots. The body on the stretcher was Abe Schine's.

"Oh, my God," I said, holding my hand to my mouth. Still picturing some kind of armed confrontation, I added without thinking, "They must have shot him."

A black man in a thick wool hunting jacket said disgustedly, "Nobody shot nobody, lady. The man had a heart attack is all. Happens every day."

"Yeah," a voice behind me chimed in. "Especially an old guy like that. What was he doin' out here anyway? Shoulda been home on a day like this."

"Shoulda been at work," a lady corrected scornfully.

"What work?" the black man challenged. "The guy was a

bum, right? All he cared about was drinking cheap wine and sleeping it off in some doorway."

I thought of the Royal Baseball Cap Company. Forty years of a man's life called "a dump" by a young go-getter in a red Ferrari. A proud, hardworking man reduced to lone picketing and egg-throwing to salvage a little dignity. I had a lump in my throat as I watched the ambulance tear away, but all I said, in a croaking voice, was, "Is he dead?"

"If he ain't now, he soon will be," somebody snickered.

"He won't make it," the lady said confidently.

"Poor old geezer." The black man with the Bronx accent gave the eulogy.

This was probably not the best time in the world to talk to Todd Lessek. I looked up at the flashcube penthouse, thought of Abe Schine's red, chapped hands, and decided to go up anyway.

The cops were just leaving, being ushered out by a genial yet grave Lessek. He was shaking his curly head and giving a perfect imitation of a man who really cared that someone had just died in front of his building.

". . . a terrible thing," I heard him murmur. "Of course, the poor guy went a little bananas after he lost his business. I didn't *want* to have him arrested for the egg-throwing, even if he *did* ruin a good suit, but hey, you can't let people get away with it, can you?" The uniformed officers agreed respectfully that you certainly couldn't and stepped into the elevator.

Lessek noticed me before they left. I could tell because his eyes narrowed and he looked ready to bite. But a nasty remark to a female visitor might spoil the more-in-sorrow-than-in-anger tone he was determined to adopt, so I got a royal welcome in front of the cops.

"Ms. Jameson," he boomed, extending a well-manicured hand, "how nice to see you again. Won't you come into my office where we can talk privately." Once again I followed Lessek through the high-tech movie set to his spacious cubicle.

Once the door closed, the welcome mat was hastily thrust out of sight. "What are you doing here?" he snapped.

"Sightseeing," I answered. "Watching them take Abe Schine's body away, for one thing."

"Was that his name?"

"Jesus! You can kill somebody and not even know his name?"

"How do you figure I killed him, Ms. Jameson? Got inside his heart and stopped up his arteries?"

"You destroyed his business," I reminded him. "Remember? Then you humiliated him. You—"

"I didn't destroy anything that wasn't already dead," Lessek shot back. "I suppose he told you his sad story, all about the flood that ruined his baseball caps? Well, did he tell you about the competition from Japan, or the polyester caps he refused to make? That guy was the stubbornest man I ever met, Ms. Jameson, and if anybody destroyed him, he destroyed himself. I offered him good money for his space," Lessek said indignantly, doing a creditable imitation of Paul Newman accused of something he didn't do. "Top dollar. He could have relocated, or retired, like everyone else in this building. You ask Jack Pearl what he thinks of me. You ask Al Wong, the importer from the second floor. They took my money and were happy to get it. But not this Schine. With him, it was eggs, it was creosote, it was trouble. So..." He shrugged an eloquent shoulder. "He asked for trouble, trouble he got. Now, if that's all you came for, Ms. Jameson..."

"It's not," I said, sitting uninvited in a tubular chair and crossing my legs. "I've been thinking about the last conversation we had, and I decided we had some unfinished business."

His face took on the complacent smile I'd expected. "Do you really want to make a fool of yourself again?"

"Would I sound like a fool if I told you a friend of mine is keeping certain documents for me?" I kept my voice steady in spite of the surge of excitement that ran through me. "Documents that show you and Ira Bellfield are partners?" I paused and looked him in the eye. "I wonder," I said idly, leaning back in the chair, "if Jesse Winthrop at the *Village Voice* would be interested in those papers?"

Lessek was shaken but still smooth: down but not out. He shrugged. "I suppose that bastard would print what you've got. Anything that creates jobs, he's against. Him and that liberal rag of his."

"You wouldn't mind?" I asked sweetly, calling his bluff. "You don't think some of your big investors would be bothered by the things you and Bellfield have done? You don't think the city would drop you so fast—"

"I've got friends," Lessek replied stubbornly. "I'm connected where it counts. The waterfront deal's too big; nobody can stop it now."

"Bullshit," I shot back. If we were in George V. Higgins territory, I could speak the language too. "Deals like yours aren't set till the cement starts to pour. The city can pull back any time it wants to, for any reason or for no reason. If that partnership stuff gets printed, people who are dying to be seen with you now won't even return your phone calls. You'll have this building because it's yours outright, but all the rest . . ." I trailed off and waved a hand at the skyline view of the waterfront. "I wonder if Helmsley or Trump would like to take over the development," I speculated, one eye on Lessek's reddening face.

My fantasy had come true; my prediction had been accurate. This time Todd Lessek didn't laugh. He reached into the pocket of his tailored jacket. It took me a minute to realize that the shiny metal thing he pulled out and pointed at me was a gun.

18

I sleepwalked through Lessek's office, feeling its unreality closing in on me as we proceeded toward the elevator. I was wading, my leg muscles straining against the pull of powerful waves. The gun in Lessek's pocket loomed on the edge of my consciousness like a hawk circling a rabbit.

We stepped out of the building into a blast of January cold. The sun was lower in the sky; the lights on the bridge cut through the late-afternoon gloom. The excitement was over, the crowd gone. I flinched as I felt the gun in my ribs, then walked mechanically in the direction indicated by Lessek's empty hand.

We came to the pedestrian stairway under the bridge. In summer, it was filled with walkers, lovers holding hands, photographers, and people deftly hoisting ten-speed bikes up and down the steps. Now, not even the muggers braved the strong wind that sliced across the bridge from the silver river below.

We started up the stairs. I needed no further prodding from the gun; I simply walked.

When we reached the first stairs lifting us from the approach ramp to the actual bridge, Lessek halted, ordering me to do the same. I did, facing him with a stance of bravery I hardly felt. My knees were having trouble holding me up, and the cruel wind brought tears to my eyes.

"This is it," Lessek said in a tight voice that strained against the wind. "Now we can talk."

"Talk?" my voice was harsh with fear, a seagull's cry. "Is that all you want to do?"

He nodded impatiently. "Of course," he replied, "I just didn't want to have this conversation where it could be overheard. My fucking office is a nest of wiretaps and bugging devices. Up here"—he gestured with his gun at the sweep of bridge, the famous Gothic arches, the luminous webbing of cables, the sunset glow of the Manhattan skyline behind us—"up here, nobody can hear what we've got to say." Given the whistling wind and the steady hum of traffic on either side of us, I had to agree with him.

"I see your point," I shouted over the din. "So what is it you want to say?"

"Let's talk price," he began, his voice cracking as he tried to lift it over a particularly vicious gust.

I threw up my hands, disgusted at being unable to hear. "Let's go up the stairs," I called. "We'll be away from the traffic and we can get out of the wind."

Lessek nodded his agreement and we walked, stiff-legged, up the stairs and along the windy wooden ramp that led to the Brooklyn pylon of the Great Bridge. By the time we reached the massive pillars, my forehead was clamped in a vise of cold, my nose was numb, and my eyes were teary. The calm of the windbreak caused by the pillars was a startling and welcome relief. So was the absence of the pistol Lessek had held on me; he must have pocketed it as we trudged along.

"That's better," I said, meaning both wind and weapon. It was far from warm, but the stone pillars, reaching up into their majestic Gothic arches, provided a refuge from the nasty wind-chill. What was more important, we could talk without shouting over the roar of traffic.

Now that we had our silent oasis, Lessek seemed curiously reluctant to talk. He looked into the distance, appearing to study the huge Jehovah's Witnesses clock that dominated the Brooklyn side of the river. Behind us, an opalescent winter sunset was beginning to turn the gray clouds into mother-of-pearl.

"How much?" he asked abruptly.

I took my chance. "We'll save the details for later. Let's talk about Linda Ritchie."

He made an impatient movement. "What about her?"

I measured him with my eyes. Gun or not, the only way to get what I wanted from him was direct challenge. Todd Lessek had no time for wimps.

"Who killed her, you or Bellfield?"

"What makes you think—"

I cut through the bluster. "You had the most to lose if Linda went public," I pointed out. "The others had prestige on the line, maybe even liberty. You had money, and lots of it, riding on Linda's discretion. And knowing her, she'd never let you forget it."

"Ira could have done something impulsive," Lessek was only running it up the flagpole; his eyes clearly showed he didn't believe a word of what he was saying.

"That's what I thought at first," I agreed. "But Ira's only got two personalities—he's a wife-beater and he's your back-street boy. So if he killed Linda, it was either a momentary impulse, or he was acting on your orders, which makes you an accessory."

"What's this 'back-street boy' stuff?" Lessek protested. "Ira understood the business. He knew there's always a Mr. Inside and a Mr. Outside. I've got the personality and the head for finance. Ira doesn't, it's that simple. Could you really see him at Lutèce or La Grenouille winding up a billion-dollar mortgage?" Lessek laughed at the incongruous image he'd conjured up. "Ira knows what side his bread was buttered on," he finished. "Even if his bitch wife doesn't."

"Norma," I remembered, "the one who landed up in the Safe Haven with a broken arm."

Lessek nodded. "Ira's a fool where that woman's con-

cerned," he said. "She nags him and nags him until finally, he
can't stand it anymore. He'd go crazy and hit her, she'd cry
and sob until he'd beg forgiveness, and they'd both jump
back on the same old merry-go-round."

I wasn't about to play marriage counselor. "Norma met
Linda Ritchie at the shelter," I prompted.

"Christ, yes," Lessek agreed. "God, I had to laugh when
poor old Ira comes running in to see me, all bent out of shape
because some broad is putting the squeeze on him over
hitting Norma a few times. I can hear him now," Lessek
laughed, imitating Bellfield's nasal whine, "'Todd, she wants a
job,' he whines at me, 'what shall I do? She says she'll tell
everybody about Norma if I don't put her on the payroll.'"
Lessek's face registered genuine amusement. "Here's a guy,"
he explained, "who Jack Newfield's calling the scum of the
earth, who's got angry tenants picketing him around the
clock, whose name is a curse word in every ghetto in the five
boroughs, and he's worried about a little bitch who's four-feet-
eight in her stocking feet. 'Ira,' I told him, 'let her talk. What
can she do to you?'"

It was a good question. I waited for an answer.

"'It's the temple,' he says. The temple, for Christ's
sake!" Lessek laughed again. "Here he is, slumlord of the
year, and he wants to be big man at the temple. He knows
damned well the rabbi and all the big shots could care less
that he rent-gouges the *schwartzes*, but let them hear one
word about him lifting a finger to big-mouth Norma and he's
out. So"—Lessek shrugged, contempt on his face—"he puts
Linda on the payroll. Biggest mistake he ever made in his
fucking life and all for the temple."

"She does seem to have learned the business pretty
fast," I remarked.

"She was one smart little cookie, I'll give her that."
There was a note of grudging admiration in Lessek's tone.
"She got right onto Duncan Pitt. And of course, she still
liked to tweak Ira every so often. Just to keep in practice. In
fact"—Lessek laughed without humor—"she finally did what
Norma always managed to do—get him so bad he punched
her face. God, was he scared! I thought he'd shit a brick, he
was so worried she'd blow his ass out of the water."

"Knowing Linda," I commented wryly, "I'm sure she got
her revenge."

"In spades. All-expense-paid trip to the Bahamas for three weeks, plus a little extra in the weekly pay envelope. She was the highest-paid real-estate broker in Brooklyn, our Linda."

"How did she catch on to you?" I asked.

"I always *told* Ira not to leave too much around the office," Lessek complained. "Trouble was, he couldn't hide things at home either, Norma being as big a snoop as she is a bitch."

"So Linda got the goods and you killed her to save your deal," I said flatly.

"Why should I kill her?" Lessek countered. "I was giving her what she wanted, wasn't I?"

"Were you?" I asked. "Maybe the money you gave her wasn't enough. Maybe she wanted more."

"I gave her more," he said simply. "And not just money, either," he added with a sly little wink.

"Presents?" I asked, thinking of the expensive trinkets Linda had flashed before her sister.

Lessek's head snapped back and he let out a crack of laughter. "I gave her a present all right," he chuckled. "I gave her Art Lucenti."

The wooden platform beneath my feet began to sway a little. I was out of my depth; the betrayals these people were capable of were beyond me. What I'd thought were realistic conclusions based on a firm foundation of logic were turning out to be naïve schoolgirl fantasies. I'd conjured up a Todd Lessek who hated Linda, who sought revenge at all costs, when what he'd done in reality was make her a silent partner.

Which explained the separate envelope. Lessek wasn't in the same category as Pitt, Pilcher, and the others. Where they paid her with money and jewelry, Lessek gave her new secrets to play with, new blood to suck.

I must have looked as disgusted as I felt. Todd Lessek immediately began to defend himself. "Hey, what could I do?" he protested, with a hint of swagger in his tone. "I mean, it was him or me, you know what I mean?" The strutting masculinity with the hint of viciousness were pure Al Pacino. Todd Lessek must have gone to a lot of movies, I decided.

"So what did you give Linda on Art?" I asked conversationally, trying to play down my personal distaste.

"He was involved in a little conflict-of-interest thing," Lessek replied. "No big deal, but you lawyers like to make mountains out of molehills when it comes to shit like that. But," he shrugged, "it was enough to get her a job on his staff. She was getting bored with Ira the henpecked, wanted new horizons. She liked working for a city councilman."

"That wasn't all she had on Art in her envelope," I pointed out.

"No," he agreed thoughtfully, "she picked up some other goodies along the way. What I'd like to know is how she got her hands on my list of limited partners. That I never gave her."

"I believe it," I said, then added, "That's how she found out about Elliott Pilcher, I suppose." He nodded.

"And Aida? Art's wife? How did she get that stuff from that drug program?" I was half thinking aloud, but some part of me must have suspected the answer, because I wasn't really surprised when Lessek said, "She didn't. I dug that up."

"Why would you—"

"Art got out of line," Lessek interrupted, his tone hard. "He's no good to me in Washington; I wanted him on the City Council, where his vote was an asset. But he goes and gets himself on the ballot without my okay. So I owed him one; I wanted to let him know he and I weren't finished, that he couldn't just walk away from me."

"Maybe he was getting sick of running your errands," I said. I still had a hard time dealing with the fact that Art Lucenti, who'd started out as a decent lawyer working on the side of poor people, had become so completely the creature of Todd Lessek. "He used to be such a good lawyer till you got hold of him."

To my surprise, Lessek smiled reminiscently. "The guy was hell on wheels. It was really something to watch him in court. I decided if he could do the job he did for peanuts, to help a bunch of welfare cheats, how much more could he do for me if I got him on the payroll? I went after him like some guys go after women. It was pure seduction."

"You offered him money," I said disgustedly.

"You think I'm stupid, don't you?" Lessek frowned as he continued. "I know you don't start with a guy like that by offering money. That comes later. What I did was, I put some of his welfare clients into one of my new gut-rehab buildings. Next thing I know, he's telling all the community groups how good I am for the neighborhood. Then I find out how ambitious he is to go into politics, and I know I've got him."

"But you like to remind him, to keep him in line. So you gave Linda Aida's criminal record."

Lessek was talking to me for only one reason—to sell me the idea that he hadn't killed Linda.

"She came to me," he shrugged. "She wanted something on Art's wife. I figured she had the hots for Art and wanted the competition out of the way."

I nodded; that fit my impression of Linda. A woman who'd insure her affair with a married man by blackmailing his wife. But how did her blackmail of Art himself fit into the picture?

"So you gave her what you had," I concluded. "Wasn't that dangerous? What if she used it when you didn't want her to?"

"Hell," Lessek replied. "Linda wants to play cat-and-mouse, better Aida than me for the mouse. Besides, I got no vested interest in Art as a congressman, remember. I don't care if he's elected or not, and it doesn't bother me at all that he gets a little pressure put on him. Matter of fact"—Lessek's capped teeth gleamed in the dull orange glow of sunset—"I let him know I had his balls in the palm of my hand." Lessek spread out a leather-gloved palm as if to show me Art Lucenti's private parts. Then, a smile crossing his face, he began to squeeze. "All you have to do," he explained, a teacher lecturing a bright pupil, "is know where to squeeze, and anything is possible."

"And you always know."

"I always know," he agreed. His subtle emphasis on the word *always* had me shivering in my coat. I was beginning to think it was me he was about to squeeze. Because I didn't kid myself; I had my weak·spot, and her name was Dawn. One hint of danger to her, and I'd be off this bridge, out of Lessek's life, and off the case, forever.

He knew it. Grinning broadly, Lessek said, "Cold, Counselor? Pretty stiff breeze up here? Or are you thinking how cold you'd be if anything happened to that house of yours?"

I started: For once, my first thought hadn't been my brownstone. I should have known Lessek would be aware of all the details of my financial life. He probably knew to the penny how much my mortgage payments were—and what a struggle it was to keep up with them.

I asked an unoriginal question. "Is that a threat?"

"Of course not," came the breezy reply. But the gloved hand holding the imaginary balls gave a convulsive squeeze. "It's just a friendly warning. In fact," he went on, spreading both his hands, "it could be considered as a choice. On the one hand"—he lifted his right palm—"the right decision could lead to an increased cash flow, permitting early payment of that mortgage of yours. On the other hand"—the left palm rose and clenched as he talked—"you could make a decision that could put you in a wringer. That could leave you out in the cold financially, and in other ways. It's totally up to you, Ms. Jameson. The ball's in your court."

"Are you offering me money?" I asked.

"Up to a reasonable amount," he agreed. "I'm sure we can come to terms."

"Maybe not," I said lightly. "We seem to have company."

As the plainclothes policemen advanced out of the shadows, Lessek took a last desperate chance. Flinging me to the ground, he began to run. He got about six feet before he was stopped.

Strong arms grabbed me from behind and propped me up. "You okay?" The voice in my ear was Button's. I opened my eyes to the welcome sight of two uniformed cops. One held Lessek's gun, initialing and bagging it for use as evidence. The other snapped handcuffs onto a snarling Lessek. They gave an extraordinarily satisfying click as he was led away.

"You were right," Button said, a broad smile lighting his face, "the DA's gonna love this. It's just what he needs to put the finishing touches on the Bellfield indictment."

"Glad I could help," I said dryly. Sweat poured down my face, in imminent danger of turning to icicles from the cold. "Now do you suppose we could adjourn to the precinct and get this wire off me? The tape," I confessed in a voice I couldn't stop from shaking, "itches like hell!"

19

Look at the co-offin
With golden ha-andles
Isn't it grand boys,
To be bloody well dead?

The Clancy Brothers, singing from the jukebox, had plenty of help on that one. They always did. The crowd at the Donegal Bay loved the idea of being the center of attraction, the laid-out star of the wake, surrounded by flowers and boozy, grieving loved ones.

I was an outsider, a Scotch-drinking Protestant. Matt Riordan, on the other hand, was home, lifting his glass of Irish and his fine tenor in a display of comradeship that was all the more impressive for being wholly genuine. He was Matty the Lawyer here, among the cops and bus drivers and civil servants, and yet his three-piece suits and educated diction didn't set him apart. They merely served to fix his identity, his role in the closely knit Inwood Irish community. They knew—and he'd proved it more than once—that his high-priced legal talents were theirs for free should young Kevin the rookie cop mistake an unarmed kid for a dangerous robbery suspect or should someone's wayward Mary Margaret get caught selling pot at the Sacred Heart dance.

It was getting late. Eyes were getting bleary, and whiskey-red noses were getting redder. But Matt Riordan was just beginning to relax. The tension lines in his face were smoothing out, the famous Riordan smile was broader, the voice richer and deeper without the strident edge of nerves. We both had something to celebrate; he'd won an acquittal and I was still alive.

Let's not have a sniffle,
Let's have a bloody good cry,
And always remember the longer you live,
The sooner you'll bloody die.

The song ended, as usual, with a rousing cheer. Riordan raised his glass to the red-haired barmaid, who nodded and smiled. I was about to protest that one more would be one too many, then decided that one too many was just what I needed.

I was in that heady state of euphoria plus exhaustion in which everything I'd done seemed to have happened to someone else. Surely it couldn't have been *me*, I now protested, who'd strapped on the Kel set recorder at the Eighty-fourth Precinct and proceeded to trap Todd Lessek into spilling his guts on tape? I, Cass Jameson, hadn't really played Cagney and Lacey up there on the Brooklyn Bridge, looking into the barrel of a snub-nosed revolver, had I? Then I recalled the world-turned-upside-down feeling of being thrown to the ground. I'd skinned my knees on the bridge walkway. Button, back at the Eight-four, had insisted on Mercurochrome. My knees, tingling under my wool skirt, looked like they had in my tomboy childhood.

"I can't believe I did all that," I said, shaking my head. "I can't believe I let Button talk me into it."

Matt shrugged noncommittally, but there was a gleam in his blue eyes. "It's what Nancy would have done," he remarked.

I fell for it. "Who's Nancy?" I asked, then laughed in spite of myself. "Is this another Nancy Drew joke?"

Riordan grinned. He'd once warned me against "playing Nancy Drew," and my reaction of mortal insult had amused him no end. He seldom lost an opportunity to kid me about it.

"And now Nancy has successfully solved another case," he said, his mouth full of bar peanuts. "What's this one called, *The Case of the Dead Lodger*?"

"That's Perry Mason," I replied automatically. To Riordan's puzzled frown, I explained, "All of the Perry Mason books use *The Case of* in the title."

A red-nosed, bleary-eyed man came over to slap Matt's back and borrow the price of a drink. After giving him a five, Matt turned to me and shook his head. "That guy," he said, "used to be a bail bondsman. Best in the business and rich as God. Now look at him—he'd drink it from a boot."

Something about the man reminded me of the ugly

burned-out hovel the Unknown Homicides called home. "At least Tito Fernandez is off the hook," I remarked. "Button told me Ira Bellfield admitted having that fire set.

"I hope you're right," I went on, "about this being the end of Linda's case. But both Lessek and Bellfield, after howling for their lawyers, denied that they had anything to do with her death."

"What did you expect?" Matt shrugged. "Full confessions? Why should they admit anything they don't have to? The important thing is that the police have to follow up on the possibility that someone besides Linda's husband did away with her."

"I guess," I admitted, "it was a kind of fantasy. That Brad would walk out of jail just as Lessek was walking in."

"Give it time, Cass," Matt Riordan advised. "Let the dank reality of life in a cell seep through to one of the bastards, and maybe he'll decide to put a knife into the other one."

"You," I said, only half-kidding, "are the most cynical man I've ever known."

He responded with a twisted smile that would have done justice to the hero in a gothic romance. "How do you think," he asked, "the Brooklyn DA's office made its case, such as it was, against the client I just got off? One of his fellow bribe-takers cut a deal. What the DA *didn't* tell the news media—but what I hammered home to the jury—was that Mr. State's Evidence got away with over a hundred thousand in bribes, whereas my poor schnook had at most fifteen thousand. It was like using the salmon to catch the minnow."

"Catchy line," I grinned.

"Highlight of the summation," he admitted with an answering smile. Then he got serious. "What do you care," he challenged, "what happens to the real killer, as long as Brad Ritchie goes free?"

He had me there. Dawn was my only concern; abstract justice was taking a backseat and I knew it. But I wasn't ready to admit it to Matt Riordan's knowing face, so I mumbled the word "cynical" again and got up to go to the ladies' room.

On the way back, wobbling slightly from an excess of Scotch, I noticed that the jukebox was playing a militant IRA song. All the mugs and glasses in the place were raised in an attitude of respectful belligerence, and at the bar, a hoarse voice cried, "I love you, Maggie Thatcher, but get your bloody troops out of my country!"

I looked over at Matt. His glass was raised, and his face

was flushed as he sang along with the words of the song. One line referred to the "land that the English stole." As he mouthed the words, all pretense of cynicism fell away, and I was looking at the face of Irish patriotism. The thought crossed my mind that the gun-running Matt had said took place at the Donegal Bay was something he knew firsthand. These Irishmen supported their case with bullets as well as maudlin ballads.

I spoke of none of this as I sat down in my chair and lifted my drink, noting dispassionately that the idealism had left Matt's face the minute he'd seen me return to my seat.

As we finished our drinks, the jukebox went into "The Wild Colonial Boy." The red-haired barmaid held up her skirt and began a jig, her varicose-veined legs looking pretty good as she hopped in perfect time to the music. The men at the bar clapped her on, and she danced faster and faster, never missing a beat. She ended in a flurry of applause, her red hair flying, her face flushed. She acknowledged the audience with a pleased curtsy. Matt Riordan blew her a kiss as we stepped out into the night.

We went to Matt's apartment. His lovemaking was uncharacteristically tender, and I thought of the idealism he suppressed so ruthlessly in his professional life, but which surfaced in the boozy patriotism of the Donegal Bay. He was a man of contradictions, Matt, and I'd spent fruitless hours trying to sort them all out. Tonight I contented myself with snuggling against his chest, accepting his kisses, and letting myself feel protected, even comforted, by his presence.

The mood was broken by a phone call. The sleepy quality in Matt's voice vanished as he spoke into the receiver. He sat up in bed and fumbled for a pencil. "Fifth Precinct," I heard him mumble. "Detective Malek. Okay. Just remember," he instructed, his voice now completely lawyerly, "no questioning until I get there, or that confession won't be anything but toilet paper. And no lineup either. I'll be there in a half hour."

He hung up the phone and turned to me, his face a study in rueful regret as he told me he had to go. But his voice was crisp, his eyes bright. He was already calculating, his head at the Fifth Precinct even as his body stood next to his bed.

"Somebody got busted?" I asked sleepily. He nodded.

"What kind of case?"

"Drugs," he replied, then frowned. "Don't ask too many questions, Cass. For your own good." He took his clothes into the bathroom and I put mine on in the bedroom.

Matt Riordan's compulsive secrecy about his clients had surprised me at first. Legal Aid lawyers routinely discussed cases, partly to seek advice from colleagues and partly just to let off steam. I'd unconsciously expected the same from Matt. But his caseload and his clients weren't society's losers but its winners. Their doings were too dangerous to discuss lightly.

I had to wonder sometimes why I continued to go out with a man whose secrets outnumbered by far the things he was willing to share with me. Large portions of Riordan's life were sealed off behind a barbed-wire fence. No Trespassing signs were everywhere, posted in several languages. Why did I keep coming back? I shrugged an answer; in spite of all that very private property, I liked the view.

Riding the subway at one A.M. didn't provide many pleasures. But there was one. Scrawled on the place where the map would have been was a great piece of graffiti: *Enola Gay*, it read, *the kiss she gives will never ever go away*.

Exhaustion hit when I got home. I fell into bed and slept like the dead until the phone woke me. It was the *Daily News* asking about Todd Lessek's arrest. I groggily gave the details the reporter wanted, then fell back into oblivion. Another bell from hell. The *Post* this time. I did it again. What with one thing and another, I got about as much sleep as Lawrence Block's insomniac spy, Evan Tanner.

Eyes gritty and head heavy, I dragged myself out of bed. Afraid to turn on the news in case I was on it, I stood in a hot shower until I began to feel alive again, then got dressed for work. I stopped into my office to pick up files and check my answering machine, and was on my way out the door when the phone rang.

It took a moment, in my fuzzy state, to recognize the thin, querulous voice. When I did, my heart sank. It was Hattie Hopkins, Terrell's grandmother.

"How could you do it?" she asked, her tone incredulous. "How could you let that boy plead guilty to something he didn't do?"

I opened my mouth to answer, but Hattie hadn't called to listen. "I suppose," she said, "I didn't have enough money for you to go to trial like I wanted. If I was a rich woman, my boy wouldn't have to do time. He'd be home with me where he belongs, not locked up with animals."

"Mrs. Hopkins," I finally raised my voice, "did Terrell tell you he was innocent?"

"I know my boy," she replied, a world of dignity in her tone. "He don't like me to worry, so he told me a lie to spare my feelings. He told me he robbed that boy, but I don't believe it for a minute. He just sayin' that to make me accept that he's going to be in jail. But I don't accept it. I don't accept it at all, and I don't aim to pay for a lawyer to put my boy in jail instead of gettin' him out like you should have done."

"Mrs. Hopkins..." I began, but the line was dead. I could sue her for my fee, I supposed, but I knew I wouldn't. She'd suffer enough, I knew, riding the bus upstate once a month to see Terrell.

I put down the phone with an exasperated clank. One more of life's disappointments I had to deal with alone, I thought. Once upon a time, I'd have rushed straight into Nathan's office or Flaherty's cubicle at Legal Aid, poured out my tale of woe and received sympathetic advice. Or at least a smile and a reminder that it was, after all, a tough business.

All through the court day, my one thought was of sleep. But even after the pleas were taken, the cases adjourned, the clients seen, I wasn't on my way home to sink into the blessed warmth of my flannel sheets. Instead, I was riding the subway to lower Manhattan to visit the law firm that represented Richard Bower's Services for Children, the agency bent on removing Arnette Pearson's kids. Today, if I could keep my eyelids open, I'd see all the records in the case. I hoped there'd be something in the piles of papers that would help Arnette; otherwise, I'd be better off going home to bed.

By a stroke of irony, the firm was located in the black building with the orange cube in front. It seemed as though years instead of days had passed since I'd met Elliott Pilcher there. Now that Lessek and Bellfield were under arrest, Elliott seemed a minor character, a walk-on in the drama of Linda Ritchie.

The firm was huge; I walked through a rabbit warren of cubbyholes, each painted pearl-gray with a maroon trim on the woodwork. The secretary I was following deposited me in a sizable law library, brought out a sheaf of papers about the size of the national debt, and asked if I wanted coffee. I nodded with eager gratitude, then opened the file.

The most recent reports were on top. I learned that the twins took classes with the Alvin Ailey school; Kwaku was regarded as a potential dancer, while Kwame came along to be with his brother. His talent was for basketball.

I flashed to Arnette, living in an SRO hotel in Brooklyn Heights. Sure, she'd get a bigger place if she had her kids, but could she send Kwaku to dance class, buy basketball shoes for Kwame? Could she give them the other extras they got from their foster parents—a nice home in Queens, schools where the teachers actually taught, classmates who thought achievement was a good idea, not something to be put down? I frowned as I thought of Kwaku fighting his way to his dance classes, of Kwame's basketball shoes being stolen from him at knifepoint. That was the reality behind the only life Arnette Pearson could give her kids.

I finished my coffee and turned to the next report. No dance classes here. Instead, I had Jomo's arrest record, Tanika's history of running away, and a detailed account of a fight between Kamisha and her new foster mother's niece. The end result was that the new foster mother, who'd had the kids for less than three months, had already petitioned the agency to remove them from her home. It was clear that the only reason the agency was holding off was that it looked better in Family Court to have all three older kids in one home. As soon as the agency won its case, the kids would be split—just as Mickey Dechter had predicted.

Another cup of coffee and two hundred pages later, my eyelids were getting very heavy. My eyes felt like pickled onions and I could hardly see the words that swam in front of me. I had pages of notes, all of them depressing. I was down to the earliest reports, before the twins were born.

And there it was. On March 14, 1976, Arnette Pearson begged her social worker for help. "Recipient made a request," the report noted in welfarese, "for a homemaker to help her with her children. Recipient feels she is under a lot of pressure and may have to leave children alone if she is not assisted in the home." There was a big red DENIED stamp over the report. But Arnette had asked and the agency had not responded. How could they go into court and convince a judge they'd done everything they could to "strengthen the natural family" when they'd denied Arnette Pearson a homemaker?

Reverently, I lifted the paper and put it on a small pile to be Xeroxed by the secretary. If only, I found myself thinking, someone had listened to Arnette Pearson, if only she'd received a small part of the help, financial and otherwise, that the agency had given the foster parents, maybe she'd still have her kids.

The thought nagged at me all the way home. The subway cars rattled, "if only"; I switched from the A train to the F at Jay street and thought "if only." I climbed the steps at the Bergen Street Station, pulling myself up by the banister, my head throbbing "if only."

If only I could to to bed! I needed sleep so badly it hurt. I could see myself climbing into my loft bed and losing myself in the warmth of my quilted comforter, but it wasn't to be. I had a four o'clock appointment with Marcy Sheldon and Dawn for a strategy session.

I could see them in my waiting room, sitting on separate couches, each reading a magazine. I schooled my features into a welcoming smile and walked through the door. Marcy greeted me with a nod and put down the *New Yorker*. Dawn neatly folded the tennis magazine she'd brought with her and put it into her knapsack. They followed me silently into my office.

Coats were taken, coffee was poured, and we all sat expectantly, waiting for someone to take the lead. It was, I knew, my job, but I was too tired to begin. Marcy Sheldon stepped into the breach, her voice cool.

"I've looked into several schools," she began, "and there's one in particular that would be especially good for Dawn. It's a Quaker school and has a very good reputation for sports as well as academics. They don't usually take new students in mid-term, but they said they'd make an exception for Dawn."

"Sounds good," I replied noncommittally. "It's in Manhattan, I suppose."

There was a distinct hesitation before Marcy clipped out her reply. "No," she said briskly, "it's near Oneonta."

"My God," I blurted out, exhaustion having destroyed all the tact cells in my brain, "that's way the hell upstate."

"It's a boarding school, of course," Marcy snapped.

"Are you crazy?" I was by now too angry as well as too tired to be polite. "Do you think a Brooklyn Family Court judge is going to give you custody of a child just so you can stick her in a boarding school somewhere?"

Marcy's face went white. Her lips tightened, and she spaced her words very carefully. "Briarwood is a *very* good school."

"I don't care if it's Harvard," I shot back. "Look"—I spread my hands, trying for a more professional demeanor— "I'm talking as a lawyer here. We have to be realistic. I know Judge Bettinger, and I know he won't buy it. You go into his courtroom talking boarding school and you'll end up visiting Dawn on Sundays while she lives with Mrs. Ritchie. Is that what you want?"

"*I* do," a low, passionate voice cut in. I turned, surprised, to see Dawn, her face determined and her fists clenched. She shot her aunt a look of pure hatred, then fixed me with a direct stare. "I want to live with Grandma Ritchie," she announced.

20

Although Dawn dropped her bombshell in a deliberately disciplined tone that echoed her aunt's, she accompanied it with a defiant toss of her head. The pose in which she sat was definitely rebellious teenager, yet underneath I sensed a child who'd been too badly hurt by too many people.

I was dimly aware that I'd handled the situation unprofessionally. Oh, the advice I'd given Marcy had been sound enough; I knew damned well Bettinger would deny us custody if Marcy proposed a boarding school in court. But the way I'd lashed out at her had been personal, not professional. It had been Dawn's friend speaking, not Marcy's lawyer. I promised myself I'd keep my roles straight in the future.

It wasn't easy. Dawn's on-edge, ready-for-a-fight look was

belied by her pallor, and the twisting, biting lips that showed her fear. What she needed was Marcy's arms around her, Marcy reassuring her that she was wanted, that the boarding school had been a bad idea. What she got instead was flat denial. "No," Marcy announced, fumbling in her purse for a cigarette. "You don't really want to live with that woman. You're just saying that because you're angry."

"Don't tell me what I want," Dawn replied with studied insolence. "You don't care what I want. You just want me out of the way. That's why you want to put me in some shitty school."

"You know I don't like you using that kind of language," Marcy protested.

"You're not my mother!" Dawn countered, her lower lip thrust out. "She let me talk any way I want, so you can't tell me what to do!"

"If I'm going to be your guardian—" Marcy began. I could have told her she was asking for it.

"But you're not!" Dawn crowed in triumph. Yet her tone was brittle, and tears seemed closer than she would have admitted. "Is she, Cass? You said the judge wouldn't let her send me to that *shitty* school."

"Briarwood is a lovely place," Marcy replied. Her eyes had the pleading sincerity she used to sell her public-relations campaigns. "Miss Farley says the tennis program is excellent. She's really looking forward to having you there."

I felt like I was losing control of the situation. Dawn was trying to use me against my own client, and Marcy was conducting a product promotion on a hurt twelve-year-old. On top of all that, my head throbbed, my eyes hurt, and my reflexes were as sound as old rubber bands.

"I can't believe," Marcy went on, her tone more-in-sorrow-than-anger, "that you want to throw away a good opportunity to go and live with that silly old bitch in Bensonhurst."

"Who's using bad language now?" Dawn taunted.

"I want you to have the best," Marcy said, reaching out her hands to where Dawn sat. "Your mother would have wanted it too, I'm sure of it. To get a good education, prepare for a good job. Meet the right kind of friends. I'm doing it for your own good."

"Bullshit!" Dawn cried, echoing my own thoughts. Her

voice cracked, and the tears began to flow. "You don't care about me! All you want is to get me out of the way so you can spend all your time at your stupid office and not feel guilty about leaving me alone!" Tears coursed down her cheeks and she caught her breath in gusty sobs that shook her whole frame. "You're just like my mom, only she left me alone so she could go out with guys. You leave me alone to go to your shitty office."

Dawn's next words were hard to understand. She buried her head in her arms like a little kid and sobbed her heart out. I finally understood one of the broken phrases that tumbled out of her. "I want my daddy," she wailed.

That got me on my feet. Guiding Dawn out of her chair, I led her upstairs, murmuring soothing but empty words. I had her lie down on my couch, put a box of Kleenex and a glass of water by her side, and went back downstairs to tell Marcy exactly what I thought of her.

But I had to do it as a lawyer. Angry as I was, quick to identify with Dawn's feelings of hurt and rejection, it was not my place to rake Marcy Sheldon over the coals as a bad aunt; I could counsel her only as a client about to make a strategic blunder.

"I meant what I said, Marcy," I began, taking my place behind the desk. "Judge Bettinger isn't going to give you custody so you can put Dawn in a boarding school. It's just not in the cards. Not in Brooklyn."

"Can we get the case transferred to Manhattan?" Marcy asked coolly.

"It's possible," I admitted with reluctance. "Manhattan judges are more sophisticated. They might agree that Dawn's educational needs would be served by a school like Briarwood. But there's more to it than that. What about Mrs. Ritchie's visitation rights? Or Brad's, when he gets out of jail?"

"*When* he gets out?" Marcy's tone was sharp. "Don't you mean *if*?"

I waved away the point. "Whatever. What I'm saying is that Dawn needs more than just a good school. What she needs—especially now—is to feel a part of someone's life, to feel important to and loved by somebody close to her." The lawyer stepped out of the room while the human being pleaded. "She needs *you*, Marcy, not Briarwood."

My thoughts flew back to the day Linda was buried. For all the phone calls and drinks dates that made up the fabric of her life, Marcy Sheldon had stood alone as her only sister entered the ground. No friend or lover had appeared to support her. Was that the truth of her life, I wondered, that she had, at the end, only "contacts"? Did she feed off her business life as a substitute for intimacy?

Marcy gazed out my window for a minute or two, taking in the cars creeping along Court Street, the black-edged city snowdrifts, the Middle Eastern restaurant across the street. Then she spoke. "It's easy for you to talk," she said. "It's not your problem."

"God, I'm glad Dawn's not here to hear this," I exploded. "All she is to you is a problem? Marcy, answer me one question. Why do you want custody? Just to spite Ma Ritchie? Because if so, let me tell you one thing right now. That's not good enough. Not for me. I can't represent you if *that's* what—"

"What would *you* do?" Marcy interrupted with a hoarse shout. Her face was distorted with anger; the mask was off. "What the hell would Cass Jameson, Miss Self-righteous, do if all of a sudden, after twenty years of living alone, *you* had a twelve-year-old girl on your hands? Would you close up your law office and go on welfare so you could stay home and play house with her?"

"Nobody's talking welfare here," I shouted back. "Don't set up straw men and then knock them down. If you've got the money for a boarding school, then you've got the money for a housekeeper or something." I caught my breath and remembered Ma Ritchie's promise to be there when Dawn came home from school. A housekeeper might not appeal to the good judge any more than a boarding school, I realized. Marcy was right; the choices were tough.

I tried a fallback position. "Do you really have to work so many hours a week?" I asked, in a gentler tone.

"If I want to be the best, I do," came the reply. Her dark brown eyes gazed steadily at me, willing me to see her as she wanted to be seen: competent professional taking her future into her own hands, seeking no favors from the world. But there was something else, a hidden force that puzzled me until I recalled the last time Marcy and I had talked. I remembered the little girl who'd seen her mother abused and abandoned, her sister turned into a spoiled princess by a daddy indifferent to herself. What lay behind Marcy Sheldon's cold calculation was naked fear.

"It's not schools, is it, Marcy?" I asked softly. "And it's not really the number of hours you work. After all, you could work seven days a week for all I care, if you'd only turn to Dawn just once and tell her you love her. But that's just what you can't do. You can't let Dawn or anyone else get close to you or they might see how vulnerable you really are."

Marcy sucked her cigarette, eyes staring blankly at the window. From the corner of one eye, a tear crept down her cheek. "Get fucked," she muttered.

I went upstairs to see how my other patient was doing. Dawn lay on the couch, tearless now, her face swollen. I brought her a cold compress from the bathroom, and watched her bathe her eyes.

"It's kind of hard for Marcy," I said lamely.

"It's not a picnic for me," she shot back. "And I'm *not* going to any boarding school."

"Look, Dawn," I began, my heart heavy. "There's something I have to be clear with you about. I represent your Aunt Marcy in court. It's my job to present the case for her getting custody."

Dawn was looking at me with wide eyes. Her face held the look I'd dreaded: suspicion. "Does that mean you're on *her* side?"

"When we started all this," I reminded her, "you were both on the same side. Or so I thought, anyway. And I want you to know that if, after thinking it over, you really want your Grandma Ritchie to have custody, then I'll give Marcy her money back and tell her to find a new lawyer. I won't help her do something you don't want."

"Will you go to court on my side?" Dawn asked innocently. "Will you tell the judge what I want?"

I shook my head. "I can't. It would be a conflict of interest." The words meant nothing to Dawn. "You already have a lawyer," I pointed out.

Dawn looked blank. "Fred Birnbaum," I reminded her. "The law guardian. The Legal Aid lawyer the court appointed to represent you. The skinny guy with glasses."

Dawn screwed up her face. "I didn't like him," she said.

"Well, he's the one who tells the judge what you want,"

I said. "Of course, you're twelve years old. You can tell the judge yourself, if you'd rather."

She nodded. "Okay," she said. "He seemed pretty nice before."

"But," I pointed out, "I have to know what you're going to say. In case it means I have to get off the case. If you really want to go with your grandma, just say so."

Dawn wrinkled her nose. "Not really," she confessed. "I just said that to make Aunt Marcy mad. She thinks Grandma's a silly old lady. And the thing is, I do too, sometimes. She fusses a lot about things that don't really matter. And she doesn't understand about tennis."

I breathed a sigh of relief. "Good," I said. "You and Marcy and I will have to work out the details, but—"

"I don't want to live with Marcy, either," Dawn said. She looked suddenly shy and said timidly, "I have another idea, if it's okay with you."

My heart jumped. Was I about to face explaining to Dawn why she couldn't live with me? It would be impossible, yet for a wild moment I pictured it working out—then realized I'd face exactly the same dilemma Marcy was in.

"My coach knows this really great place in Florida," Dawn began, her voice gaining confidence and her face glowing with enthusiasm. "He runs a school for girls who play tennis. Not one of those tacky tennis factories, or anything," Dawn explained hastily. "It's almost like a family," she added with a wistfulness that actually hurt to see. "The girls live in a regular house and go to school as well as practicing every day. Three of the girls are pros and they're not even fifteen yet. I bet they make tons of money."

I must have looked as aghast as I felt. What a mess, I thought, anger flooding me. Dawn was so starved for "family" that she'd try to find it in a Florida tennis academy that turned out fourteen-year-old "pros." Marcy, I thought grimly, had more to answer for than she knew.

"My mom even said she'd think about it," Dawn said defensively. "When I showed her the article in *Tennis Today* about Carling Bassett, she said she'd look into it after we got to Washington. She smiled at me and said she'd never realized before how good I was," Dawn added with a naïve pride.

Anger at Marcy was replaced by rage at dead Linda.

What she'd finally understood, I realized, was that there was money in the game her daughter loved. I could just see Linda as an absentee tennis mom, parking Dawn at some tennis factory for nine months a year, raking in the prize money. Dawn might turn prodigy at fourteen, with two years' intensive coaching, but what would Dawn be at eighteen? Bitter, hating the sight of a tennis racquet? Or worse, hating herself for being a has-been?

"Dawn, honey," I said in a tone I hoped sounded more reasonable than I felt, "if the judge wouldn't let you go away to boarding school, he probably wouldn't agree to Florida either."

"But this is different," Dawn wailed, tears threatening again. "This is what I want!"

"Is it?" I asked softly. Then I played a dangerous trump card. "What about when your dad gets out of jail? Do you want to be in Florida when that happens, or do you want to be here waiting for him?"

Dawn's reply was accusatory. Fixing me with a baleful red-rimmed eye, she said, "You promised you'd help him. But he's still in jail."

I thought about all the interviews I'd conducted, the leads I'd followed up. I'd been burglarized and locked in a burning building and threatened with a gun. But it was true; Brad Ritchie was still behind bars. "I tried, Dawn," I said tiredly. "God knows, I tried."

"No, you haven't." Dawn's bitten lips curled with contempt. "You just wanted to get on television. I saw you on 'Live at Five' last night, and all you talked about was that dumb Todd Lessek. You didn't say a word about my daddy or my mother either."

"They didn't ask me," I mumbled, defensive in spite of myself.

"If you really wanted to help my dad," Dawn went on, tossing her head, "you'd talk to Congressman Lucenti."

"Look, Dawn"—I tried reason—"just because he and your mother had a thing going doesn't mean he's the one who killed her."

"It was more than that. She called him to come over that night. That's why she sent me to Aunt Marcy's."

"How do you know that?" I was numb with shock, but

intrigued at the same time. "Or are you making it up to help your dad?"

"She called his campaign office. I saw her write down the number and I kept the piece of paper she wrote it on."

"Why didn't you tell the police?"

She looked at me as though I were Mortimer Snerd. "If the cops knew my mom called Art Lucenti," she explained with commendable patience, "they would have thought my dad got jealous and killed Mom because she was meeting the congressman." She sounded like a kid relating to a classmate the latest episode of "Dallas"; instead, she was talking about people she'd known, a life she'd lived.

Plus, she had a point. I could just see Button marking the phone number with his initials and bagging it for use as evidence against Brad Ritchie. Button was no respecter of persons; he'd go after Lucenti if he thought there was guilt there—but he wouldn't look any harder for it than he had to.

I gave the matter serious thought as I shepherded Dawn downstairs. If I'd known before that Linda had met Art Lucenti the night she was killed, would I have gone straight to him and skipped the others? Damned right I would have. And it wasn't too late now. I resolved to get about thirteen hours' sleep and go to the campaign headquarters as soon as possible.

Marcy's makeup and bland smile were back in place. She said she hoped Dawn was feeling better, and shook my hand in farewell. Dawn seemed to shrink into herself, like an animal retreating into its shell. They left in silence, with all the issues between them as unresolved as Linda's murder.

But I'd had all I could stand for one day. Trudging upstairs and climbing up to my loft bed, I lay my head on the pillow with a deep sigh of satisfaction. Sleep at last!

But sleep was no balm. Instead of sweet dreams, I saw Linda's murder. The screams, the blood, the knife—it was all there. But that wasn't the scary part. What had me waking in a cold sweat was that the face that gloated over Linda's dead body belonged to Dawn.

"How many?" Dorinda asked, her ladle poised to pour. It was six-thirty A.M.; the Morning Glory had a half-hour to go before opening, but I'd slept twelve hours and wakened at six, starved.

"Three," I replied promptly. Then I reconsidered. A little of Dorinda's industrial-strength pancakes (every whole grain known to man) goes a long way. "Make that two," I amended.

"How did yesterday go?" Dorinda wondered, as she ladled dollops of batter onto the sizzling griddle.

I told her. "As far as I'm concerned," I finished disgustedly, "if Marcy loses this case, it'll be what she deserves. It may also be the best thing for Dawn. Ma Ritchie may be Willy Loman, but at least she loves the kid. What goes on in Marcy's heart is anybody's guess."

The pancakes were beginning to resemble NASA photos of the moon. Pockmarks cratered the surface, and I could smell a faint burning odor, but Dorinda just stood, spatula in hand, a dreamy expression on her face.

"You know," she remarked, "I wasn't always a vegetarian."

"What in hell does that have to do with anything?" I demanded. "And for God's sake, turn those pancakes."

When the pancakes were safely turned, Dorinda explained, "Randy was this guy I went with after I left Fernando."

"Was that the filmmaker or the poet?"

"Fernando was an actor," she replied with a touch of impatience. "Randy was a tofu salesman."

"You're kidding." I grinned, diverted in spite of myself. She shook her head. "He was macrobiotic."

I pointed to the pancakes; Dorinda took the hint and scooped them onto a plate. When she handed me a choice of syrup or honey, I waved at her to leave both and finish her story.

"I was still eating meat then," Dorinda explained, "but I was interested in going vegetarian." She paused and frowned at the memory. "But the funny thing was, that here was a guy who could really have helped me, and yet every time we ate out together, I insisted we go to a place where I could get meat.

"I mean," she went on, her voice stronger, "here I was, interested as hell and yet resisting it at the same time. I think I was afraid that if I really gave vegetarianism a chance, it would change my whole life. And I wasn't ready for that. Not then."

I got the point. "You think Marcy's coldness is just a way of resisting Dawn?"

"It could be," Dorinda insisted. "It could be that if she ever really let go, the dam would burst and a whole flood of love would flow out."

It was a charming thought, but Dorinda hadn't been there when Marcy Sheldon had told Dawn about the boarding school. I shook my head and ate the rest of my pancakes in silence. This was Brooklyn, I reminded myself, not Hollywood. This wasn't a TV movie of the week, with all the problems of the world solved in two hours as the credits rolled and the music swelled.

21

The rest of the morning wasn't much of an improvement. The sky was that yellow-gray peculiar to a New York January. I was better rested, but still hung over with the shock of Dawn's announcement. My mood wasn't helped by the thought that today was the day Arnette Pearson was going to lose her kids.

I could see the outcome in Glenda Shute's complacent face before the arguments even began. She and the agency lawyer exchanged the kind of smiles worn by all the movie social workers who came to take Shirley Temple/Jackie Cooper/Ricky Schroder to a "decent home."

I flashed Mickey Dechter a quick glance of (with luck) discreet camaraderie and was shocked at her appearance. Haggard, as if the court were deciding her fate along with that of Arnette Pearson. She reminded me of Dawn on her anguished court days. I found myself apprehensive as I looked at her. When we lost—as we surely would—would her thoughts be of the Pearson kids, or of three foster children in far-off Tennessee?

I stepped up to the bench, Arnette at my side. She was still wearing the black karate outfit, and her hair looked wilder than ever. She gave the impression of being tensed to the limit, poised for a kung fu kick at the bench if she lost the case.

Arnette's face was a Masai mask, impervious to pain. At her side, her hands were balled into fists. I reached out with my right hand and cupped it around her left fist. The skin felt leathery, the sinews as taut as a bowstring. I squeezed until she opened her hand, then she clasped mine with a grip that threatened to cut off my blood supply. It didn't matter; what counted was the link, the lifeline.

"If it please the court," I began, launching into the arguments Mickey Dechter and I had perfected in secret sessions. I wasn't supposed to be talking first; the agency was the petitioner. But that was part of my strategy. Before the smooth, gold-chained agency lawyer could go into her pitch, I wanted the judge to know the mother whose rights she would be terminating.

I painted word pictures: Arnette at seventeen, giving birth to Tanika alone, having been cast out by her religious mother. At eighteen, still alone, pregnant again with Jomo. Her affair with a Black Power advocate who called himself Lumumba and who left her life after fathering Kamisha.

Three kids under five, no husband, and a life of endless waits in endless welfare lines and clinics. Wanting more, she wangled a grant to go back to high school for her diploma. When Kamisha was hospitalized for pneumonia contracted in a heatless apartment, she was forced to quit. The grant was never renewed.

I talked about Jerome, the man Arnette had left her kids for. He was a man with plans, a man who represented hope, a way out. Her leaving the children with her newly reconciled mother had been a stab at a secure future with a man willing to support the whole family once he'd made it. The problem was, he didn't. Arnette returned to New York, to find the kids in foster care.

She also found herself pregnant with the twins. Enter the agency. Even though she'd been reinstated as the custodial parent, Arnette was now under direct supervision by social workers who offered plenty of criticism and little support. I read from the records I'd seen in the agency office to make my case. Black marks went onto Arnette's record whenever she ran out of food between welfare checks, but no help in increasing her grant or dealing with Social Services was ever forthcoming. She was turned down in every request she ever made to the agency, yet she was constantly under pressure to do better by her children. Her challenges to the agency, her demands for more help, were counted against her in the agency's reports.

I took the court on a verbal tour of the agency's visiting rooms—the one-way mirrors through which Arnette was studied like a bug on a slide, the foster mother's competitive ploys to capture the children's attention during Arnette's visiting time, the subtle disapproval of Arnette's lifestyle that surfaced in little digs that went into her record. No wonder, I concluded, that the visits slowed and then ceased. Was this, I asked rhetorically, the agency's idea of "strengthening the bonds of the natural family," which was what the law mandated?

I ended with a plea for time—the only thing we could realistically walk away with. I asked for a six-month adjournment during which Arnette could visit and plan, and recement the bonds between herself and her kids.

I sat down knowing we'd lost. Glenda Shute's face as she turned to the agency lawyer said that *now* she was ready to hear something that made sense.

What she heard was the standard agency line. Whatever the agency had done or failed to do in the past, the only question before the court was, what was the best interests of the children *now*. She started in on her glowing account of the benefits of adoption.

I jumped to my feet and interrupted, risking the court's wrath. Angry, I exposed the truth about the three older children: that there was no hope of adoption for them, that they were on the verge of removal from their present foster home, and that the only reason they were still together in that home was to impress the court. I finished with a point Mickey and I had argued about. I asked the court to enter separate orders—one for Kwame and Kwaku, releasing them for adoption, and one for Tanika, Jomo, and Kamisha, granting the adjournment.

It was a legal impossibility, and I knew it. How could the court rule that Arnette was an unfit mother as to two kids but fit as to the other three? And yet, watching the whole loaf slip away, I had to reach out to grab a half if I possibly could. I owed it to Arnette and to the social worker who followed my words with anguished intensity.

We lost. It took a lot more words and a few supercilious looks from Glenda Shute, who seemed to blame me for daring to make the effort to stop the agency's well-intentioned plans for the Pearson kids. When the words were pronounced, I felt the hand in mine squeeze so hard I thought my own hand would come off. Then Arnette abruptly cut the connection, flinging my arm against my side. She stalked out of the courtroom with a door-slamming bang that reminded me forcibly of Brad Ritchie.

Her hallway performance continued the parallel. Squaring off at me, Arnette raked me up and down with contempt blazing in her eyes.

"Shoulda had me a *black* lawyer," she said. "The Black United Front, that's who I need now. I gotta *do* something behind all this racist bullshit, you dig?"

"We did everything we could," I said, stepping in front of my client. It was an instinctive movement to shield the social worker, who was brushing away a furtive tear. Despite my efforts, Arnette saw the gesture. "What *you* got to cry for?" she taunted Mickey. "It's *my* kids they done stole."

I'd been where Mickey was. I knew the pain of wanting to help, of knowing what to do to help, but of being unable, sometimes forbidden, to do it.

I looked straight into Arnette's angry eyes. "God knows," I said, "you've seen a lot of people in your life who said they were going to help you and then gave you the shaft instead. But Mickey isn't one of them. She risked her job to get me into this case. I think you owe her an apology."

Arnette was ready to walk. I could see it in her eyes, hot with fury. But I knew the anger was a mask, that deep underneath was a hurt so big it couldn't be expressed without tearing her apart. Rage was safer than grief. She looked at the ground. "I'm sorry," she mumbled grudgingly.

Mickey nodded her acceptance, but her face still held a vulnerability that bothered me. She was taking our loss far too hard.

I turned back to my client. "The three older kids," I began, my tone deliberately businesslike, "do they know how to reach you?"

She nodded. "They got my mama's number. They call once in a while."

"Good. Because I know for a fact they're leaving the

foster home they're in now. Maybe the new foster mothers will let you visit them or let them visit you, even if it is against the rules."

"Best I can hope for, I guess," Arnette conceded. Then her face brightened into a near-smile. "Hey," she said, "they their mama's kids. They don't hold by the rules too much."

That had been the easy part. "But the twins"—I swallowed as I said the words—"I'm afraid they're gone forever. Those parents will never let you see them."

"I know," she sighed. "Sometime it seem like a dream that I ever had them. They been gone so long, it's like they never was part of me noway. I be used to it."

I wished her luck and watched her walk down the hallway toward the elevators, then I turned toward Mickey. "It's a tough business," I said. She managed a wan smile but no answer.

As we walked toward the ladies' room, I asked her the question uppermost in my mind. "How can you do it? If it kills you this much—"

"I can't." She shook her head. "Not anymore. It gets worse and worse the more I do it. I can't separate my clients from Loretta and Holly Ann and little Michaeline—"

"Michaeline?" I must have missed something, I thought. "Who's Michaeline?"

"Me," she replied with a small smile. "I didn't get to be Mickey till I went to college and my friends told me Michaeline was a white-trash name. I tried to tell 'em I *was* white trash, but . . ."

We walked into the lavatory. After we each used the facility, we stood in silence for a minute, each leaning against a sink. I surveyed the graffiti. A gang calling itself the Real Home Girls had done a major decorating job. First they'd spray-painted their names: Sweet Apple, Shaqueen, Brown Sugar, Honey Dee, Cookie T., Diamond Lou, and Lady Love. Then came their motto: *We all about love, sex, and puttin' bitches in check.*

My thoughts flashed to Arnette Pearson. She had the same gritty tenacity I'd seen in so many of my clients over the years. She'd need it through the lonely nights and doubtful days of her bleak future.

On the opposite wall, also done by the Real Home Girls, was the following ghetto haiku:

Million Dollar Girls
Chillin' Hard
In a Zillion Dollar World

I was about to call Mickey's attention to the lines when she asked, "Did you ever see that movie, *King of Hearts*?"

"Sure," I replied, startled. "It's a classic antiwar film." In the story, inmates from a mental asylum take on the roles of villagers driven out by German bombs during World War I. The crazies turn out to be a lot saner, and certainly more human, than the rest of us.

"Do you remember the part where the inmates are going back to the asylum?" she asked. There was an intent look on her fact that told me we were talking about a lot more than movies.

"As they approach the gates," she went on dreamily, not waiting for an answer, "each of them begins to drop pieces of clothing. The beauty leaves her picture hat, the general drops his sword, the bishop his mitre, until they're all just lunatics again." She turned and faced me, pain in her eyes. "That's how I'm starting to feel when I come to work in the mornings," she confessed. "As though on the way I have to leave pieces of myself behind. I'm less and less human every day."

Ira Bellfield. Duncan Pitt. Todd Lessek. Elliott Pilcher. Art Lucenti. Especially Art Lucenti. Hadn't each of them done the same? Cutting off parts of themselves in the name of profit or advancement until there was nothing left? They must have left some trail, I thought, borrowing Mickey's metaphor and picturing a road littered with the virtues and qualities each man had left behind as he turned himself into a success.

Mickey was talking again. "I met this woman," she said, "when I was working at Willowbrook. You know Willowbrook?"

I nodded. The treatment of mentally retarded patients there had become a national scandal.

"Well, this woman and I were busy signing patients out so they could get community-based care," Mickey explained, lapsing momentarily into jargon. "But then I noticed a funny thing. This woman I was working with, who'd been a social worker for thirty years, had actually signed some of the same patients *in* twenty years earlier." Her face wore a look of intense conviction that reminded me of a few antiwar marches I'd been on. "In, out, it was all the same to her." She fixed me with her warm brown eyes and said in a low voice: "I'm ready to leave social work if that happens to me."

"God," I said at last, "I feel as though I'm listening to a record of myself." My thoughts traveled back to the long, soul-searching conversations I'd had with Nathan. The ones in which I'd threatened to quit law and go into photography full-time.

"You?" Mickey's voice was skeptical. "You seem so gung-ho."

"I bounced back," I replied wryly. "Having my own practice, not to mention my own mortgage payments to make, gave me a new perspective."

"I'm not sure that would work for me," she said wistfully, looking away. "Adding responsibilities to the ones I've already got."

"Responsibility," I echoed, "but without authority. That's the real problem, isn't it? Knowing what needs to be done, but not being able to do it either because you haven't got the resources or it's against policy."

"True," Mickey agreed, a rueful smile of recognition on her face. "It makes me doubt myself as a social worker when the fact is I'm damned good when I'm allowed to be." She was silent a minute, and I had the feeling she was trying to decide whether to share a secret.

"I've been taking classes," she confided at last, "in divorce mediation. That's—"

"I know what it is!" I exclaimed. "I just finished a bar association seminar on alternatives to litigation."

Mickey laughed. "I thought lawyers didn't believe in alternatives to litigation."

"This lawyer does," I replied firmly. "Especially in Family Court. There's a lot to be said for working things out instead of going for the jugular in court. Particularly when kids are involved."

"The only thing that bothers me," Mickey confessed, "is whether I know enough about the law to be a good mediator. I mean, I know people. I know how to help them get in touch with their feelings without letting their emotions take over. But I don't know the tax laws, or—" She broke off and smiled apologetically. "Why are you lettin' me run off at the mouth like this?"

I smiled one answer and gave another. "Because I've got an extra office to rent," I said. While she digested that, I added, "And I do know the tax laws and the estate-planning implications of divorce. In fact, I think that together you and I would make one hell of a good divorce mediator. Plus," I went on, "we'd each have our own clients apart from the mediation practice. That way we'll have something to fall back on if everyone in Brooklyn suddenly decides to stay married."

Helping felt good. I liked the warmth of her answering smile, the sparkle in her brown eyes as she began to plan with me. We stood in the ladies' room a good half hour, building our caseload, setting our priorities. The prospect of sharing had me excited as the prospect of independence had her.

Finally, Mickey stopped, looked at her watch, and said, "I have to run. I was due in Part 5 an hour ago."

A sudden doubt assailed me. "You really think we can do it? Work together?"

She looked toward the graffiti-sprayed wall. "What the hell," she replied. "Aren't we million-dollar girls?"

I laughed, and walked into the hall with my new partner.

22

"Why in the name of God," Detective Button exploded, "didn't that damned kid tell me this before?"

"She was afraid," I said, quiet in the face of Button's anger. "Afraid you'd think it was another motive for her father."

"Isn't it?" he challenged. "You're the one who told me Brad Ritchie flipped out when he heard his ex-wife was making it with the congressman."

"I'm not so sure," I said thoughtfully.

"What do you mean, you're not sure?" Button snorted.

"You were in the courthouse when it happened, weren't you?"

I shook my head. "That's not what I mean. I'm not sure Linda was telling the truth. I'm not sure there was an affair."

"You mean because of the blackmail."

"How the hell did you know—"

Button leaned back in his chair and let out a rich chuckle. "Because you just told me," he said, enjoying his cunning. "But, hey, it wasn't so hard to figure. We already know the deceased was putting the squeeze on half the people in New York—"

"Not to mention Brooklyn," I murmured.

"—so now you come to me talkin' 'bout Congressman Lucenti and I got to wonder what busy little Linda had on him, don't I?" His shrewd, hard eyes told me he expected the whole story and he expected it yesterday.

I showed him the contents of Art Lucenti's file from Linda's papers. He looked it over, then whistled. "Guy must be shitting in his pants," Button remarked, "since we got Lessek and Bellfield. He's just waiting for the other shoe to drop. And now," he added cheerfully, "that you've seen fit to tell me about this here phone call, I'd best go drop a shoe on the honorable congressman."

"Wait a minute." I held up a restraining hand. "Let me go with you." I tried to make it sound like a request instead of a plea.

Button raised his eyebrows to the ceiling. "Why?" he asked.

The answer I gave him was true if not complete. "Because I feel guilty," I said. "Dawn Ritchie didn't tell me about that phone call so I could come running to you with it. She meant it to be a secret. I feel responsible. If Lucenti isn't thoroughly checked out—"

Button's face was impassive, his voice cold. "Are you going to accuse me of giving him a break because of who he is?"

"No," I said, and meant it. "But you've got an indicted suspect in the can already. It wouldn't be hard to let Lucenti skate out of this with a little fancy footwork."

"You're kind of messing up your metaphors there, Counselor," Button grinned. "But the answer's no. This is official police business—no kibitzers."

"I might remind you," I pointed out, my voice dropping to a chilly tone, "that I didn't have to tell you anything. I could have confronted Lucenti on my own and not—"

"So why didn't you?" Button challenged. "And don't try to convince me you suddenly saw your civic duty, because I won't believe—"

"Oh, come off it, Detective," I interrupted. "How the hell could I go waltzing into Lucenti's headquarters demanding that people tell me their innermost secrets in strictest confidence when I've just been plastered all over the media as the woman who got Todd Lessek on tape? Who'd talk to me? I'm a walking Abscam, thanks to you."

Button eyed me speculatively, his brow creased with thought. "You know," he said at last, "that's not a bad idea. Not bad at all."

"What's not bad?" Then a horrible thought struck me. "Oh, no," I protested, "you're not going to wire me for sound again, are you? That tape itches like hell."

Button smiled sweetly. "Only when you sweat," he pointed out.

"A lady never sweats," I countered absently.

"I know. I had a grandmother too." He leaned his backside against his desk and smiled at me in a fatherly fashion I found thoroughly repellent. "No, what I'm thinking is this. Congressman Lucenti's up to his ass in lawyers. The minute I get to his door, he's gonna be on the phone talkin' 'bout warrants and calling the mayor and demanding to know who told us about this here phone call he's supposed to have made."

"I see what you mean."

"But if you're there with me," he went on, his eyes gleaming with anticipation, "it's a subtle way of saying, 'You play ball with us or you're gonna be looking at yourself on the six o'clock news and you won't like what you see.'" The smile that accompanied his words was positively sharklike.

"All that," I commented sarcastically, "just because I'm there?"

Button gave me a look of feigned innocence. "Hey," he protested, "*I* can't be threatening the man. That might violate his consitutional rights, or something, wouldn't it, Counselor?"

"Or something," I muttered. But it didn't really matter;

the important thing was I'd be inside Lucenti's headquarters and in a position to get my own questions answered.

As we drove on the Brooklyn-Queens Expressway in Button's unmarked car, he hit me with the one question I'd been hoping he'd forget to ask. I should have known forgetting wasn't in his repertoire.

"Is there anything else in those files," he asked with deceptive casualness, "that I ought to know about?"

"No," I answered firmly, having decided long ago that Aida Valentin Lucenti's pathetic criminal past was something no one, least of all the police, ought to know about.

In the immortal words of Dick Cavett, politics bores my ass off. There's something about a room plastered with posters of the smiling candidate that seems to me irrevocably phony. Yet I had to admit, looking around Art Lucenti's campaign headquarters—soon to be transformed into his neighborhood office—that Art had a perfect political-poster face. An open smile, dark wavy hair, laugh lines around the eyes offset by a strong masculine jaw that spoke of unbending integrity. He was shown laughing with a senior citizen in a yarmulke, buying bread from a beaming Italian matron, holding a jump rope while two black girls did Double Dutch routines, sitting in solemn conference with a group of Puerto Rican teenagers wearing anti-drug T-shirts. Each picture showed a side of Art I had to respect. Too bad, I thought, that other photos hadn't been displayed as well: Art selling out his tenant clients by secretly working for Todd Lessek, Art cutting himself in on the waterfront deal, Art paying blackmail money to Linda Ritchie.

I watched while Detective Button flashed his ID at the girl behind the desk. He seemed amused at her flustered speed as she dashed into the congressman's office to inform him of the official visitor.

The congressman wasn't nearly as impressed as his underling. He strolled out of his office, stretched out a hand in instinctive political fashion, and invited us into his sanctum.

"This is Ms. Jameson." Button indicated me with a wave of his hand. "She's here at my request."

Art's smile never faltered, but there was a hint of irony when he said, "We've met. At Linda Ritchie's funeral, wasn't it?"

I nodded. I wasn't sure I had a speaking part in Button's little play.

"I have a few more questions about Mrs. Ritchie's murder," Button began. I was irresistibly reminded of Columbo, who kept coming back and coming back with his "few more questions" until he'd thoroughly trapped his quarry. The image of Button as a black Peter Falk almost put a grin on my face. I clamped my jaws shut and listened.

"A sad business," Art sighed. His heart was no longer in it; hypocrisy had tired him. Or perhaps the arrest of his pal Lessek had replaced the tragedy of Linda's death in his thoughts.

"New evidence has just come to my attention," Button went on smoothly, "and I thought I'd better check it out. I wouldn't want anyone to say"—he glanced at me pointedly—"that the police were treating a congressman any differently from any other citizen."

Art got the message. The quick look he gave me from under his long eyelashes was shrewd and penetrating. He licked his lips and said, "Of course, I'm always willing to cooperate with the authorities."

"Good. A witness has come forward who says Mrs. Ritchie called you here at your office the night of her death and asked you to come to her apartment. Is that true, Congressman?"

"Who"—Art bleated, pale and stunned—"Who is this witness?" He looked at me, and this time his eyes gleamed with malice. The smooth political façade had cracked. "And what is she doing here? I think I'd better call my lawyer," he concluded, his voice gradually moving from bluster to decisiveness.

"By all means," Button said, gesturing toward the phone on the cluttered desk. "Go ahead and call. As for Ms. Jameson, she represents the family of the witness I mentioned."

I gave Button full points for guile. As Marcy Sheldon's lawyer, I supposed I could be fairly represented as the attorney for Dawn Ritchie's "family," but the way Button put it was misleading in the extreme. A fact that bothered me not at all as I looked into Art Lucenti's scheming face.

"Congressman," Button continued with inexorable logic, "we can and will get the phone company's records for the numbers in this office. If a phone call was made on the night

of the murder on one of these phones to or from Mrs.
Ritchie's number, we'll find out about it. If I have to do it
without your assistance, I will, but rest assured your lack of
cooperation will be duly noted."

If Art Lucenti had been a lesser mortal, the line would
have been "We can do this the easy way or the hard way." I
began to sense that part of my function here was to stand as a
symbol of the perils of the hard way. The arrest of Todd
Lessek had to be much on the congressional mind this
morning.

Art Lucenti's thought processes weren't moving very
swiftly, I thought unkindly, attributing the delay to the absence
of political advisors to weigh the pros and cons with him in
some smokey back room of the mind. But finally his eyes met
Button's, and he said, "Okay." Then he flashed me a contemptuous glance and said, "But I'll talk to you alone. Not to
her."

I opened my moth to protest, then sat back complacently.
That was the advantage, I thought, in coming with the cops.
You couldn't be thrown out.

"Please wait outside, Ms. Jameson," Button said blandly,
ignoring my fury. There was a hint of steel in his voice that
had me moving, however reluctantly, out of my chair. The
fact that I was contemplating murder apparently bothered
Button not at all.

By the time I hit the outer office, with its clacking
typewriters and smiling posters, I was mad as hell. I should
have known better, I thought sourly, pacing around the
cluttered office in my rage, than to trust a cop!

No wonder, I told myself with angry hindsight, that
Button had been so agreeable to my coming along. He'd
known instinctively that the minute things got interesting,
Lucenti would have me evicted. I looked wistfully at the
closed door. What was going on in there? I wondered. Was
Art stonewalling, was he baring his soul, was he turning on
his formidable charm? But that particular commodity, I thought
wryly, had been singularly lacking when I'd left the room.

My reflexive pacing was interrupted by the woman
who'd inspected Button's ID when we'd first come in. "Would
you like some coffee while you're waiting?" she asked.

The woman looked to be around thirty, though her
unfocused face and fluffy hairstyle made her seem younger. A

fuzzy pink sweater and heart-shaped locket added to the effect, which was less dewy youth than gauche adolescence.

I responded to the question as I always did, with an enthusiastic acceptance and a silent hope that the coffee would be drinkable. It wasn't.

"Good coffee," I lied, swallowing it with a grimace I turned into a smile. Maybe politics is catching.

The woman smiled back, and I was struck by the oddness of her mouth. She had a full, sensuous lower lip, but her upper lip was a taut line that suggested a desiccated New England spinster. Her lips looked as though they belonged to two different people—people who wouldn't like each other very much.

"I'm Donna Healy," she said, sitting down next to me on a straight-backed chair. "I've been with the congressman since his first campaign. It's hard not to worry when . . ." Her eyes strayed to the closed door, behind which her boss was facing Detective Button's no-doubt thorough cross-examination.

Donna Healy. I was sure I'd heard the name from Linda. Then I recalled bitchy remarks about one of Art's aides who'd been in love with him since the year one, but whom he treated with casual disdain. Linda, I remembered with distaste, considered the whole idea irresistibly funny.

"Detective Button's hoping the congressman can help him find whoever murdered Linda Ritchie," I explained.

"But didn't her husband—"

"That's what the police thought at first," I answered coolly, "but that was before they found out she was blackmailing everyone she knew—including the congressman."

Whatever I'd expected from Donna Healy—outraged denials, tearful sympathy—it wasn't what I got. "I knew it!" she cried excitedly. There was a flush of triumph on her unformed face, a light of vindication in her pale blue eyes. "That explains everything," she went on happily.

I caught up with her. Linda had played her little game with Donna as she had with Brad, convincing the lovesick girl that Art was giving her the special attention Donna had hungered for for years. It was, I realized with a suddenness that stopped my breath, a stunning motive for murder. And Donna had just as much access to the phones as her boss did. But would Linda have arranged to meet her co-worker at her own apartment?

"That's why he was taking her to Washington, wasn't it?" Donna asked shyly. "Linda tried to hint it was because he couldn't stand not to be with her, but I didn't believe it." Yet something in her tiny voice told me she had believed it, and it had hurt her very much.

"I always dreamed of working in Washington with Art someday," she went on. "I always knew he'd get there, even when he was only a district leader. But then we won and instead of me he picked Pete Lo Presto as his legislative aide. He said I'd be more effective in the neighborhood office, but..." Her voice trailed off.

"And his taking Linda was the last straw," I prodded sympathetically.

She nodded and swallowed hard. "But I should have known not to believe Linda about the other stuff," she said. "Art would never be unfaithful to his wife." The assertion was tempered by a good measure of regret. "He never looks at other women."

"That's not what Linda wanted people to believe." I fueled the flame of Donna's anger. "You weren't the only person she gave the wrong impression to."

This time the strange lips twisted in unmistakable bitterness. "From the day Linda first came in here, she was trouble. Little sly insinuations about how much she knew, or how she and Art did this, or Art told her that. She made such a big deal about it every time she spoke to him."

I took a shot in the dark. "Did they ever go into corners together and talk? Or meet secretly?"

Donna rolled her eyes. "She used to break in on him when he was in the middle of something and go into her helpless act. He'd ask her to wait till he was finished, but somehow she always got him to leave what he was doing and go with her."

I began to wonder about Donna's alibi for the night Linda was killed. It was far out, but Button's betrayal still rankled, and I had a quick fantasy of finding the real killer while he fooled around with the congressional red herring. But it was all too obvious that Donna's dream of a relationship with Art would in no way have been advanced by the death of Linda Ritchie. Not with the beautiful Aida around. Still, it was worth a question.

"The night Linda died," I asked innocently, "you weren't here, by any chance?"

Donna Healy's mouth tightened, and her eyes narrowed. "How did—" Then she broke off, her pale eyes widening as she remembered something.

"I *was* here," she explained. Looking toward a closed door at the rear of the office, she added, "But Her Highness sent me away."

It took a minute. "Mrs. Lucenti," I murmured, nodding sympathetically. "Did she say why she wanted you to go?"

This time the sneer wasn't merely the product of Donna's incongruous lips; she meant it. "She *said* she wanted to be alone with Art so they could work on his new committee assignments. As if that dumb PR knew anything about congressional legislation," she finished with a snort.

"Then why . . ."

Donna leaned forward, a conspirator's smile on her face. "She wanted me out of the way," she said triumphantly.

Even allowing for Donna Healy's obvious bias, there was something here that needed following up. "Was there anything about a phone call that night?" I asked tentatively.

"Was there ever!" Donna replied, still in a teenage secret-sharing mood. "I heard them talking about it the next day. Art left the headquarters early because Pete Lo Presto called, only Pete said he never called at all."

"So the congressman was out somewhere alone the night Linda died." I was thinking aloud, but my thoughts were taking the wrong direction for Donna Healy.

"You mean," she corrected sharply, "that Aida got Art out of the way. If anybody from here killed Linda, it was her."

"Why didn't you tell this to the cops?" I asked. "You certainly aren't covering up for Mrs. Lucenti."

"I wouldn't lift a finger for that lazy bitch," Donna agreed. "But Art asked me not to say anything, so . . ." She shrugged.

"Maybe he's telling the truth now," I said, glancing at the door to Art's office.

"I hope so," Donna said, flashing a look of hatred at the door behind which Aida Lucenti sat. "She deserves anything she gets."

"What makes you say that?"

"Not only is she as lazy and dumb as all her kind, she

hasn't even got any feeling for her own family." One look at Donna Healy's desk, covered with graduation pictures, first Communion photos, baby pictures, showed what a cardinal sin ignoring family was in her book.

"They go to Puerto Rico once a year to see her relatives," Donna went on. "But Art *makes* her go. She said last year it made her sad to see how poor they were, but he said it would look bad if she neglected them, so they went. She won't even stay in their house," Donna confided, a superior smile on her lips. "She has to have a fancy hotel with a swimming pool."

I pretended to think about Donna's accusation. "And she turned down that job, too," I recalled.

"That shows you how lazy she is," Donna commented. "She nagged Art over and over for something she could do to help his campaign. Of course, the best thing she could do would be to give him a divorce, but..."

I gave the remark the perfunctory laugh she expected, and Donna went on, "So he told her about this job on the mayor's commission and she got real excited about it. She couldn't wait to start, only then the bad publicity happened. Then when that was over and he'd fought like a tiger to get her accepted, she up and says she's not interested anymore."

"Perhaps all the publicity made her nervous," I pointed out.

"That's what she *said*," Donna countered, "but what she really wanted was plenty of time to go to the beauty parlor or the health spa without having to work. Art tried to convince her, to show her how bad it looked, her backing out after he fought so hard to get her the job—which was her idea in the first place!"

"How did she get along with Linda?"

"Linda hated her," Donna said simply. "She called her all kinds of names behind her back."

"What about to her face? What kind of relationship did they have?"

Donna shrugged; now that the conversation had moved from Art to Aida, her interest was waning noticeably.

"Were there any of those private conversations like she had with Art?"

Donna's forehead puckered with thought. "I did see a note once," she finally confessed. "I always knew," she added cattily, "that Aida was illiterate, but even a Puerto Rican ought to be able to spell *Linda*, don't you think?"

"So they wrote notes," I said. "They didn't talk to one another?"

"Not like Linda and Art."

Which made sense, I thought. If Linda wanted the illusion of intimacy with Art, she'd engineer private little meetings that would have the extra advantage of driving Donna Healy up the wall. Her treatment of Aida, too, was reminiscent of her previous pattern of tormenting Duncan Pitt with phone calls to his wife. If ghetto-educated Aida Valentin Lucenti·was uncomfortable with written English, then Linda would demand notes—and then probably show them to Donna to get a quick laugh. I was suddenly tired of Donna's juvenile jealousy.

"You said Mrs. Lucenti's here?"

Donna nodded. "She's probably doing her nails," she added waspishly, "while her husband covers up for her with the police."

23

Aida Valentin Lucenti was not doing her nails, or much of anything else, when I walked into the little room. She sat at an empty desk, her eyes not quite focused on a pile of dust-covered campaign signs in the corner of the room, drumming expertly manicured fingers on the scarred desktop.

"Well?" she asked sharply. "Have they arrested him yet?"

Taken aback, I said the first words that occurred to me. "Should they?"

"Look, don't cop an attitude." The worried frown that creased her forehead took the edge off the ghetto-blunt words. "Just tell me what's going down, okay?"

"I don't know," I answered, making for the only other

chair in the room. "Honestly," I added, lifting a haphazard pile of invitations to a long-ago fundraiser. Putting the pile on the desk, I said, "They threw me out as soon as things got interesting," and sat down.

Something in my face must have told Aida she'd come on a little strong. Stopping her rhythmic drumming, she waved a hand deprecatingly. "Don't mind me," she said with an attempted smile, "it's just my nerves. I hate to think of Art having to go through all that on top of everything else."

"You mean on top of Todd Lessek's arrest?"

Aida's face tightened. Her trademark dark glasses hid much of her face, but the rest closed up behind unmistakable security gates. "What happens to Mr. Lessek," she pronounced coldly, "does not concern my husband in the least." She opened a gold cigarette case and took out a cigarette with an air of indifference spoiled by the slight tremor of her hand.

"Then why," I asked ingenuously, "do you think the police will arrest your husband?"

She gave me a distinctly unfriendly look. "You should know," she replied with a disdainful shrug. "You're the one who stirred up all the trouble." She tapped the cigarette against the gold case, then lit it with a matching lighter.

"What I want to know," she continued, breathing smoke, "is why? Why are you trying to destroy my husband?" The businesslike tone, the hard face, were wholly at variance with her dusky skin, her sensuous figure. She was like a tropical princess, unaccountably attired in a pinstriped business suit.

The accusation stunned me. I just sat and stared at this women whose cool words were like ice on a volcano of deep emotions.

I went on the attack. "Where were you," I asked calmly, "the night Linda was killed?"

At first I thought the volcano was about to explode. Then she smiled and said, "Here," looking around at the empty room. She went on to explain, confirming what Donna had said. "We had work to do. Art's got a lot of bills to study to get ready for his committee work in the House. We were going to get in a pizza and work late, like we used to do when he first went into politics." There was a slight, reminiscent smile on her face, and I had a quick vision of a romantic young couple eating take-out food and working together on a common dream. It was hardly the picture as painted by jealous Donna Healy, but I could see it clearly enough that Aida's words rang true.

"Then the phone rang," she went on. "I knew it was trouble because Art took it in the other room." She gestured toward Art's private office. "Then he came back and said he had to go out for a while, but he'd be back."

"Do you know who called?" My heart was pounding, but I tried to keep my voice steady.

Her mouth twisted into a wry smile. "I thought I did. He gave me the impression it was Pete Lo Presto, his new L.A. Legislative aide," she explained with a slightly condescending smile. I didn't mind; it probably wasn't often that ghetto-educated Aida Lucenti got a chance to show off her knowledge.

"Did Art tell you it was him?"

"Not in so many words," she admitted. "But he let me believe it. So I stayed and worked—"

"Alone," I pointed out.

"Alone," she agreed.

"And the phone call—did Pete Lo Presto make it?"

She shook her head, and looked at the ground. "No," she said. "He wasn't even home. I found out later he was at the club all night, planning a dinner to pay off Art's campaign debts. And he told me Art hadn't been anywhere near the club that night."

"You think your husband got a call from Linda Ritchie, went over there to confront her, and ended up killing her?"

No answer. From a woman of her passionate loyalty, the failure to defend was a confession.

Finally, words came, spoken flatly through a dry throat. "Why should he kill her?" Aida asked. "He was giving the little *puta* what she wanted."

"Maybe he got tired of paying Linda off," I suggested. "Maybe he was afraid she'd never stop and he'd be bled dry."

Aida's face was blandly indifferent; my arrow was wide of the mark.

"Or maybe she wanted more than money," I went on, thinking of Donna Healy's reference to secret meetings. "Maybe she wanted Art himself."

Aida snorted her contempt. "She was a fool—a bitch and a fool," Aida proclaimed. "Art had no desire to make love to a child-woman." Sexual pride enveloped Aida like a musky perfume.

"Maybe not," I shot back, "but if the alternative were exposure—"

"Then of course, he would have done it," she shrugged. "Did you think," she added, the taunting note dominant now, "that he would kill to protect his virtue?"

"Would he kill to protect his wife?" I asked. "Would he kill to protect you?"

Bull's-eye. I had the dubious satisfaction of watching the complacency leave her face, to be replaced by a perfect mask. A hollow tree without a solitary bird to cheer its bleakness.

She recovered quickly. "Why should he have to?" But the voice was a croak.

"Because of this." I pulled the last of the blackmail material out of my purse and put it on the desk. Gray-faced, Aida turned the pages with trembling fingers, then faced me and asked, "The police—do they know"—her scarlet forefinger tapped her criminal record—"about this?"

I shook my head.

"I understand," she sighed, her tone weary. Her shoulders sagged; the body she so meticulously maintained with her regular sessions at the spa was suddenly limp, flabby. "*Now*," she nodded with certainty, "now you are ready to name your price."

I decided to go with the moment. "I understand," I began, carefully noncommittal, "that there are lots of opportunities for a lawyer in Washington. Not to mention," I went on, noting the cynical gleam in my companion's smile, "on the federal bench." The thought of becoming a judge has never appealed to me, but I'd begun to wonder just how high a price she would pay—or convince Art to pay—in order to bury her past.

"I'm sure something can be arranged," she purred. She was in control again, the color back in her cheeks, the hollow look replaced by a sleek confidence. "Just so long as the police know nothing of this."

"They don't," I said crisply. "Button would kill me, but they don't. And they aren't going to and you don't have to bribe me. I'm not a blackmailer."

The surprise on her face was accompanied by a flash of anger. "Then why are you playing games with me?"

"I'm not," I sighed. "I only want one thing, and that's the person who killed Linda Ritchie. It's clear that you and your husband had reason to want her dead. Look what you were willing to give me to keep your past quiet. Wouldn't Art have gone after Linda if he'd known what she was doing to you?"

As I watched Aida Valentin Lucenti search her soul for an answer, I knew I was looking at a tormented human being. Her face was ashen, her melon-tinged lips twisted in agony. She stared at the pile of dusty posters, her fingers again doing their unconscious drumming.

She'd already answered the question, I realized, whatever she chose to say. I wondered whether she would put her reply into words, or let her body speak for her. Finally, she turned to me, her face a mixture of resignation and pleading. "He might," she whispered, "he might."

It was like glimpsing an enormous room through a tiny peephole. Behind the glossy façade, under the hard-seeming exterior, was a terribly frightened woman. She, as much as I, as much as Detective Button, had come to believe that Art Lucenti had killed Linda Ritchie.

The Flaherty living room had seen a hasty clearing of children. On the colorful rag rug lay a Cabbage Patch doll that must have been Jenny's, a chemistry set I couldn't believe Chris was old enough for, and a pull toy of baby Andy's. From upstairs I could hear the sounds of reluctant kids being put to bed—splashes from the bath, cries of "Where's my Teddy?" and, from Chris's room, a plaintive plea to pipe down so he could hear "Knight Rider."

Pat, lowering his bulk onto the chintz-covered sofa, smiled apologetically. "The joys of fatherhood," he joked.

The kids had left the downstairs TV on. In spite of myself, I was drawn to it. Pat saw my eyes stray to the screen and kidded, "You and Todd Lessek won't be on tonight, Cass. That's yesterday's news."

"It's not that," I responded absently, my attention caught by the news story. "Here it comes." I pointed as Peter Jennings showed the clip.

Flaherty grunted his understanding as the tape rolled. Hundreds of paralyzed veterans were demonstrating in Washington to protest budget cutbacks. They carried signs demanding access to public buildings and increased aid for the disabled. I scanned the screen for a familiar face.

"Your brother went to the demo?" Pat asked interestedly.

I nodded. "He said he was going. With his roommate Gene Kavanaugh and their companion. They have a special van."

The vets were orderly, even cheerful, in their militancy. They wore parts of uniforms—Army jackets, caps, even Green Berets, dotted the crowd. Most were wheelchair-bound; some, like my brother Ron, were quadriplegics, unable to move their own chairs. They were either motorized or pushed by buddies. The signs read BUILD RAMPS, NOT BOMBS, and ACCESS NOW! A spokesman talked, his voice cracking from the cold, of the way vets felt about being denied access to housing, to public buildings, to veterans' benefits, in the country for which they'd given so much. I was moved, and I tried to see Ron in the crowd, but I saw only people who reminded me of him.

"How's he doing?" Pat asked, "since he left the VA hospital?"

I turned and smiled. "Great," I replied, "really great. He's heavily into computers. He's got one of his own, and he's taking classes at Kent. They've got a special computer program for the disabled. Plus he's into ham radio. He can't get out of his chair, but he can talk to Switzerland." I shook my head in admiration.

"And," I went on, warming to the subject, "he and Gene have a new attendant. He's a real character. His name is Zack and he's a Vietnam vet who went from drugs to Jesus, so you never know whether he's going to say 'Praise the Lord' or 'Fuck you' in any given situation." I joined in Pat's appreciative laughter. "Zack and Gene are both born-agains; Ron says it's like living in a revival meeting, but they really seem pretty happy together."

"You saw him over Christmas?"

"Yeah," I said, looking away. Christmas was a minefield of emotions. Happiness is relative, and I still felt a searing pain when I saw my once-tall brother folded into an electric wheelchair. I wasn't ready to talk about it, not even to as old a friend as Pat Flaherty.

"I think Art Lucenti killed Linda," I said abruptly.

"I thought you had your money on Todd Lessek," Pat

replied. He went along with the change of subject with a grace I was grateful for.

"If I did," I smiled wanly, "I guess I lost it. Lessek's hanging tough, denying it all. So's Bellfield, and he's already admitted every other crime in the book."

"Why would Art kill her? Because he was being blackmailed?"

"Or because he found out Aida was." My enthusiasm was returning, my voice becoming animated as I began to make my case. "You and I may not think her record was so bad," I explained, "but for Art to see her put through hell in the press—"

"What about Nilda?"

"Who's Nilda?"

"Nilda Vargas, Aida's co-defendant."

"Nilda—oh, the name I saw written on Aida's rap sheet. What about her?"

"You really don't know, do you?"

"Know what? Pat"—I was getting exasperated—"what are you talking about?"

"I can't believe you don't know. Nilda Vargas was notorious, for God's sake."

"Why?" I all but shouted, my patience exhausted.

"She killed people."

24

"My God." I stopped the bentwood rocker and tried to take it in. "Who'd she kill? And where is she now?"

"She's dead," Pat replied in a flat voice unlike his own. "Died of an overdose. As to who she killed—I don't remember names or anything. There were too many, for one thing." His mouth twisted. "The papers called it a 'crime spree.' They nicknamed her and her boyfriend 'the South Bronx Bonnie and Clyde.'" Pat's tone was sarcastic and bitter. "I can't believe you don't remember it!" he exclaimed. "It was a huge media circus. The Son of Sam of its day."

"Just what 'day' are we talking about?"

"Oh, God. Nineteen seventy, seventy-one. Somewhere in there."

"I was probably still in college in Ohio," I reminded him, "not paying much attention to the New York crime scene."

"It was her being a girl that caused the publicity storm," he explained. "Otherwise, it would have been a routine story. Nelson Rodriguez"—he had begun to assume a lecturing tone—"was the leader of a two-bit gang called the Savage Machos." He cleared his throat. "Nilda Vargas became his girl. She was good at roles, Nilda—she played one for me, all right," he added, with a note of anger I couldn't understand. "Only for me she played the good little client, always coming to court on time, going to see her probation officer, that kind of thing. With Nelson, she played gang sweetheart, Macho Deb all the way—leather miniskirt, gang colors—the whole bit. Down to going with him on his robberies. Small businessmen, mostly on the Grand Concourse, and there were plenty of liquor stores, delis, cleaning stores, just ripe for the picking. The Machos would make the customers hit the floor and when they had the money, they'd shoot everyone in the head. Didn't matter if they were young or old or pregnant women or how much they begged them, the proprietor would get it. Didn't matter that he'd given them all he had without a fight; he was dead the minute they walked into his place."

"Jesus," I said. "Nice people."

"Yeah," he agreed sourly. "Finally, one of the victims lived. He led the cops to Nelson Rodriguez and the gang."

"Including Nilda Vargas?"

"Nilda was never caught," he explained. "Her body was found a few months later in a shooting gallery. Dead of an overdose."

"And she and Aida were co-defendants," I mused out loud. "So in addition to her criminal record, Aida faces guilt by association with Nilda Vargas."

"It gets better," Pat said. His face was chalky white above the red beard; the freckles that dotted his face in summer had faded. "It wasn't widely known, but Aida Valentin was living in the abandoned building where Nilda died."

"So Aida harbored a fugitive? A little accessory-after-the-fact stuff?"

Pat's answering smile was sardonic. "The penal law prefers to call it criminal facilitation."

"Is it enough to kill for?"

Pat shrugged. "Maybe," he replied. "Put it together with the rest of the stuff, picture it splashed all over the *Post*. If it had come out during the campaign, Art would have been spending a lot of time defending his wife instead of getting elected."

"But that brings it back to the damned election!" I hit the arm of the chair in frustration.

"What's that mean?"

I gave him the same reasoning Duncan Pitt the fire marshal had laid on me. "Which means," I concluded, "that Art had a hell of a motive to kill Linda before November, but a pretty weak one in January."

"Maybe it just piled up," Pat suggested. His face was drawn in thought. "This Linda liked to turn the screws, you said?"

I nodded, recalling her many petty cruelties.

"Does Art know Linda was blackmailing Aida?" Pat asked.

I thought about it. "No," I said definitely. "Aida seemed very concerned that Art shouldn't know."

"Does Art know about Aida's past?"

I shook my head slowly. "I don't think so," I said. "I don't have any reason, just a feeling."

"On the other hand"—Pat was beginning to sound like a Jesuit—"Aida may think she's kept her secret, but what if Linda told Art the truth—and Art went berserk when he realized Linda was squeezing Aida?"

"I like it," I said, my mind conjuring up a sharp visual memory of Aida, sitting in the dusty little room, brooding on the possibility of her husband's guilt. "I could see that. Art's got a kind of old-fashioned machismo that says you take it on the chin for yourself, but you die to protect the womenfolk."

"The note you mentioned," Pat began slowly, "what if Art found one, realized what Linda was up to—"

"The note!" I cried. I calmed down and told Pat about

Donna Healy's supercilious amusement at Aida's poor spelling. "But what if the name wasn't *Linda* spelled wrong, but *Nilda?*" I finished in triumph. "That would prove Aida was being blackmailed over the Nilda business."

Pat wasn't with me. Not entirely. He gazed into his fireplace with a faraway expression on his face. "God, Nilda," he laughed. "Even dead thirteen years, that girl's trouble. The shortest miniskirts and the tallest platform shoes in the South Bronx—and that was saying something. She was sharp and funny. I swear if she hadn't become Nelson's girl, she could have been anything she wanted to be."

"Sounds like you had more than a lawyer-client relationship," I commented.

"We were all pretty gung-ho in those days," he answered with a smile. "We were going to save the South Bronx single-handed. You may be too young to remember."

What I remembered was an idealistic college student who'd gone into the tomato fields of Northwest Ohio to help the migrant farmworkers and had gotten a bigger dose of radical politics than she'd bargained for. "I remember."

"Okay. Then you know how we all felt. Part of it was that the traditional distance between lawyer and client made no sense in that context. We were close to our clients as people, and proud of it. So when Nilda started hanging around the office, doing me favors, bringing me little things, it seemed okay. I was glad that she was going to school and seeing her probation officer and staying out of trouble because she wanted my approval. What I didn't see"—he looked away, his face deadly serious—"was that she wanted something else—something I couldn't give."

"Like what?" I thought I knew, but I wanted it from him.

"She was a ghetto kid," he explained. His face was pinched and his voice tight. "She knew more about sex at fifteen than I did at twenty-five—and my two years in the seminary didn't help one bit. I was a naïve idiot and the only person in the office who didn't see what was happening.

"It was Christmas," he went on, clearing his throat. "We had a tree in the office. Red and green balls and somebody's leftover Christmas lights. Nilda hung two Christmas balls from her ears like huge glowing earrings and then pranced and danced all around the office, her little ass bouncing under that skirt. She was all over me, Cass. Perching on my desk, sitting in my lap, running her fingers through my hair. Even I had to get the picture. Everyone kidded me about her anyway, but finally I couldn't stand it. I told her to keep her hands to herself. She got mad, called me filthy names in Spanish, and stormed out of the office. The next thing I heard," he said with a shrug, "she'd started going with Nelson Rodriguez. No more school, no more probation—just meaner and meaner crimes."

I sounded a skeptical note. "All that, just because you—"

"Just because I rejected her as a woman?" Pat's tone was harsh, but it was directed at himself as well as me. "Because that's how *she* saw it. She was a kid under all that sex—a kid with her first crush on an adult male who should have known how to handle it. But I didn't. I made it worse."

· I said nothing, but I hoped the look I was giving him expressed my sympathy. I decided it didn't and reached out my hand. He took it with a rueful smile.

"I tried to talk to her," Pat went on, his voice tight, "but she was finished with me. She just laughed and called me *maricón*." Spanish for "queer." It figured.

"It sounds to me," I said tentatively, "as though the real problem wasn't that she came on to you, but that you responded. You wanted her, but you couldn't admit it to yourself."

Pat's face reddened and he snapped, "Thank you for the pop psychology, Cass, but I've managed to figure out that little insight all by myself."

It was my turn to blush. "I'm sorry," I said. "I didn't mean to sound like a smartass."

Pat sighed. "I remember at the time feeling good that I'd withstood temptation. Saint Patrick of the Slums wrestling with the devil." He gave a wan, bitter smile. "It was only later—much later—that I realized how in saving my own soul, I'd lost Nilda's."

There wasn't much more to be said. I thought about the young Pat Flaherty, the young Nilda Vargas, the young Aida Valentin. None of my thoughts, however, seemed to bring me any closer to the killer of Linda Ritchie.

Then it hit me. A chill ran through me in spite of the fire in Pat's fireplace.

"Pat," I croaked, "what if the woman we think is Aida Valentin Lucenti is really Nilda Vargas? What if she's not dead?"

"Too much TV, Cass," Pat protested, waving a pudgy hand. "That's crazy."

"Is it? What about—"

"Cass!" Flaherty was getting angry. "I knew them!"

"How many years ago?" I shot back. "You said yourself that Aida's changed."

"Yes, but not . . ." he broke off, lost in thought.

I pressed my advantage. "That would explain her running away from you at the fundraiser," I urged. "She was afraid you'd recognize her close-up."

Pat remained silent. I continued to think out loud. "It fits, Pat, it really does. Remember those discrepancies in Aida's application to the drug program? They make sense if you realize that *Nilda* was trying her best to remember the details of *Aida*'s past. It also explains how she became the star of the drug program—she was never an addict to begin with!"

Other details began to come back to me, details Donna Healy had put her own interpretation on, but which now had a new significance. "It explains why Mrs. Lucenti's not too keen on visiting the relatives in Puerto Rico. They're Aida's family, but she plays the Nuyorican so they think she's just Aida gone Anglo."

When Flaherty finally spoke, it was with a hollow voice that told me he was taking the possibility very seriously. "It was summer when she died," he said, "and the body was there for over a week. Bodies swell in the heat, and the maggots come. Not to mention the rats." I had the distinct feeling this was not the first time he had thought about a body rotting in a South Bronx tenement. "Nilda's mother was a junkie," he continued, lifting anguished blue eyes to meet mine. "She'd have identified anything they put in front of her as a daughter."

"And the medical examiner does a fingerprint check only when he hasn't got a family member's ID," I remembered. Pat gave me a funny look, but said nothing. Then I recalled the rats: no fingers, no fingerprints.

"All she had to do," Pat said, "was switch their clothes and identification. They looked enough alike that they could

pass for one another if you didn't know them," he added.
"And jewelry," I agreed slowly. It was a grisly thought. One
girl pulling earrings out of dead ears and putting them into
her own, then putting her own gold rings through the holes
in the dead girl's ears.

"Pat," I exclaimed, "when did Nilda die?"

"August." He frowned with concentration. "August—
somewhere around the fifteenth. I remember going to church—
holy day of obligation."

Whatever that was. "Aida applied to the drug program
on the eleventh of August," I said.

"But could she really pass herself off as Aida?" Skepti-
cism was returning to Pat's face and voice.

I gave it serious thought. "She'd have Aida's birth certifi-
cate and her Medicaid card. She deliberately went to another
borough, where she wasn't known. And—"

"And she changed her looks," Pat finished. "New hairstyle,
modeling classes. She didn't look like the old Aida *or* the old
Nilda. She was okay as long as she didn't get busted."

"Fingerprints!" I all but shouted. "That's it! That's the
clincher. That no-show job that caused all the fuss?" Pat
nodded. "She *had* to quit that job. They were after her to
come in and be fingerprinted. It's routine."

"It's routine"—Pat shook his head—"unless you happen
to be wanted for murder under another name."

I took my thoughts one step further. "Linda," I said
confidently. "I'll bet that's what started her wondering—and
snooping. She was working for Art when the whole no-show
job thing blew up. She must have sensed that Aida was
afraid, and, with her instinct for the jugular, she decided to
find out why."

"But how would she have known about Nilda?" Pat
asked. It wasn't an objection, I realized, just a question.

I answered it with one of my own. "Did Nilda Vargas
have adult arrests? On-the-record stuff, not sealed?"

Pat nodded.

I explained. "There was a second NYSIIS number scrawled
on Aida's rap sheet along with Nilda's name. Linda could
have checked it, seen Nilda's record, and her physical description, and—"

Pat interrupted. "You know those dark glasses Aida
always wears?"

Puzzled, I nodded.

"Nilda's eyes were green," he said with finality. "Bright green in a dark Spanish face. You couldn't miss them."

25

Eight inches. School-closing weather in the city; a dusting back in my snowbelt Ohio hometown. I sighed and stretched my arms to the ceiling. No lazy Saturday for me. Shoveling was the first priority. The last thing in the world I could afford was a lawsuit.

I went for my coat, but before I put it on, I looked long and hard at the telephone. To call or not to call. To warn or not to warn. I'd been through it all with Flaherty the night before.

"We could be wrong," he'd said quietly, his face troubled. I'd felt a rush of pleasure at the "we," but I also heard the pain in his voice. "And if we are, if everything in her past is raked up for nothing..." He'd broken off and looked at me with a face full of misery. "I'd feel like a first-class bastard," he said, his voice low.

I remembered being sharp with Flaherty, reminding him that Nilda Vargas had been no saint, and that somebody had killed Linda Ritchie. I hadn't said in so many words that I was going straight to the cops, but I'd implied it.

Now I wasn't so sure. The theory that had seemed so brilliant the night before looked pretty thin in the light of morning. Maybe Aida Lucenti *did* deserve a chance to explain. I picked up the phone.

I put it down again. What, I asked myself, was I planning to say to her? And what if the phone was answered not by Aida, but by Art? Part of me still considered him the prime suspect; I didn't think he'd appreciate my interest in him or his wife.

My afternoon in Lucenti's headquarters came back to me. I'd picked up a flyer from the edge of Donna Healy's desk. I fished it out of my purse and read that Art was planning to appear at a rally to save a neighborhood firehouse in Fort Greene. I smiled sourly; given his track record, I decided wryly, Todd Lessek probably had plans to turn the firehouse into a luxury co-op.

Then I remembered Donna Healy's bitchy remark about Aida's penchant for coming to the office in the early morning. At the time, I'd assumed she did it to see Linda in private, but now I wondered whether instead it was a way for Aida to be close to her husband's work without running the gauntlet of jealousy put up by all the Donna Healys who worked for Art.

I dialed again, a different number this time. I let the phone ring a long time and was finally rewarded with a "hello" that had a definite tinge of Spanish.

"Mrs. Lucenti?" I asked, getting a murmured yes in response. I plunged ahead. "This is Cassandra Jameson. I was in your husband's office yesterday?" I made it a question although I was sure there was no danger of her forgetting.

"I remember," she replied in a voice that was cool, ironic. I could picture a touch of amusement on her face.

"I'd like to talk to you again," I said. "There are some new developments we should discuss." I was talking, I thought with an inner smile, as though the phone were tapped. The smile left my lips when I realized it probably was.

"I don't believe we have anything more to say to each other." She said it nicely, still with an undertone of amusement.

"Oh, I think we do," I countered softly. "You see, I talked to Pat Flaherty last night. He told me all about a girl you and he used to know—Nilda Vargas. Of course," I added insinuatingly, "you knew her better than he did—a lot better."

Silence. The sound of breathing. Maybe a heartbeat, but that may have been imagination.

Then the question. "Have you told anyone else?"

"No," I said, keeping my voice level. "I wanted to talk to you first."

"Come here," she ordered, her tone ragged. "Right away."

"As soon as I can," I promised, putting down the receiver with a bang.

I could have won a gold medal for Olympic speed-shoveling. Eight inches never disappeared so quickly.

I dashed back into the office to deposit the shovel and take a quick trip to the bathroom. I almost ignored the ringing phone, but then picked it up, thinking it might be Aida Lucenti.

It wasn't. It was Marcy Sheldon, sounding more agitated than I'd ever heard her.

"Cass, is that you?" Her voice was strident. "Cass, it's awful. I don't know what to think, what to do. You've got to help me."

"Marcy, I'm on my way out. Can I call you—"

"It's Dawn," she wailed, cutting off my protests. "She's run away."

My first thought was: Not now! My second was that it didn't surprise me in the least. Dawn must have felt so alone, so rejected ever since she'd heard Marcy's plan to send her to boarding school. Running away must have seemed the only alternative. But now, I decided reluctantly, was hardly the time to lecture Marcy Sheldon on her shortcomings as a guardian.

"Where'd she go?" I asked. "Florida?" I was thinking of the tennis academy she'd described with such longing.

"Of course not!" Marcy snapped. "How could a twelve-year-old get to Florida?"

If she didn't know, I wasn't going to tell her. "Did she leave a note?"

"Yes, I have it here. She says—"

"Can you read it to me?" I interrupted. "I'd like her exact words."

I got Dawn's words but with her aunt's exasperated, I'm-wasting-precious-time-here tone of voice.

"'Dear Aunt Marcy,'" she read, "'You and Cass don't care about my daddy being in jail for something he didn't do, but I do. I care a lot. So I'm going to find the man who killed

Mom, and then the police will have to let Daddy go. P.S., When he gets out, I can live with him. Love, Dawn.' "

It took me a minute to get over the hurt of Dawn's "you and Cass." How could she, I wondered, lump me in with the aunt who threatened her with boarding school? Then I realized that in her eyes I too had promised but I hadn't delivered. I guessed that made me about even with Marcy.

"I wonder where she's gone," I mused aloud. "And what she means by—" I broke off as an awful thought struck me. "Do you suppose she'd try to find Art Lucenti?"

"Why would she do a crazy thing like that?" I didn't let Marcy's scornful tone bother me; it was clear she was worried as hell.

"She thinks he killed Linda," I explained. I did some fast thinking. With any luck, Dawn would have gone to the Lucentis' house, or even to Detective Button. But there was a chance she was headed for the same place I was—Art Lucenti's campaign office, where she'd meet the woman who might or might not have killed several people under the name Nilda Vargas. It was becoming more imperative than ever that I get the truth.

"After all I've done"—Marcy's words held all the bitterness that choice of words usually conveys—"she wants to live with that worthless father of hers."

"You can bet he won't send her to boarding school," I shot back.

I regretted the words as soon as I'd said them. Maybe Marcy's coldness was the root cause of Dawn's running away, but now wasn't the time to discuss it.

"I'm sorry," I said at once, cutting into Marcy's passionate defense of her position. "I shouldn't have said that."

"You know," Marcy said after a pause, "when this is over, I think maybe I'd better hire another lawyer."

"That's fine with me," I said crisply, trying not to think about the prospect of never seeing Dawn again. "But meanwhile, there's something you should know."

I told her everything—Art, Aida, Nilda—the whole sordid package. It wasn't easy—I had to talk through a minefield of interruptions, denials, accusations. Yet frustrating as it was, I knew I was doing the right thing. Marcy had a right to know the danger Dawn might be in. And if part of me hoped that the thought of such danger would soften Marcy's frozen emotions, then so be it.

"Listen, Marcy," I concluded, "I'm on my way over to the headquarters right now. If Dawn calls you or comes home, *don't*, under any circumstances, let her go to Lucenti's. And," I added, taking a deep breath, "if I don't call you in two hours, get the police. Two hours," I repeated, "not before and not after."

I hung up before I could get more arguments. Then I called the number on the firehouse flyer. No, Congressman Lucenti wasn't there yet. Yes, he was still expected. Yes (with a sigh), a message could be left. I lowered my voice and tried to sound impressive as I told the message-taker that Art was urgently needed at his office. His wife, I said ominously, was in trouble and needed him right away. My urgency seemed to impress; I was assured the congressman would get the message the minute he walked in the door.

Next call: the Henry Street Car Service. Yellow cabs don't cruise Brooklyn looking for fares; everyone calls the car service. Including the crooks—I'd once represented a gang of armed robbers who'd made their getaway in a car-service vehicle and then wondered why they were so easily traced. It was smart thinking like that that had netted them five-to-fifteen apiece.

I jumped into the car as soon as it pulled up and gave the address. Adrenaline rushed through my body. I felt as if I were starting to pick a jury in a felony case. I had the same sense of being in a complicated game where brains and nerve were equally crucial, that same anything-can-happen feeling, that same smell of adventure in the air. I tried to tell myself it wasn't healthy to enjoy the feeling, but it didn't help. It was what street cops felt; it was why they loved wearing the tin.

I paid the driver with a perfunctory smile, then got out and forced myself to walk instead of run toward the campaign office. The door was locked; I knocked loudly and waited, tapping my foot with impatience.

Aida Lucenti opened the door a crack, then opened it wider and let me in. Her face looked haggard under the oversized sunglasses. For a wild, hysterical second I wanted to rip them off her face and reveal her green eyes.

I didn't. I didn't have to. Her face told me the truth. It was an exposed face now, the makeup and the contoured cheekbones insufficient to gloss over the street-smart South Bronx toughness.

"Good morning, Mrs. Lucenti," I said formally, then added, "or should I call you Nilda?"

26

If there's one thing I know on God's green earth, it's how to talk to skells.

She began with bluster. "Nilda's dead," she announced with a sullen, defiant edge to her voice. Her stance was wary, at odds with the designer suit and blood-red silk blouse.

"Don't bullshit me, Nilda," I said with bluff good humor. Speaking not to the sophisticated façade but to the scared ghetto kid inside, I went on, "It's like I tell my clients. You can fool some of the people all of the time and all of the people some of the time, but you can't fool your lawyer any of the time."

"What proof you got?" she challenged, beginning to walk around the room. Her movements were lithe, sinuous, unthinking—like a cat's. "I tell you what proof—none." She rapped her knuckles on the passing desk for emphasis. "And I tell you why—there's no proof 'cause there's no truth."

I watched her with a deliberate stare that started a tiny blush across her dusky cheeks. "You know," I said conversationally, "you really are beginning to sound like one of my criminal clients. The kind who never says he isn't guilty—he just says the cops didn't see him do the crime. I'll tell you what I tell them: It's not much of a defense. Besides," I added, looking at my purse on the floor, "how do you know what I can and can't prove?"

"Prove it, then," she snapped, resuming her pacing. A caged panther in an Anne Klein suit.

"What's the point?" I asked, my tone deliberately weary. "Your fingerprints will tell the whole story. Either you're really Aida Valentin or you're not." I shrugged my indifference to the outcome.

She stopped moving. As still as an animal in hiding, she whispered, "They can't fingerprint me unless I'm under arrest. That's the law."

"Good," I approved. "You'll make a terrific jailhouse lawyer, Nilda."

"Stop calling me that!" There was a note of near-hysteria in her voice that told me I was coming close to provoking the mental state I wanted her in.

"The only problem with that reasoning," I continued in the same unhurried voice, "is that you could be arrested any minute. If not for the murder of Linda Ritchie, then on the old Nilda Vargas warrants. The cops could arrest you, print you, and then"—I locked eyes with her—"if you're really Aida, you get an apology from the mayor and a nice big lawsuit for false arrest. On the other hand, if you're Nilda..."

I didn't have to finish. The despair in her face told me mayoral apologies wouldn't be necessary.

She started pacing again. Faster this time, with stiffer, more constricted movements. It was as if the panther had been moved to a smaller cage.

Finally, she confronted me. The defiance was back in her face in full force, but I was experienced enough to know it masked surrender. "Okay," she announced, "so I'm Nilda Vargas. That doesn't men I killed Linda."

"What about that phone call—the one that got your husband out of the office?"

"It was from Linda," she replied. "He lied when he told me it was from Pete."

"Is that what you told the police?"

Her melon-tinted lip curled with contempt. "Of course not. Do you think I would betray him?" She was genuinely indignant. It was either a sincere belief that Art was guilty, or a very clever acting job by a known killer. As far as I was concerned, the jury was still out.

"Why don't we sit down?" I suggested, "and talk about your legal position?"

Nilda seemed reluctant to give up her freedom to move, but she docilely sat on a hard chair next to the desk. I went behind it and sat in the swivel chair. The lawyer-client relationship having been reinforced, I got down to business.

"If you didn't kill Linda," I began, "then all you have to worry about are the old warrants."

"All I have to worry about," she repeated with a sardonic laugh. "Lady, those warrants weren't for shoplifting. They were for murder."

"It was a long time ago," I pointed out. "Who knows whether the DA could make out a case or not anymore? Witnesses die, cops retire. There may be no statute of limitations on murder, but that doesn't mean the DA's got an automatic conviction."

"You think I could beat the cases?" I tried not to smile. I'd heard those words many different times in many different contexts, but never from a woman who dressed better than I.

"I didn't say that," I cautioned. "I'd have to know more. But there could be a good chance of pleading to manslaughter, at least. Who's still around from the gang, for one thing? They could help you or hurt you, depending on whether any of them needs a break from the DA's office."

She wrinkled her forehead in thought. "Nelson's dead," she said, no part of her conveying the slightest hint that she was talking about her former lover. "He got stabbed upstate. I don't know about he rest. But a lot of them were junkies and they were all into fighting and shit like that, so they could be dead too."

"Well, that's the first step," I said. "Find out what kind of case the DA has. Then there's the question of what you did—you personally, not the gang—to cause those people's deaths. Did you ever take part in the killing?"

She shook her head. Behind the dark glasses, her eyes were wide. "I was too scared," she said in a small voice. "I tried not to let Nelson see because he wanted his woman to be strong, but it made me sick. All I wanted to do was run away and throw up, but I had to stand there and look anyway. Because that was what Nelson wanted."

"And you always did what Nelson wanted," I said wryly. Not my favorite defense: The devil made me do it. But then I considered Nilda's sultry good looks, suitably toned down by her business clothes. Young impressionable girl, mother a junkie, led astray by an older man. An older man who happened to be a vicious killer who liked an admiring audience for his crimes.

I recalled Pat Flaherty's remark, "She was good at roles,

Nilda." She'd been a Galatea in search of a Pygmalion. First Pat, then Nelson, then the rising young lawyer Art Lucenti. For each she'd unearthed and developed a new personality. What I wondered was, how far had she gone to prove to her killer lover that she was his kind of woman?

"I suppose you were afraid of Nelson sometimes," I murmured.

Nilda picked up her cue; she'd be great on direct. "Of course," she said, her voice low. "He said he'd kill me if I tried to leave him. He said no woman ever walked out on Nelson Rodriguez."

"And did you," I asked, "try to leave?"

"Once," she whispered. "He cut me." She looked up, her face pleading. "I could show you the scar," she offered.

I shook my head. "Not now," I replied, abstracted by the vision of Nilda in the witness box, modestly unbuttoning her silk blouse to reveal a nasty, jagged scar. *"Ladies and gentlemen of the jury, Nilda Vargas* tried *to leave the depraved killer who made her an unwilling partner in his crimes—and look what he did to her! Is it any wonder, ladies and gentlemen, that she never tried again?"*

I stepped out of my imaginary courtroom and fixed Nilda with a confident smile. "So far," I said hopefully, "we've got three possibilities. One: The People have no case after all this time. Two: You weren't guilty because you were acting under duress. Three: A motion to dismiss in the interest of justice. You tell the court all about how you've gotten your life together and led an exemplary existence since the crimes were committed, and ask the judge to throw out all the charges."

"You mean . . ." Hope began to dawn in the drawn face. "I might not go to jail?"

"It's possible," I said. "I'd have to know a lot more before I could be sure, and even then there are no guarantees, but it looks pretty good."

"I'd kill myself before I'd go to jail." She said it in a matter-of-fact voice that carried its own conviction. From what I'd seen of her compulsive pacing, it was the simple truth.

"But," I went on, a stern quality entering my voice, "you *do* have to turn yourself in to the police. You have to tell them who you really are."

She turned away. I expected an argument, but what I got was a whisper. "I have to tell my husband first."

"Of course," I replied. I'd been willing to bet Art still thought the woman he married was Aida Valentin, and now I knew I was right.

"I need some time," she went on, her voice intense. "I have to think."

"How much?"

I wasn't sure how much I was willing to give. I kept hoping Art Lucenti would walk in the door and help me with this.

A knock on the door had both of us jumping out of our skins. I turned to see Dawn Ritchie's face, looking anxious but determined, peering through the glass.

Things happened at once. Nilda went for the door with a speed that left me behind. I was only halfway out of my chair when she yanked the door open. The look on her face made it clear she intended to get rid of Dawn as quickly and as rudely as possible. Which was all right with me; the last place I wanted Dawn was in the company of Nilda Vargas.

"Cass!" Dawn's face was a study in shock. "What are *you* doing here?"

"What I've been doing for some time now," I replied acidly, "trying to find out who killed your mother so I can get your father out of jail."

Dawn had the grace to blush. "I thought you'd given up," she murmured, her eyes on the ground.

"I know you did. You were wrong." I gave her a penetrating glance, trying to convey some sense of urgency. Then I said sharply, "Now get the hell out of here."

A man stepped up out of the shadows. I turned hoping to see Art Lucenti, but the man approaching the door was dressed in blue. Cop blue.

Fury gripped my soul. Nearly shaking, I grabbed for Dawn. Damn Marcy, I thought, hoping I could get Dawn out of there and send the cop away before Nilda panicked.

It was too late. Quick as a cat, Nilda blocked my way, and hissed, "You bitch! You called the fucking cops! You lied to me!"

"No," I shouted. "It wasn't me, it was Dawn's aunt. I told her—"

It was a mistake to mention Dawn. Nilda made her move so quickly she was like a blur, over to where Dawn stood.

The cop stepped up to the door. "I'm looking for a Dawn—" he began, then stopped cold as he saw Nilda.

I looked, and my heart turned sick. Nilda grabbed Dawn in a choke hold, pulled something from her pocket, and flicked it into a gleaming knife. Holding the knife to Dawn's throat, she shouted, "Get the fuck out of here! Come one step closer and she's dead!"

27

"Nilda, are you crazy?" I ran toward her, the unwisdom of calling someone holding a knife "crazy" not apparent to me at that moment.

"Get back, bitch," Nilda cried, "or I'll kill her!"

"Don't do it, lady," the cop begged. His raised hands were trembling and his voice cracked. He had the veiny red nose of the chronic drinker.

Nilda turned toward him, yanking Dawn with her in a swift motion that looked vicious but was probably just nerves. "Get out," she shrieked. "Get out and don't come back."

"I'm gone," the cop said. He backed out the door as though leaving the queen, then turned and ran. Toward the nearest phone, I hoped.

"Nilda, what the fuck?" Shock, fear, and rage were equally mixed; my voice sounded raucous in my own ears. "I thought we were talking! I thought you were going to turn yourself in. I thought..." I broke off at the hint of triumph in Nilda's manic smile. Rule number one: Skells will break your heart.

"Oh, God," I said, deflated by my sudden understanding, "you *did* kill Linda."

Dawn, already pale and trembling as if in a deadly fever,

began to whimper. Nilda cuffed her on the side of the head. I winced, but Dawn stopped her keening noise.

"This still makes no sense." I said the first thing that came into my head. "There's no future in it, Nilda. What do you expect to gain?"

"I'm not going to jail," Nilda replied, her calm tone belied by the uncharacteristically high pitch of her voice. "No matter what I have to do, I'm not going to jail."

She meant it. Taking a hostage may have been a drastic move, but I could see now that Nilda had been desperate, convinced that the cop had come, at my instigation, to put the finishing touches on my brilliant deduction that Aida Valentin and Nilda Vargas were one and the same person. She hadn't planned to escape jail at the point of a knife, but she'd do it that way if she had to.

Calm was my weapon, that and my mouth. "Flaherty was right," I said casually. "You're a hell of a natural actress. You almost had me convinced you were the loyal wife covering up for her guilty husband. The funny thing is, I would have given you the time you asked for. The time you'd have needed to book passage to South America, I suppose. What I wonder is"—I gave her a penetrating look—"would there have been one ticket or two? Were you planning on leaving Art or taking him with you?"

No answer. The hand holding the knife was rigid. It appeared rock-steady, but I suspected the stiffness was a rigidity born of pure fear. The blade was so close to Dawn's neck that one hard swallow would nick the skin.

"Nilda," I said in a tone I worked hard to soften, "can you move the knife a little, please?"

She glanced at me as though I'd proposed an impromptu trip to the moon. I suspected that she was afraid to make the smallest concession, afraid she'd lose her nerve completely and sink into submission. "No," she said curtly.

"Nilda"—the same coaxing voice—"she can't breathe. Look, move it an inch, *one inch*"—my voice grew intense with pleading and hope—"and it'll still be close enough to"—I broke off, not really interested in finishing the thought.

"You telling me what to do, bitch?" The challenge was pure skell, but I had the feeling Nilda'd taken the attitude out of mothballs. Her days as a Savage Macho Deb were a long time past now, and her aggressiveness sounded forced.

"I'm asking, Nilda," I said quietly. "In fact, if you want me to, I'm begging."

She moved the knife. I sighed with relief; Dawn, released ever so slightly from her prison, began to swallow convulsively. "Thank you," I said to Nilda, who nodded with a curtness that I sensed masked her own relief.

Art. He was my ace in the hole, my hope. I had to wrench my mind away from Dawn's tensed muscles and strained face and concentrate on Art and Nilda.

"As I was saying"—I tried for the casual tone—"was Art supposed to drop everything to run off with you to Costa Rica or wherever?" I added a taunting note: "How's his Spanish, Nilda? You think he'd have been thrilled to give up being a congressman to play Sydney Greenstreet in some tropical hole?"

"Art loves me." Nilda tossed her head. "He'll go with me." She said it confidently, but I didn't buy her assurance for a minute.

"Maybe he will and maybe he won't," I countered, "but the point is, you couldn't be sure. That's why you killed Linda, isn't it? You weren't sure what Art would do once he found out he wasn't married to Aida Valentin."

"Shut up," Nilda said, her hand beginning to shake. The knife was still an inch away from Dawn's neck, so I pushed my luck—and hers.

"Maybe there's more to it than that," I suggested. "Maybe that charming little story about innocent little Nilda corrupted by evil Nelson Rodriguez wasn't the whole truth, and maybe there are a few people still around and ready to testify who remember it differently."

No answer, but the sullen set of Nilda's mouth told me I was making progress.

"Then again," I went on, "who's to say Aida's death was an accident? It was pretty convenient for you—maybe you made sure she got some bad dope."

"Shut up!" Nilda shook with rage, her voice a scream. She thrust the knife against Dawn's neck. Even now, I could see she had no real will to hurt, but Dawn jumped and a tiny dot of blood appeared on her white neck. Her huge eyes were a prayer.

"Hey," I protested, "don't get carried away. After all, it's not what *I* think that counts. It's what Art thinks. And I wonder how he's going to feel if he walks in here and finds his beautiful wife holding a bloody knife in her hand with a dead kid on the floor."

I could see at once that Dawn was horrified by my choice of words. I probably wouldn't have cared to have them videotaped for posterity myself. But Nilda got the point. The knife flew away from Dawn's throat. This time Nilda left a good three inches, and the knife shook perceptibly.

The phone shrilled. All three of us jumped, then Nilda cried, "Don't touch it!"

"It might be the cops," I pointed out. Nilda's eyes grew wide. "What did you expect?" I asked her. "They've probably got the place cordoned off and surrounded by now. But they may have Art. Think about it."

Nilda didn't have to think very hard. "Pick it up," she ordered, "and bring it over to where I can hear every word."

I obeyed. My legs were so rubbery, I had to grab onto a desk or two to carry me to the phone. I hoped Nilda didn't notice; my strategy depended on my being—or seeming to be—the one in control. I brought the phone to where Nilda sat, picked up the receiver, and held it between us.

"Cass?" Detective Button barked my name, but I could hear an undertone of concern that warmed me.

I looked at Nilda, intentionally reinforcing her need to seem in charge. Only after she nodded did I respond. "I'm here," I said crisply.

"Congressman Lucenti's here," Button said. "Shall I send him in?"

Nilda nodded. Behind her closed face, I felt a surge of hope. Art was coming; Art would make it all right.

I felt the same way, staking everything on Art's abiding love for the woman he'd married. The gamble was that I was staking Dawn's life on whatever would be left after Art Lucenti's illusions had been stripped away.

"Yes," I told the phone, responding to Nilda's eager nod. "Send him right in." I hung up the phone and tensed myself for the next round.

Art came in like gangbusters. His "What the hell is going on?" could be heard even before the door was open. As he swung it wide and strode into the room, he boomed, "First I get a message that my wife needs me. Then the cops tell me some cockamamie story about a hostage. What the—" His jaw fell open, and the words stopped when he saw the knife.

"My God," he breathed, the take-charge masculinity evaporating like an April snow. "Aida?" The deep voice quavered, and a shadow of doubt crossed the handsome face.

Nilda didn't reply. She might have been a statue in her rigidity. It was as if his glance, his voice, could break her. He repeated the name, "Aida?" He ended on a high note of uncharacteristic uncertainty.

No answer. It was, I supposed, difficult to tell your husband that he'd been calling you by the wrong name for thirteen years.

"Shall I tell him?" I asked Nilda gently.

"I'm talking to my wife. Haven't you made enough trouble already?"

"Art, please," Nilda begged. "Listen to her."

Art reached her in two strides. Standing over her, he said forcefully, "If this is about that crap Todd Lessek showed me—"

He broke off as Nilda and I both shouted, "What?"

Art rounded on me. "That prick showed me Aida's criminal record. He had some fairy tale about Linda Ritchie digging it up, but I knew better. He wanted me to know where I stood with him." I recalled the bitter cold day Lessek and I had stood on the Brooklyn Bridge and I'd watched Lessek crush Art Lucenti's imaginary balls. I was learning now that Art hadn't had the naïve faith in Lessek that the developer had thought.

"I told him what he could do with it then," Art said, turning back toward his wife, "and I still mean it. Let it come out. Who cares? All that matters is, I'm proud of you and I don't care where you came from or what you did."

It was a lovely speech. The only problem was that he wasn't talking to Aida Valentin. It was time somebody told him that, and it looked like it wasn't going to be Nilda. She shot me an agonized glance. I sympathized; Art's touching profession of support was about to be severely tested.

I didn't dare take my eyes off Nilda, but I said matter-of-factly, "She wants me to explain. It's a long story, and it'll be easier if you just listen, okay?"

I could hear an impatient huff, but I had his attention. "Aida had a friend in the South Bronx," I began, "a friend named Nilda Vargas. Nilda started running with a gang and got herself in a lot of trouble. Wanted for murder, that kind of thing."

"What's that got to do with my wife?" Art challenged. "You can't blame her for what her friends did."

"This is going to take longer if you keep interrupting." I sighed. "The point is, Nilda Vargas is supposed to be dead. The rest of the world thinks she died fifteen years ago. Only a few people know the truth—that Nilda is alive and that Aida Valentin is the one who died."

Art's eyes widened, and he paled. He looked at Nilda with an expression of horror. "Then—" He choked on the words and started again. "You mean, my wife—"

I nodded. "Is really Nilda Vargas," I finished. "And she's wanted for murder."

Three women waited. I sensed a subtle realignment, subtle yet as dangerous as a shifting fault line. I was on Nilda's side. It was the two of us, with Dawn's silent, terrified presence between us, against Art Lucenti. We had to win him, had to keep him in the office, on Nilda's side, or it would all be over. If Art turned away, walked out the door, abandoned Nilda, then Dawn would die and Nilda would follow. She would have no further reason to live and no reason at all to spare Dawn. Yet underneath the fierce pose I sensed the truth: Nilda did not want to kill anyone. What she wanted was for Art to take the knife away and embrace her as he always had before. I hoped to God, for her sake as well as for Dawn's, that he could do it.

"My God," Art said again. It was beginning to sound like a prayer. "Wasn't there a man?" he asked. "Nelson something?"

"Nelson Rodriguez," I responded helpfully. "He was the real killer. A gang leader."

Art nodded. "I remember the news stories." His handsome face was settling back into its customary lines of command and complacency. I had the feeling he was engaging in the same lawyer-think I'd used before Nilda'd gone nuts and whipped out her knife. He was weighing the possibilities, picturing Nilda walking out of court a free woman, after winning a motion to dismiss in the interests of justice.

Part of me wanted to risk staying with the illusion. Let Art think the old charges were all Nilda had to worry about. What difference did it make as long as he got the knife away from her? But I knew the truth would have to come out. Nilda's tense pose, her manufactured defiance, showed me that Art hadn't passed the final test. She would not relinquish her weapon or her hostage until he did.

How to put it? Oh, by the way, your wife killed Linda Ritchie as well as all those other people. The difference was that the others were faceless, nameless, and could be blamed on Nelson Rodriguez. Linda had happened now, had been killed by the woman Art had known and loved for thirteen years, not by a phantom teenager in a gang jacket and a miniskirt.

"Linda found out," I said baldly. "She was blackmailing Nilda."

Art turned green. For a moment I thought he was going to throw up. "Oh, God," he said again, then he faced his wife, who visibly trembled with anxiety.

"Why?" he asked, his voice choking. "Why couldn't you tell me? You know I'd have helped you if I'd known."

That was just what Nilda Vargas Lucenti hadn't known, I thought, as I watched her face relax.

"Didn't you trust me?" he asked, bewildered.

Nilda looked down. Her eyes seemed fixed on the knife she held in her hand, but I doubted she really saw its gleaming edge. "You changed a lot, Art," she replied softly. "I wasn't sure how much."

Art's eyes narrowed. "What do you mean, I changed?"

"You were so idealistic," she said, "when I first saw you in the office. You used to spend all day in court and then come back to the office, drop your files on the desk, and jump into a gypsy cab to go to a rent-strike meeting. I loved you for what you were doing to help people." She took a breath and went on. "Then you started doing what Todd Lessek wanted instead of what you knew was right."

"You never said anything," Art protested.

"It was what you wanted," she announced simply. "I didn't want to be the one to get in your way."

I put my oar in. "It wasn't easy for her," I pointed out, "being the wife of a well-known man and a fugitive from justice at the same time."

I looked straight at Art Lucenti. The pain and betrayal that had filled his face were fading now. A sober sadness was taking its place. Slowly, with agonizing clarity, he was giving up the illusion that he and Nilda could walk out the door and resume something like their old life.

"She never tried to talk you out of it, did she?" I pressed. "She was there for you, Art—what are you going to do for her?"

No answer. "She molded herself to you, to your world. The right clothes, the right people. For years she was what you wanted her to be. You never even bothered to find out who she really was, for God's sake. She sacrificed for you— what are you willing to sacrifice for her?"

Art gazed at his wife with naked longing. Then he turned toward the door, as if weighing his choices.

"Art." I said the words I'd been hoping to avoid. "Nilda's a skell. By rights, her first, second, and third thoughts ought to be for herself alone. But she's *here*, not in Costa Rica or someplace, because she wants you by her side."

Time stopped. Art looked long and hard at his wife. I hoped to God he was seeing the woman he loved as well as the tough gang kid, the disheveled hostage-taker, the knife-murderer. Finally, he sighed and reached out a hand. It trembled slightly, but it came right up to the shining blade. "Aida," he said gently, "give me the knife."

It glinted in her hand, but she made no move to lower it. Her eyes were fixed on his face, as if trying to sense a trick.

"I'll hire the best damned lawyer in town," Art promised. "You won't go to jail if I have anything to say about it. A lot of people owe me a lot of favors, and I'll collect on all of them if I have to."

Still no movement from Nilda. "It's your only chance," I pleaded. "Think about it, Nilda. Art loves you in spite of what you did in the past. But what do you think he'll feel if he has to stand there and watch you cut a child's throat?"

Dawn flinched. The idea hadn't done a lot for me either. But the very brutality of the thought made Art wince and Nilda saw it. Very slowly, the knife blade began to lower, glinting in the fluorescent lighting. Down, down, down it came until it hung limply at her side.

Art took it from her unresisting fingers and gently laid it on a table. Then he reached out and stroked her hair. "I love you, babe," he said softly, "in spite of everything."

I walked over to Dawn, who still sat motionless. "It's over," I said, a little numb myself. "It's over."

The cops were a flood of blue. In the maelstrom, I saw Button shepherding Marcy Sheldon. Her face was pinched with anxiety, but there was no sign of tears.

My eyes followed her over to where Dawn sat, her lips working, her body still. Looking into her niece's deathly pale face, Marcy asked, her voice steady, "Are you all right, honey?"

Dawn looked up, her eyes slowly focusing on the figure in front of her. "I'm fine," she said in a small voice. Suddenly, without a sound, her face crumpled. She turned and buried her head in her aunt's stomach, her chest heaving with sobs. Her arms went around Marcy's waist, and she hugged as tightly as though the tiny woman were a life preserver.

Marcy's façade cracked. Looking down at the sobbing child, she burst into tears herself, hugging Dawn and crying incoherently. They began to rock together, a keening sound coming from them. Out of the wailing, I heard the words I'd longed for Marcy to say: "I love you, Dawn. I'll never send you away." Dorinda had been right. The dam had burst, and the flood of love that poured out filled my heart with hope and my eyes with unshed tears.

I turned toward the Lucentis. Nilda's face was tear-streaked too, and she pulled her arms away as a uniformed cop tried to put handcuffs on her. Art reached out but was restrained in a curiously soothing gesture by Detective Button. "No," Nilda moaned. "I can't go to jail, I can't." There was a desperate undertone to her protests.

Near tears himself, Art Lucenti turned to Button and asked a question I couldn't hear. Nilda was still sobbing. "I'll die," she said. "I'll die in jail. Art, help me. Please help me." She reached out her arms, only to be restrained by a bluecoat.

Button pursed his lips and nodded. As the uniformed cops parted, Art walked over to his wife and reached out his arms for one final embrace.

It happened as a blur of sound and motion. A muffled bang, a body falling in slow motion. A look of utter astonishment on the face of a young cop. Pain and then a smile—an incongruous genuine smile—on the face of Nilda Vargas Lucenti. Inarticulate grunts and hands reaching toward the tottering body. Scuffling feet rushing toward the man with the gun. A look of inexpressible sadness on Art Lucenti's face as he lifted the gun to his mouth and pulled the trigger.

28

"Men have died from time to time, and worms have eaten them," my mind quoted, "but not for love." In the week since I'd seen Art Lucenti's head splattered like a watermelon across the floor of his headquarters, I'd thought a lot about love.

Love had started it all. Harry Sheldon had loved his little Linda as no man should love a daughter. He'd created a woman whose need for love was insatiable, who made childishly enormous demands upon an adult world that finally refused to play.

Love had sucked me in; only my feelings for Dawn Ritchie had induced me to look for Linda's killer. And yet I couldn't escape the knowledge that my withholding of Aida Valentin's criminal record had put Dawn in danger. It had probably caused the Lucentis' deaths as well; the thought that they had chosen death over disgrace was only partial compensation for the guilt I felt.

Now it was up to love to redeem itself. I hoped, for Dawn Ritchie's sake, that love would be strong enough for the job.

I wasn't at all sure I was strong enough. My palms itched with sweat, and my heart pounded. My own office library suddenly seemed a strange and slightly sinister place. I hadn't been this nervous since the day I'd first stepped into a courtroom.

Maybe it was because I'd known Dawn's family too long and too well to expect a miracle. Or maybe I'd finally understood that it was one thing to theorize glowingly about mediation and quite another to make it work. Underlying everything was the sick feeling of apprehension I'd had since the Lucentis died—as though everything I touched was bound to turn to death and failure.

Marcy Sheldon seemed to share some of my doubts. "Do you really think they'll come?" she asked for the third time. I wasn't up to answering again, so Mickey Dechter replied reassuringly, "They said they would."

"Daddy will," Dawn asserted, adding the age-old incantation of childhood: "He promised."

The library door opened. Dawn's face became a huge grin. "Daddy," she exclaimed happily, "you came!" Turning to her aunt, she said, "I told you he'd come."

Jail hadn't mellowed Brad Ritchie. He slouched into the room, his face wearing its usual defiant pout. On seeing Dawn's joyous welcome, his eyes dropped as though he'd been accused. Then he raised his head and smiled at his daughter with a boyish charm I'd never seen before. "For you, baby," he said simply.

As Brad settled into his chair, his muscular legs sprawled in front of him, I felt a surge of hope. He might still look like a high-school kid bent on defying the teacher, but the fact remained, he was here. Whatever baggage he'd brought with him, he'd made the trip.

Which was more than could be said for his mother. The empty chair between Marcy and Mickey seemed to mock my plans for the session even as Brad's presence gave me hope. I'd learned enough from my partner the social worker to realize that Ma Ritchie, by coming late—or, perhaps, not coming at all—was making her first move in the dominance game she would play with Marcy Sheldon. The only question was whether she would play that game here in my office or save it for court.

Mickey Dechter and I had planned the seating arrangements as though we were hosting a summit meeting. We'd deliberately put Dawn between Brad and Marcy, hoping to foster a sense of sharing. Our decision was vindicated almost immediately, as Dawn glanced shyly from father to aunt, seeming to will them to accept the larger symbolic meaning of the fact that she sat between them. Brad smiled affectionately at her, acknowledging Marcy with a brief nod. Marcy looked away, uncomfortable. Then she fumbled for a cigarette, looked back at Brad, and managed a wan smile.

Marcy was dressed, as usual, in a petite man-tailored suit, but a scarf at the throat and a softer shade of lipstick added a new femininity. But the difference in her went beyond clothes. There was a less rigid look to her posture and a new grace to her gestures. At times, a tentative smile crossed her features, only to disappear at once, like the Cheshire cat's.

The library door opened and Viola Ritchie bustled in,

filling the air with breathless apologies. In order to avoid the appearance of Brad and his mother ganging up on tiny Marcy Sheldon, we'd seated Mrs. Ritchie between Marcy and Mickey Dechter. Without so much as a pause in her flow of words, the older woman walked to the empty chair, tipped it, and began dragging it over to where Brad and Dawn sat.

The best-laid plans and all that. Mickey and I shared rueful smiles and tacitly agreed not to press the point. It was enough that Mrs. Ritchie was here.

"I'd like to start," Mickey began in her curiously soothing voice, "by welcoming everyone and thanking you all for coming." I smiled at this Southern touch. "Cass and I appreciate it and we promise to do everything in our power to make it worth your while. I think I ought to start by saying a few words about what mediation is—and what it is not." She looked at each person in turn as she spoke, her candid eyes seeming to invite an equal candor.

"Mediation is not a substitute for the Family Court proceedings that some of you are already engaged in," she said. "The judge will still have the final say as to the custody matter. However," she went on, looking first at Mrs. Ritchie and then at Marcy, "the fact remains that no matter what happens in that courtroom, each of you has a unique role to play in the life of our young friend here." The special smile Mickey gave Dawn was returned with a relaxed confidence I'd never seen the child display before.

"What we'd like to accomplish here," Mickey went on, "is to try to work out accommodations between the parties so that, whatever happens in court, no one feels cheated and everyone's needs are taken into account. It's in the best interests of everyone, but especially those of Dawn, that we work together as much as possible. Which brings me," she added, "to another statement about what mediation is *not*. We are not here to practice therapy, by raking up the past or opening old wounds. Our one objective is to discuss the issue of Dawn's custody and visitation."

For some reason I couldn't fathom, Micky's calm, reasoned words—which had Marcy nodding in unconscious agreement and even Brad looking receptive—were making me increasingly nervous. At first I couldn't figure out why, but then I began to notice a strange feeling. I found myself—surely for the first time in my professional life—wishing there were a judge in the room. I was an advocate, trained to represent one client to the best of my ability, trained to present my case before the court and then wait for a verdict. However committed I might be in principle to mediation, the truth was I felt ill at ease, as though my legal skills were worse than useless in this new forum I'd chosen.

It was Ma Ritchie who came to my rescue. "I'm not sure," she said uncertainly, "that I really ought to be here without my lawyer."

I jumped in gratefully, eager to play the role I knew so well. "We discussed that, Mrs. Ritchie," I pointed out calmly. "I said that your lawyer was welcome to be here, but that this was just a preliminary discussion. Everything that's said here will be confidential. If there is some kind of agreement by the end of the session, your lawyer and I will draw up a formal stipulation. You won't sign anything or commit yourself without his okay."

I continued telling Viola Ritchie what she already knew. "I talked to Mr. Kretschmer," I reminded her, "and he was willing to let us go ahead without him."

"Well, all right." Mrs. Ritchie feigned reluctant agreement, but the complacent smile on her face told me she'd never intended to leave the session. "I'll stay—for my granddaughter's sake."

Mickey Dechter resumed her opening remarks. "Each of you," she began, her voice deepening, "will continue to be a part of Dawn's life—and therefore of each other's lives—for a long time to come, regardless of the outcome of the court proceedings. I'd like to hear from each of you as to why you feel Dawn should live with you. Everyone will have a chance to talk, so please don't interrupt. Who'd like to go first?"

There was only the tiniest pause before Marcy Sheldon's businesslike voice filled the room. I had the usual sinking sensation I experienced whenever my client took the stand, going beyond my ability to shield him from hostile questions. I felt like an anxious mother watching her toddler's first steps, hoping that she wouldn't fall down and cut herself on broken glass.

Professionalism has it uses. Marcy gave the same slick, well-organized, crisply presented performance she would have shown a prospective client with a million-dollar account. And yet, the sidelong glances she gave Dawn were anything but cold. "I used to think," she concluded, looking straight at me, "that being the best at what I do was the most important thing in the world. It was my highest priority, and it got all my energy and attention. Now," she explained, her well-manicured hands twisting together in the only sign of nerves she'd shown, "I've found something more important to me than being the best. I can still be good—damned good—and work a lot less. The energy and time I free up will go into only one thing—making a good home for Dawn."

It was a nice speech. But I began to suspect, looking at Dawn's unmoved face, that it wouldn't be enough. I recalled sitting in Dawn's bedroom the night Linda's body had been carried out of my house. Dawn had been ready to cast aside everything and everybody she knew and loved in order to follow Brad to almost certain poverty in Miami. Now that he was free to petition for her custody, wouldn't Dawn's first choice be life with her adored father?

Mrs. Ritchie thought so. She went for the jugular with her opening statement: "Now that my son's been cleared of his wife's murder," she announced confidently, "there's no reason Dawn can't live with us." She went on to paint a rosy picture of home life. Hot meals, church on Sunday, freshly laundered clothes hung on the line to dry; it all sounded too good to be true.

It *was* too good to be true, I decided, as I listened to Ma Ritchie's honeyed voice. Her dangerous tongue conjured up an impossible "Little House on the Prairie" version of family life. And yet, to a twelve-year-old raised by a selfish mother, separated from a flawed but loving father, it must have sounded like heaven. Especially since Mrs. Ritchie was careful to emphasize the time Brad and Dawn would spend together, the things they would share. By the end of her recitation, Dawn's eyes were shining with anticipation. Marcy Sheldon, noting the eager look on her niece's face, sat plunged in gloom.

But there was something wrong with the picture. Marcy's wasn't the only long face at the table. Brad Ritchie seemed to sink lower in his chair as his mother wove her spell.

I thought about Willy Loman. Like Ma Ritchie, the salesman had lived on dreams, building impossible futures for himself and his sons. I had the feeling that, like Willy, Viola Ritchie was long on dreams and short on realities.

"And that's why I'm sure," she concluded, "that Dawn will be perfectly happy living with us."

"Us?" I challenged, finally seeing the flaw in Mrs. Ritchie's gem of a presentation. Turning to Brad, I asked, "Were you really planning to live with your mother for the next six years? Till Dawn's eighteen?"

Brad looked uncomfortable. Glancing first at his daughter, whose eyes pleaded with him, and then to his mother, whose whole face was a demand, he mumbled, "For a while. Till I get my act together."

"And then?"

"I guess I'll take care of Dawn on my own," he replied, sounding less than certain. Straightening up, he began to think out loud. "I can get a job and an apartment. We'll be fine. We don't need—"

"Who'll stay with Dawn while you're at work?" I confronted him. "Who'll take her to her tennis matches, Brad? Hell, who'll *pay* for her tennis matches?"

"Cass"—Mickey's voice was no longer soothing—"this isn't an adversary proceeding."

I shot Mickey a look one partner should never give another. Then I glanced at Dawn. The look of relaxed anticipation had left her face and was beginning to be replaced by the tense, pinched look she'd always worn in court. I felt bad for her, but I knew the fantasy world the Ritchies lived in was no place she could really call home.

"Mickey, I have to . . ."

My partner held up a restraining hand, then turned to Brad. "Mr. Ritchie," she said firmly, "your daughter's future is too important to rest on a wish or a hope. Are you sure you can handle having Dawn with you twenty-four hours a day, seven days a week? Being totally responsible for all the decisions that have to be made in a twelve-year-old's life?"

While Mickey talked, her questioning calm but relentless, I flashed back to all those Family Court appearances. To the first day I'd seen Brad and Linda in their "Come to Daddy, Dawnie"/"No, stay here by Mommy" routine. To the innumerable motions Brad and his lawyers had filed, litigating and relitigating every detail of Brad's visitation. To the final day, when Brad had threatened to do what it turned out he hadn't done after all—kill the wife who'd withheld his

child from him. After all that, I thought, how could he say no
to Dawn now?

Brad looked at his daughter. The love, the plea in
her eyes were painful to see. Finally Brad dropped his
eyes. "I'm sorry, honey," he said, his attempt at a smile
a twisted grimace. "I guess I'm just not a very good
father."

Dawn swallowed hard, then reached out her hand and
touched his strong arm. "It's okay, Daddy," she whispered. "I
understand. And you *are* a good father," she added passionately, looking around the room as if daring anyone to contra-
dict her.

I was stunned. Brad's frank admission was the last thing
in the world I'd expected. It was so different from the
position he'd taken when Linda was alive. When Linda was
alive . . . was that, I wondered, the key? Had the constant
custody battle been a way of maintaining a link with Linda as
much as a real fight over Dawn? Now, with Linda dead, that
game was over. And Marcy, unlike her sister, had no plans to
take Dawn out of the city.

Sheepishly, yet with clear relief, Brad shook his head.
"I love her," he told Mickey. "I want to be with her
as much as I can. But," he added with a touch of sadness, "I know my limits. I know there's things I can't give
her."

"That's why you need your mother, Brad," Viola Ritchie
cried. "Let me help you!"

"You know it won't work, Ma," Brad pleaded for understanding. "Me and you never could live together for too long.
You know that."

"That was in the past," his mother countered. "This time
it'll all be different."

The age-old cry, I thought. This time it will be different.
Brad shook his head. "No, it won't, Ma."

Ma Ritchie was down but not out. "What makes you
think," she asked, turning toward Mickey and me, "that I
can't take care of my granddaughter by myself? So what if my
only son doesn't want to live with his own mother?"

"Ma!" Brad protested.

"Mrs. Ritchie," Mickey began.

Viola Ritchie rose in her chair. "We'll see what the judge
has to say," she promised. Picking up her pocketbook, she

fired a parting shot. "I'm going to get custody with or without my son's help and that's that."

Her departure left a palpable, uncomfortable silence. It was Dawn who broke that silence. In a small voice, she asked, "Will I have to live with her?"

It was a good question. I opened my mouth to give my best legal analysis of our chances in court, but Brad Ritchie beat me to the punch. "Don't worry, honey," he said firmly. "You won't have to live anywhere you don't want to."

The anxious frown left Dawn's face, replaced by a grateful smile. For once, I thought, Dawn had found in her father the strength she'd been looking for. "Then if I can't live with you," she announced, "I'd like to stay with Aunt Marcy."

If Marcy Sheldon had any feelings about being second best, she covered them with a broad smile. I answered the unspoken question in her eyes.

"I always thought," I explained, "that Mrs. Ritchie's best hope was for both Brad and Dawn to live with her. Since that's not going to happen, and since Brad will support Dawn's decision, our chances look pretty good. Bettinger's one judge who pays a lot of attention to the wishes of the child."

Marcy nodded, then stood and took the coat Mickey handed her. Dawn pulled on the new fawn-colored ski jacket, so different from the tattered pink one she'd worn that day in Family Court when Linda had walked out the winner. "I'm hungry," she said with childish directness. "Can we get something to eat before practice?"

"Sure," Marcy replied. Looking at me, she asked, "Is there a place around here you'd recommend?"

Even as I extolled the virtues of the Morning Glory, I was aware that something was missing. The big issues had been settled, even better than I'd hoped, and yet I felt no elation.

Then I noticed Brad Ritchie. He stood in the doorway, his leather jacket open, his face a study in indecisiveness. His eyes were fixed on Dawn. He looked forlorn, like the kid nobody wants to play with watching the others run and laugh.

I had a sudden idea. "Marcy," I began, "did Dawn say she was practicing later?"

Marcy nodded, stopping her progress toward the door.

"How do you think she'd feel about an audience?"

"She'd probably love it," Marcy replied, an indulgent smile on her face. "The truth is, she's a little show-off."

Dawn blushed and ducked her head, but she wasn't displeased by the description. "Would you and Mickey like to come?" Marcy asked.

"We both have clients to see this afternoon," I said smoothly. "But maybe Brad would like—"

"Daddy, yes!" Dawn gave an excited squeal. "Please come. I made a big improvement in my backhand since you saw me last. You won't believe it."

"If it's okay with your aunt," Brad mumbled, scarcely daring to look at the tiny woman.

I'd boxed Marcy Sheldon in as neatly as I had Brad Ritchie that day in Family Court. I had the same guilt level: practically none. It was true that Marcy couldn't say no without putting out Dawn's smile like a candle. And yet, Mickey had been right. All the adults in Dawn's life were going to have to stop acting like kids and start working together. They might as well, I decided, start now.

Marcy rose to the occasion, inviting Brad to lunch with a gracious social lie. "I'd have asked you before," she explained, "but I thought you had other plans."

"Dawn's tennis must take an awful lot of your time, Marcy," Mickey Dechter said in a thoughtful tone.

"The understatement of the year," Marcy laughed. "But it's worth it."

"Wouldn't it be nice if there was someone who could help you with all that? Someone who'd take Dawn where she has to go, and talk to her coach, and do all the little things that must be hard for someone as busy as you?"

It was a nice try, I thought wryly, giving my partner a grateful glance. But it didn't look as though Marcy was going to buy it. There was a doubtful frown on her forehead; Dawn's tennis had been so important to her for so long that it was hard for her to think of letting go. And yet, the hopeful look on Brad Ritchie's face showed that he too could see where Mickey's thoughts were taking her.

"It *would* make things easier," I remarked. "Be honest." Then I lowered my voice so that only Marcy could hear. "And be generous," I urged.

Marcy Sheldon's Cheshire-cat smile appeared, and this time it stayed for a while. "I think it's a great idea," she said warmly. "I can use the help, and it will give Brad and Dawn time together."

The hug Dawn gave her tiny aunt nearly knocked her over, but it didn't look as though Marcy minded very much. Brad Ritchie, too excited to stand still, walked over and put his arms around his daughter. "Let's go eat," he suggested. As they left the office, Dawn regaled her father with a ball-by-ball account of a match she'd won in Westchester the week before.

It took me a minute to realize that the sick feeling I'd had since Art Lucenti put the gun in his mouth was gone. The sun had finally broken through the clouds that enveloped me. I had done for Dawn what I'd set out to do; I'd given her back her father.

I smiled as I recalled the truth I'd learned at the Friday's Child Day-Care Center: It's never too late to have a happy childhood.

ABOUT THE AUTHOR

CAROLYN WHEAT is herself a former defense attorney with the Legal Aid Society in Brooklyn. Her first novel, *Dead Man's Thoughts*, was hailed by *Library Journal* as "literate, witty, with a realistic, serious depiction of life in court, on the streets, and in jail, as well as characters who have real depth and honest emotions," and was nominated for an Edgar as the best first mystery of 1983.

Kinsey Millhone is . . .

"The best new private eye." —The Detroit News

"A tough-cookie with a soft center." —Newsweek

"A stand-out specimen of the new female operatives."
  —Philadelphia Inquirer

Sue Grafton is . . .

The Shamus and Anthony Award winning creator of Kinsey Millhone and quite simply one of the hottest new mystery writers around.

Bantam is . . .

The proud publisher of Sue Grafton's Kinsey Millhone mysteries:

Special Offer
Buy a Bantam Book
for only 50¢.

Now you can have Bantam's catalog filled with hundreds of titles plus take advantage of our unique and exciting bonus book offer. A special offer which gives you the opportunity to purchase a Bantam book for only 50¢. Here's how!

By ordering any five books at the regular price per order, you can also choose any other single book listed (up to a $5.95 value) for just 50¢. Some restrictions do apply, but for further details why not send for Bantam's catalog of titles today!

Just send us your name and address and we will send you a catalog!